Praise for the Suspense Novels of Daryl Wood Gerber

"This was a fast-paced action-packed drama that immediately grabbed my attention, quickly becoming a page-turner as I could not put this book down."

—Dru's Book Musings

"The frantic plot will keep readers on edge."

—Kirkus Reviews

"The novel's plot is thick and the prose is more than rich enough to sustain it. Its shifting perspectives will give readers an even greater sense of excitement as the many pieces of the puzzle fall into place. Readers will be shocked by this exciting, fast-paced thriller's twists and turns."

—Kirkus Reviews

"Daryl Wood Gerber has proven again to be a gifted storyteller and one to watch in this genre. An absolute must-read!"

—Escape with Dollycas

"This is an edge-of-your-seat, can't-put-it-down thriller. If you like Dan Brown's thrillers you will want to read this!"

—Goodreads

"*Day of Secrets* is an action-packed, suspense-filled, riveting book. I was glued to this story, could not put it down, and didn't want it to end."

—Goodreads

Books by Daryl Wood Gerber

The Cookbook Nook Mysteries

Final Sentence
Inherit the Word
Stirring the Plot
Fudging the Books
Grilling the Subject
Pressing the Issue
Wreath Between the Lines
Sifting Through Clues
Shredding the Evidence

The French Bistro Mysteries

A Deadly Éclair
A Soufflé of Suspicion

Suspense

Girl on the Run
Day of Secrets
Desolate Shores
Fan Mail
Cold Conviction

Writing as Avery Aames

The Long Quiche Goodbye
Lost and Fondue
Clobbered by Camembert
To Brie or Not to Brie
Days of Wine and Roquefort
As Gouda as Dead
For Cheddar or Worse

COLD CONVICTION

DARYL WOOD GERBER

BEYOND THE PAGE

PUBLISHING

Cold Conviction
Daryl Wood Gerber
Copyright © 2020 by Daryl Wood Gerber
Cover design and illustration by Dar Albert, Wicked Smart Designs

Beyond the Page Books
are published by
Beyond the Page Publishing
www.beyondthepagepub.com

ISBN: 978-1-950461-81-3

*To Dru Ann Love, for your fabulous blogging,
your undying support for the mystery community,
and for the inspiration you gave me for this story.*

Acknowledgments

"We all lose somebody we care about and want to find some comforting way of dealing with it, something that will give us a little closure, a little peace." —Mitch Ablom

Writing a book can be a solitary process. Authors spend a lot of time, nowadays, staring at a computer. But I, personally, lean on my community to give me guidance, support, and inspiration.

Thank you to my family and friends for all your support.

Thank you to those who have helped make this suspense series a success: my publisher, Beyond the Page, including Bill Harris and Jessica Faust; my cover artist, Dar Albert; and my agent, John Talbot.

Thank you to my talented author friends Krista Davis and Hannah Dennison for your words of wisdom and encouragement.

Thank you to my early readers—you know who you are—for your enthusiasm for my suspense novels as well as your keen eyes at catching mistakes.

Thank you to all my readers, including librarians, for taking this journey with me. I have had a blast writing about Aspen while delving into the reasons she left her career as a therapist and became a private detective. I have grown to love the cast of characters that populate her world, and in the process, have learned so much about myself.

Chapter 1

I awoke with a jolt, heart pounding. A nightmare hadn't startled me. What had? I ran my fingers through my hair and peered at the bedroom window, which was open a crack. When I slept, I liked to drink in Lake Tahoe's crisp, pine-scented air. To calm myself now, I listened to the distant swish of the lake's waves lapping the shore and the breeze whistling through the pines. There was no other sound. Not even a nocturnal critter skittering on the cabin's rear patio.

The cordless telephone jangled.

My insides reeled. I struggled to a sitting position, switched on the lamp on the nightstand—the clock read two a.m.—lifted the cordless telephone's receiver, and pressed Talk.

"Aspen, I didn't do it," Rosie rasped.

My older sister, an addict who was known to ramble. Had I sensed she would call? Was that why I'd awakened?

I stifled a yawn. Yesterday had been a long, trying day. Today, Wednesday, was going to prove even longer if I didn't get more sleep. "What are you talking about, Rosie?"

"It wasn't my fault." She didn't slur her words. She sounded sober. And she was pacing. I heard her lumbering footsteps. "It wasn't my fault," she repeated, her voice barely a whisper.

I pressed the receiver tightly to my ear. "Speak up. What wasn't your fault?"

Cinder, my rescue dog, gazed at me from the foot of the bed. I signaled for him to settle down.

"I don't know who killed Mom and Dad," Rosie said.

I winced. Rosie may have sounded clearheaded, but she had to be on something. Heroin probably, her drug of choice. "Rosie, nobody knows who did it. The case went cold. Remember?"

Our parents were murdered in their home fourteen years ago. According to the Atherton police, my father had come upon an intruder in the dining room. The robber had shot Dad first and then Mom when she'd tried to save him. The police had interrogated a ton of people—family, friends, neighbors, Rosie's associates as well as

Dad's and Mom's clients. All had been cleared and the weapon never found.

"Let it go," I said softly.

"You've always blamed me."

"No—"

"You did. Everyone did. But it wasn't my fault."

At the time of the murder, Rosie had been clean for a year. She'd recently given birth to Candace, my niece. However, in view of her past, which had included stealing from our parents to help pay for her next fix, Rosie had been the obvious suspect. Except she'd had an alibi. A verifiable alibi. As did I. I was in my first semester of college and had been in class.

"It wasn't Antoine, either," she said. "Or anybody else I knew. You know addicts. They talk."

I'd once been a therapist. Yes, I knew addicts.

"No one talked." My sister slapped something hard. "I don't know who killed them."

"Okay. I hear you. I believe you. Go to sleep."

"I can't. You've got to—" She hiccupped. "You've got to—"

"I've got to *what?*"

For a month, the police had interrogated Rosie. A freshman, I was barely able to keep my head above water, let alone intercede on her behalf. When the case went unsolved, she fell into despair and returned to heroin to ease her problems. Over the ensuing years, her daughter had paid the price, struggling with her self-confidence as well as a battle with bulimia. I still couldn't believe I'd been able to gain custody of Candace nearly two years ago. Today, she was healthy, happy, and thriving in high school.

"You can find out who killed them," Rosie said. "I know you can. The police were . . . *are* useless."

The memory of the phone call from Detective Sergeant Evers hit me squarely between the eyes. *"Miss Adams."* He'd sounded official but kind. *"We're sorry to have to tell you, but—"*

"You can find out the truth," Rosie said. "Please."

I scrubbed my neck, itching to end the call. "It's over, Rosie."

"You're a P.I. It's your job."

A few years ago, at the tender age of twenty-eight, after my failed marriage and the anguish of trying to save struggling teens had broken me, I'd moved to Lake Tahoe to work for my aunt, who owned a detective agency. I'd started as a gofer, process serving and such. As of six months ago, I'd become a full-fledged private investigator. At my core, I was a problem solver; I wanted to help people find clarity.

"I need you to prove it wasn't my fault. If I could see my way clear of guilt, maybe . . ." Rosie's words drifted off.

"Maybe what?"

"Maybe I could get clean. Pull myself together. Stop being a loser." My sister sucked back a sob.

So did someone else.

I whipped my focus to the right. Candace stood in the doorway, a cordless phone receiver in her hand, her eyes glistening with tears. Pajamas hanging on her lithe frame, she reminded me more of *me* at that age than her oversized mother, although she was close to her mother's height. She'd grown another two inches in the past few months. Her auburn hair had grown, too, and was usually silky and wavy. Right now, it was a rat's nest. How much had she heard of my conversation with her mother? All of it, I imagined. She was a light sleeper.

"Please, Aspen," Rosie begged. "I'm having nightmares. I see their faces."

Please, Candace mouthed.

"Aspen, I never told the police something," Rosie said.

I held my breath.

"When I arrived there that day . . ."

Rosie had been living in Redwood City at the time and working as a waitress at a diner. She'd never married—she didn't know who Candace's father was—and had to put Candace in day care in order to hold down the job. That day, she'd gone on an interview to work as a customer service representative, a telephone-type job expressly designed for stay-at-home parents. The interview had been in Morgan Hill, a thirty-minute drive from Atherton. After the interview, on the way to pick up Candace at day care, Rosie had decided to stop by our parents' home first and run a load of laundry. They were supposed to be out of town on a trip. She'd have the place to herself. In and out.

Wrong. She was the one who'd found them. She'd called 911.

"When I arrived there," she began again, "Mom was alive."

"Alive?" The word leaped out of my mouth.

"Yes, but her eyes were closed and she was bleeding out, and there was so much—" Rosie didn't add *blood.* "I didn't press her chest. I was too afraid I'd . . ." She cleared her throat.

Afraid she'd speed up our mother's death. Got it.

"In her last breath, Mom said, 'You'll never get it.'"

"She spoke?" My heart thudded. "What did she mean? Get what?"

"I don't know. I think . . ." Rosie slurped back tears.

Candace tiptoed to my bed and scrambled under the covers with me, her ear glued to the receiver. Cinder belly-crawled to her. She rubbed his ears with her free hand.

"I thought *it* was the inheritance," Rosie said. "It had to be. She . . . and Dad . . . meant to cut me out of any inheritance."

"They cut me out, too." Almost all of our parents' wealth had been left to our heirs—Candace and whatever child I might have, should I have any.

"Right," Rosie said with an edge, "but I didn't know that at the time. I felt so rotten, knowing how much Mom hated me."

"She didn't—"

"I let her down. I broke her heart. So, I kept silent and didn't mention what she'd said to anyone, but now, I'm wondering if I might have misunderstood her words."

"Misunderstood how?" My voice crackled with tension.

"Remember I said her eyes were closed? Maybe she didn't know it was me. Maybe she thought she was rebuking the robber. Whoever killed Mom and Dad stole the silver tea set and silverware, but maybe there was something else the robber was after."

"Like what?"

My father had been a defense lawyer and, being one-quarter Washoe Indian, had handled a lot of volatile Native American–related cases. My mother had worked as an interior designer. They hadn't been poor by any stretch of the imagination, but they hadn't been rolling in dough. They hadn't kept piles of cash lying around the house, and my mother hadn't worn expensive jewelry; she'd liked arty, colorful pieces.

"'You won't get *it*,'" Rosie reiterated.

"It," I echoed. "What is *it*?"

"It's haunted me, Aspen. All these years."

"I understand, but—"

"There's one other thing, an angle that came to me an hour ago. That's why I'm calling. I know you have their hope chest, so you probably already know this, but there's a gun in it." Over the years, Rosie had rummaged through everything our parents had owned. "I never touched it. I drew the line at holding it, but what if—" She sucked in air.

"What if *what*?"

"What if the killer used it on Mom and Dad?"

"You're just now telling me this?" I barked.

Candace whimpered. The dog, too.

"I'm sorry," Rosie wailed.

With Rosie sinking into personal despair after our parents' deaths, I hadn't had the composure to handle the estate by myself, so I'd asked the estate's attorney, the bank executor, and my mother's best friend and business partner, Tammie, to pack up our parents' house. I'd had the wherewithal to set aside a number of items to sell immediately, the proceeds to go into trust for Rosie's and my heirs, and Rosie had taken a few items for her personal use, all of which were now long gone, sold off to pay for her addiction. I'd also tagged a few items that I'd known I would want after graduation—snowshoes, Native American paraphernalia, a couch, a lamp, and the hope chest that my grandmother had crafted as a wedding gift for my parents. With my blessing, Tammie had put my selections and the remainder of the household and clothing items into a storage unit that we'd booked for a pittance. I'd only visited the unit once to collect the tagged items.

I gazed at the hope chest at the foot of my bed, a feeling of dread washing over me. Before the movers had carted it and the other items from my parents' house to the storage unit, I'd tried to go through the contents, only to realize that I wasn't emotionally ready. Touching the linens and childhood mementoes my mother had kept had knocked me for a loop. Since then, I'd been too afraid to open it. Was there a gun in it? And if there wasn't a gun, what did that mean?

"Why would the killer use it and put it back?" I asked.

"I. Don't. Know." Rosie howled.

Candace recoiled.

I said, "Okay, Sis, calm down."

"I think it was Dad's," she said. "He probably bought it for protection. You know how many ticked-off clients he had."

Our father had represented clients from a variety of tribes, ranging from wealthy casino owners to the destitute in need of a fair shake. My mother had blamed Dad's father for his bleeding-heart attitude. Although his father, Jonathan Adams II, had continued to run the family lumber business, he had lived his life driven by social causes. He had demanded the same from his boys.

"Like I said," Rosie continued, "around midnight I got to thinking. What if Dad didn't have the gun for protection? What if he'd purchased it because he'd gotten involved in something illicit?"

"Dad? Not a chance. He was as honorable as the day is long." Our father had been tough and could be distant, but he had been devoted to his clients, his causes, and our mother.

"Want me to look in the hope chest?" Candace asked.

I covered the receiver's mouthpiece. "No!"

Defensively, she raised her hand. "Don't wig out."

"Please, Aspen," Rosie went on. "Do this for me. Get the police to reopen the case or do your own investigation. If I get clean and stay clean, maybe Candy and I could—" Rosie clicked her tongue.

She didn't have to finish the thought. I knew where her line of thinking was headed. Maybe she could be reunited with her daughter. Maybe they could be a family again.

I petted Candace's hair. Although I doubted her mother could go straight and I worried about the mental well-being of my sweet niece if Rosie wanted to fight me for custody, I said, "Yes. I'll do it."

Chapter 2

For fourteen years, I'd replayed my parents' deaths in my head. If only they hadn't been home. If only I'd opted to live at home instead of on the Stanford campus. If only Rosie hadn't surrounded herself with so many dangerous people. Did I blame her for their deaths? In my heart of hearts, yes. I'd tried my best not to hold her responsible, but I'd been young, impressionable, and disconsolate. I didn't believe for a second that she'd pulled the trigger, but I believed that someone she had known, thanks to her seedy lifestyle, had robbed and killed them.

"Where do we start?" Candace rolled onto her side and curled her knees into her abdomen.

"*We* don't start anywhere," I said, taking the reins of the conversation. "It's the middle of the night. You need to sleep. You have school tomorrow."

"But—"

"No buts. Bed. Sleep. Hop to it. You know your mother. She's stewing over something that she can't control."

"You said you'd help."

"And I will. In the morning." I tapped the tip of her ski-jump nose— a family trait—and kissed her forehead. "You can sleep here if you want."

"No, thanks." She slithered out of bed and trudged to the doorway. Pausing in the arch, she peeked over her shoulder. "Don't you want to know the truth?"

"As much as you do, but remember, sometimes learning the truth isn't possible."

• • •

At five a.m., no longer able to lie still, I bounded out of bed and stretched. Catching a glimpse of myself in the mirror—drawn olive skin, bloodshot eyes, downturned mouth—I knew I'd need more than one cup of caffeine to get me going. I threw on a nubby red sweater and jeans, brewed a pot of coffee, let Cinder out for a romp in the crisp air, and returned to my bedroom, cup of coffee in hand.

I stared at the hope chest, a beautiful piece of cedar furniture that Grandma Patrice had crafted. She had been a gifted artist and carpenter and had passed her appreciation of the art down to my mother. Me? I couldn't draw a stick figure without messing up, although I could whittle. My boyfriend, Nick Shaper, a detective for the Placer County Sheriff's Department and talented woodworker, had commented once on how lovely the chest was, its front engraved with the words *Love Never Fails*.

Candace slipped into the room as silently as a wraith. "Open it," she whispered. She'd donned a robe over her pajamas and was wearing a pair of bunny-faced slippers. November mornings could be nippy. Lake Tahoe had had its first snowfall two weeks ago, the last week in October. She drew closer. "Please."

I knelt and twisted the key in the brass lock. I opened the lid and drank in the woodsy balsamic aroma of cedar. Memories of my grandmother scudded through me. She'd had strong arms and had always smelled faintly of varnish.

"Aspen," Candace said, "please keep going."

"Okay."

At the top lay my pink baby blanket, hand-knitted by my mother. Beneath it, Rosie's yellow blanket. Our mother had used the finest merino wool yarn. I removed the blankets and set them on the floor to my right.

Beneath the blankets were two anti-tarnish bags. One held a silver bowl etched with my initials; the other held a bowl with Rosie's initials. Seeing them made me catch my breath. I had been certain that Rosie had stolen them and hawked them at a pawnshop. I set them beside the blankets and continued.

I removed a stack of pale pink onionskin envelopes, tied with pink ribbon. The faint scent of lavender clung to them. I spotted two sachets beneath them.

Candace held out a hand. "May I read them?"

I gave them to her.

She untied the ribbon, peeled off the top envelope, and pulled a sheet of matching stationery from within. I watched as she read silently. After a long moment, she said, "Aw."

"What does it say?"

"It's a letter from Grandma Lily to her grandma telling her about the first thing she cooked for Grandpa Jim after they got married."

My mother hadn't been much of a cook. Grandma Patrice had managed the kitchen.

I said, "She must have taken back the letters after Nana died. What did she make?"

"Pot roast. She wrote that it tasted like shoe leather." Candace giggled and sorted through the rest of them. "They're all letters between Nana and Grandma Lily."

I blinked away tears. "Let's keep moving."

Candace set the letters beside the bags holding the silver bowls and settled onto the floor, legs crisscrossed. "What're those? Under the sachets. More letters?" She motioned to another stack. The topmost envelope was plain, the return address smudged.

I removed the sachets and handed the stack to her. Then, intent on finding the gun Rosie had mentioned, I continued to remove items. There was an assortment of swimming and diving ribbons—I'd been the swimmer and Rosie the diver. For two years, prior to entering high school, we'd joined a local team. I dug deeper and found a dreamcatcher similar to the one hanging over my bed and a keepsake leather photo album, acid-free by the feel of it.

Flipping it open, I saw photographs of relatives: my father and his brothers, my grandfather and my grandmother, and my great-grandfather. There were no pictures of great-grandmother Blue Sky. A full-fledged Washoe Indian, she had refused to allow her image to be captured by a camera. She had permitted someone to draw her once. She'd been a handsome woman with long black hair and skin the color of cashews, but her most intriguing features were her entrancing eyes and prominent cheekbones.

Next, I discovered a white wedding veil and wedding dress, wrapped in what appeared to be dry-cleaner plastic. The dress was my mother's, I supposed. It wasn't mine. I'd given my wedding dress to a small chapel that helped the poor find a moment of wedded bliss, hoping whomever wore it might find the happiness that had eluded me.

Beneath the dress was a red-and-white quilt. Grandma Patrice must have made it. Each stitch was perfect. The word *Love*, in the same font as on the hope chest, had been stitched into the framework multiple times.

"Aspen," Candace said, "listen to this." She was browsing through the correspondence. "'My love, I treasure you more than life itself. James.' Isn't that romantic?"

"It is. Mom and Dad met during the summer at Meeks Bay. They'd both worked there." Meeks Bay was a recreation and camping area on the west side of Lake Tahoe, not far from where I lived.

"And this one," Candace continued. "'Lily, you are as beautiful as a sunrise.'"

My heart wrenched, in a good way. My parents had shared a unique love. I felt that way about Nick. Would we last? We lived in the present; we hadn't talked about the future.

"Listen to this: 'Dearest Lillian, we are so happy to have you join our family. Your spirit is ardent, and your heart is courageous. James could not have found a more beautiful bride. With love, Blue Sky and Jonathan.'"

Tears pressed at the corners of my eyes as emotions churned inside me. Why hadn't my mother shown me these letters when I was growing up? I'd known that my ancestors had adored her, but their words, in writing, made me choke up with pride.

"Uh-oh." Candace frowned. "I found one from my mom."

"What does it say?"

"'Give it a rest, Lily. Your wayward daughter, Rosie.'"

I rolled my eyes. "Late in high school, your mother took to calling our mother Lily. To change the dynamic, I'm pretty sure. Mom was always asking your mother to go straight."

Candace shuffled to the next letter, written on green floral paper. "'Dear Lily, I hope you can help.'" She frowned. "This one isn't from my mom."

I peered at her. "Who wrote it?"

She skimmed to the end. "I don't know. There's a pretty *M* engraved on the top. I think a page is missing. Whoever wrote it marked this page with the number one."

"Does the writer say help with what?"

Candace said, "It says, 'My mother might be sick. I hate what she's doing. She—' It cuts off there."

I slipped the letter from Candace's hand and examined it. The cursive writing was elegant. I flipped over the sheet. Nothing on the reverse side. The letter must have mistakenly found its way into the pile. Not unheard of. My mother's office had often been a mess.

"I wrote letters like that," Candace said. "But I never mailed them."

"Who did you write?"

"You." She ran her lip between her teeth. "I tore them up."

I set the letter aside and swooped her into a hug. "I'm sorry I let you stay in that situation so long."

"It's okay. You didn't know."

As a psychologist, I should have seen the signs.

Candace pressed apart, gathered the letters, set them into a pile, and put them beside the chest.

I peered at the stack. *Mother.* The initial *M.* The elegant cursive writing, as if done by an artist.

"Yoo-hoo." Candace flicked her fingers in front of my face. "What are you thinking?"

"I was wondering whether Mia, my mother's partner's daughter, might have written the letter and, if she had, what my mother's response was," I said. "Growing up, Mia and your mom spent a lot of time together. Anything Mia did, your mother wanted to do. When Mia took up long-distance running, so did your mom. When Mia took up guitar, Rosie did, too. When Mia learned to shoot a bow and arrow, Rosie wanted to become an ace. They were inseparable until—" I hesitated.

"Until Mom got hooked on drugs," Candace stated, like an adult assessing reality.

"Mia followed the rules. Your mother drew outside the lines." I clapped my hands. "No more walking down Memory Lane. Whatever Mia and my mother did or didn't hash out is old news. Moving on."

I removed a selection of baby outfits from the hope chest. Pink elephants. Yellow giraffes. Clearly, my mother had selected one color theme for my sister and another for me.

By the time I reached the bottom of the chest, there was only one thing left—a foot-square cedar box, its lid carved with flowers. There was no gun.

Candace said, "The box is beautiful. Open it."

"I would if I could."

"Isn't it a box?"

"It might be. Or it could be a work of art." I explained how Grandma Patrice had made all sorts of boxes. Some you could open; some you couldn't.

I twisted the box right and left, checking for seams or any indication there was a lid. I shook the box and heard something move inside. Not with a clack or jolt, suggesting that whatever was inside was nestled in some kind of padding. I searched again for a seam and found a tiny square button at the lower center of the right side. I pressed and the lid clicked open. I lifted it and stared at the contents.

A Colt .45. Wedged into black velvet.

Chapter 3

While Candace showered to get ready for school, I inspected the Colt. I didn't own a gun, but I knew my way around firearms. I'd trained at a range. My aunt and Nick had both encouraged me to do so. The safety was on. The magazine was empty. There were no bullets in the cedar box. Was the gun a keepsake?

As I returned the gun to the cedar box and set the box at the bottom of the hope chest, questions roiled in my mind. If the killer had used the gun, why not steal it? Why empty it of bullets and return the gun to the hope chest? And another thing . . . why put all of the other items neatly on top of it? Wouldn't the killer have been in a hurry and dumped the things inside?

A half hour later Candace, looking dazed, sat at the picnic-style table in the dining area as I made us a hearty breakfast.

The sun was rising as I sat down to eat. Striations of gray and orange clouds decorated the sky. I stared at my scrambled eggs and my stomach lurched. I wasn't hungry, but I knew I needed fuel. Candace pushed her food around with her fork but didn't take a bite. Out of view, I could hear Cinder chowing down on his kibble and slurping water. He hadn't a clue what was going on. Oh, to be a dog.

"What are you going to do with the gun?" Candace set her fork down.

"I'm going to leave it where it is and talk to Aunt Max about it. And I'm removing the hope chest's key."

She huffed, chin jutting forward. "I wouldn't touch the gun. Ever."

"I believe you, but I don't want any of your friends to gain access."

"Waverly's the only person I've ever had over." The moment Candace and Waverly had met, they had become fast friends. They both loved skiing and books, and yes, boys.

"Rory," I stated.

"Get real. He's come to pick me up once. Okay, more than once. But he hasn't stayed." The edge in her voice was challenging.

I didn't take the bait. Instead, I downed a bite of my eggs. They tasted bitter. Off. They weren't. It was me. My taste buds. But if I ate,

Candace would eat. I forced down another bite and gazed out the window at the distant view of the lake.

Why had my father owned a gun? At first, his business had done well, allowing him to invest in a family vacation home at Rubicon Bay, but ultimately, a few ticked-off clients, as Rosie had called them, had refused to pay and the business had flagged. Dad had been forced to sell the vacation home. Had one of his clients threatened Dad or the family? Or, as Rosie had suggested, had our father gotten mixed up in something criminal in an effort to recoup his losses?

No, I didn't believe it. I couldn't believe it. Dad had walked the straight and narrow.

"Shouldn't you have the gun checked out?" Candace asked.

"I will. But I want to research its provenance first."

"Its what?"

"Ownership or previous ownership." Maybe the gun had belonged to my father's father or grandfather. Or perhaps my father had received the gun as payment. If that were the case, I wanted to make sure it hadn't been used in a crime other than, and hopefully not in, my parents' murders.

"Oh, right," Candace said. "The police do it all the time using the serial number."

I smiled at my niece. She watched a lot of crime shows on television. Like me, she enjoyed solving puzzles. But she was naïve. "Aunt Max claims it doesn't always work that way," I said. "People think there's a master list somewhere, like for guns all over the world, starting with the number one, but there isn't."

"Really?"

"No, ma'am. There is no big computer keeping track of every serial number. It's not like the VIN number on a car."

"The what?" Candace squinted.

I explained what that was. She was learning to drive. "There is no national database of guns, no centralized record of who owns what. This is one of the main issues between gun rights activists and their opponents. There is the National Tracing Center and, on any given day, agents run a thousand-plus traces. They sort through enormous record books that gun stores are required to keep."

Candace said, "TMI."

I understood the verbal shorthand: *too much information*. I locked my lips with an imaginary key and pointed to her food. "Eat."

• • •

After dropping Candace at school, I drove home and made a beeline for the bedroom. I hadn't returned all the items to the hope chest. I'd set many in piles against the far wall. I retrieved the pen and pad beside my bed and knelt on one knee beside the chest. Cinder crowded me and whimpered. I nudged him away and commanded he lie down. He did. I unlocked the hope chest, lifted out the gun box, opened it, and removed the gun. I peered at its serial number. I knew from experience that numbers could often be misread. Zero versus the letter *O*, the numeral one versus the lowercase letter *l* or the small-cap *I*. I jotted down the number meticulously. I even took a picture of it with the camera on my cell phone.

As I was setting the gun in its case, my phone rang. Rosie.

"Did you find it?" she blurted out before I could say hello. This time her speech was slurred. "The gun?"

"Rosie—"

"Did you?"

"Yes."

"What are you going to do? What's next? I want to help."

"Not when you're loaded."

"Don't be a self-righteous—" She cut herself off. At least she had the sense not to denigrate me. Assailing me with verbal attacks would not win her points. "Sorry. I . . . you know . . . I . . .." She clicked her tongue. "Touch base when you have a plan." She ended the call abruptly.

I closed the gun case lid, ready to return the case to the chest, when I noticed something on the left side of the box. A second smaller button. I removed the gun from the case, set it carefully on the floor, and depressed the button on the box. A slim drawer popped out. Within was a receipt for the Colt .45 from a gun shop in the Bay Area. The receipt was made out to Grayson Baxter—Grandpa Gray. My mother's father.

Grandpa Gray, a man of English-Scottish origin and educated on the East Coast, had moved west with Grandma Patrice when he'd landed a job at General Motors in the San Francisco Bay Area. He could tell the most terrific stories. Bald-faced lies, my grandmother had kidded, but I'd listened intently to each one. Sadly, Grandpa Gray had died penniless, his bad business decisions as well as his gambling addiction destroying him and taking their toll on our family.

I stared at the gun and thought of my mother. How had she felt about inheriting it? She had been a peaceful soul, as artistic as her mother, and driven by the will to create beauty in the world. Why had she kept it? Why hadn't she mentioned it to me?

Rosie was right. I needed to learn more.

Chapter 4

I hooked a leash onto Cinder and headed out for a walk to clear my mind and to breathe in the sweet citrusy aroma of the sugar pines.

"What am I going to do, dog?" I said as I closed the door and we trotted down the steps. I couldn't go off half-cocked. I doubted the Atherton police would reopen the case purely because I asked. Other than finding a gun in my parents' hope chest, I had no new evidence to compel them to do so. I needed a plan of attack, a way to cajole them into letting me have a look-see at the case file. Maybe they'd missed something that only I, a family member, might notice. Granted, the passage of time didn't make leads easier to follow, it made the search harder, but I had to try.

My aunt Max sent me a text. I stopped next to a tree to read it: *RU coming in?*

I responded: *Soon.*

Seconds later, Nick sent me a text: *Been thinking about you. Everything OK?*

Nick and I didn't have ESP, but we were often in sync. We'd been dating ever since he—*we*—had solved the murder of my friend Vikki. After the debacle of my marriage, I hadn't believed I could love anyone again. But Nick was different. He was intense yet fun and filled with integrity. With his help, I'd been able to guide Candace back to health. Not many men would have given so much of themselves.

I replied: *Sort of. Got time to talk?*

My cell phone rang. Nick. I stabbed the Accept button. "Hey."

"What's wrong?" Nick asked, his voice gentle, coaxing.

I told him about Rosie's call. "I think I should go to Atherton, as promised, and at least review the file. Maybe the police missed something."

"But you don't think so."

"I didn't press the police to do more because I was young and new to college and . . . I trusted them." I didn't add that one of the reasons I hadn't trusted Nick when I'd first met him was because of the lack of results in my parents' case. "Rosie was useless."

"What about your mother's business partner?"

"Tammie nagged the police for a long time. At least six months. Before working with Mom, she'd worked as a bookkeeper for a law firm that specialized in criminal defense cases. She and Mom met when the firm collaborated with my father on a case." I pulled Cinder to a stop beneath the boughs of a pine tree. "She knew the ins and outs of the legal system and gave the police all sorts of guff, but when the case went cold, she gave up. She, like everybody else, had a life."

"I'll go with you," Nick said.

"No. You don't have—"

"I want to. I've got some vacation time stored up."

"Which we were going to use to take a trip to Napa."

Nick chuckled, low and warm. "Eleven months from now. Plenty of time to rack up extra days by then." He said something to someone in the background. "Aspen, I've got to go. I'll pack a bag and meet you at your place by dusk."

"Thank you."

He blew me a kiss and ended the call.

Cinder tugged on the leash and yelped. He wanted a free run. I took him to the cabin. Even in dog-friendly Lake Tahoe, dogs were required to be on a leash unless on their own property. I released him and he tore to a tree to torment an unsuspecting pair of squirrels. While he gallivanted, I called my neighbor, a crafter who ran her business out of her house.

"Jewel," I said, "it's me. I've got an emergency. I have to go to the Bay Area. My aunt will watch Candace," I said, although I hadn't asked her yet, "but Cinder can be a handful—"

"Bring him over. You know my little mutt loves him." Jewel had a warm voice and a warmer heart. "Anything else I can do to help?"

"No, thanks," I said. "I really appreciate this. I promise I'll return the favor."

"That's what neighbors are for."

An hour later, I strode into the Maxine Adams Detective Agency, located at the north end of the lake in Incline Village. Although the agency was housed in a quaint cottage outfitted with couches, reading chairs, and lamps, beneath its homey veneer it was a top-notch operation. My aunt had made sure that we had up-to-date computers, the latest software, and state-of-the-art security devices.

Neither of our two veteran investigators were in. Both worked late hours.

Rowena, our chatty receptionist, popped off the couch. Though she was nearly seventy, she didn't look fifty. Good diet, plenty of water, and a glass of wine each night did the trick, she'd confided. She had secured her frizzy hair with a claw-style clip and had dressed warmly for the weather in a wool sweater over corduroys. "What a surprise," she said, as if I didn't show up five days a week.

Honestly, the surprise was Rowena being present. She rarely came in to work, yet my aunt paid her a handsome salary. I figured she had dirt on my aunt—something to do with Max's behavior during college. They'd been roommates.

"Well, well, look what the cat dragged in." My aunt, who due to a minor medical scare had been on a serious paleo diet, had dropped one hundred pounds. Now, a svelte one hundred and ninety-eight, she looked positively radiant in a plum sweater and jeans tucked into boots. No more muumuus for her. "Paleo blueberry muffin?" She entered from the small kitchen holding a plate of treats. "Grain-free, dairy-free, gluten-free, and refined-sugar-free."

"Not hungry."

"What's going on?"

"What isn't?" I countered, my humor lackluster.

"Sit. Spill."

The moment my parents were killed, my aunt and my uncle Matthew, who died from a heart attack a few years ago, had reached out to Rosie and me. Rosie had wanted nothing to do with them. Max, in particular. Our aunt could be judgmental and not shy about sharing her opinions on everything from politics to books. I adored her. Her humor was fine-tuned, her brain superb.

I filled her in on Rosie's urgent call and me finding the Colt .45.

"Do you think the robber used it in the murders?" Max asked.

I outlined all the reasons why I thought that was a long shot—the gun being in its case and the hope chest items neatly folded on top of it.

"Give it to me." She held out a hand, expecting me to cough up the gun. "I'll find out more about it. Have it tested."

"I locked it in the hope chest. For now."

"All right." She set the treats aside and sat at the round table in the center of the room. "Join me."

I did.

"What's really troubling you?" she asked.

"Why didn't Mom tell me about the gun?"

"I'm sure she had a good reason."

"You knew my grandfather better than me." I was eleven when he died of pneumonia and other complications. "Why would he have had it?"

"It was probably a Baxter tradition. His father was a hunter."

"I didn't know that."

Max's mouth turned up. "Your grandfather was a terrific guy. Sure, he had his drawbacks, but he was a kind man. And funny? Could he ever tell a mean story. *Mean*, in a good way. He made everyone laugh."

Not everybody. I recalled a few quarrels between my grandparents after we'd bought and moved into the house that they had owned. Doozies, my mother had called the spats. My parents had purchased the house to help pay off debts Grandpa Gray had racked up. During one of the fights, Grandma Patrice—she was no shrinking violet; she could swear like a truckdriver—had dubbed him a good-for-nothing. Had she known about the gun? Of course she had. She'd made the box it was in.

Max tapped the table. "Go to Atherton. I'll assign your current case to Yaz and Darcy." Yaz Yazdani and Darcy Doherty were two of the finest investigators around. Darcy was a wizard at financial searches. Yaz, because of the hit-and-run incident that had killed his lover, was dedicated to tracking down perps and making sure justice was served. "They'll get the job done."

I had been tailing a man whose ex-wife hadn't been receiving support checks. A landscaper, he claimed to be out of work. In truth, he was doing plenty of jobs and getting paid cash under the table. I had documentation. Max said we needed more before his ex-wife could haul him into court.

"Have you called the Atherton police?" Max asked.

"That's next on my agenda."

She rose from her chair. I stood, too.

She gripped my shoulders and peered into my eyes. "Don't expect closure."

"I told Candace the same thing. Speaking of which, could I ask for a favor?"

"Yes, I'll watch her."

Relief washed over me. "She has school every day until the Wednesday before Thanksgiving."

"That's two weeks away. Do you figure you'll be gone that long?"

"I don't know. I hope not. I'll pack a bag with food she likes. She's dutiful with homework. You won't need to press her. And she's neat, so you won't have to ask her to—"

"Relax." Max clasped my hand. "I've raised a child. She'll be fine. I'll bring my granddaughter over on the weekend to entertain her."

"Candace probably has plans with Waverly. She'll be heartbroken if she has to cancel."

"I'll make sure she obeys her curfew." Max moved to Rowena, who had returned to her post at the reception desk and seemed busy, though I was pretty sure she was surfing news sites. She, like my aunt, enjoyed being on top of current events.

I strode to the desk I shared with Darcy and Yaz, settled in front of the computer, opened the Internet browser, and pulled up the telephone number for the Atherton police department.

After locating it, I called and asked for the Investigation Division. Detective Sergeant Quincy took the call. I asked if Detective Sergeant Evers was available. Quincy informed me that he'd retired. Disheartened, I asked Quincy if I could set an appointment tomorrow to meet with whomever might be in charge of cold cases. He said it was he and asked what this was in regard to.

"The double homicide of Lily and James Adams fourteen years ago." Their names caught in my throat. "I'm their daughter, Aspen Adams."

Quincy said he was sorry for my loss and, as anticipated, inquired whether I had new information to share. I answered in the negative but asked if he had time to meet and respond to a few questions anyway. He told me to arrive at ten a.m.

Next, I checked my cell phone for Tammie Laplante's contact information. Finding it, I drew in a deep breath and tapped in her number. I reached her voicemail.

"Hello, it's Tammie Laplante, Interior Motives Designs. Thank you so much for your call. I look forward to serving your needs. Please leave your name and number at the tone, and if you feel the need to repeat them, please do. You will have plenty of time. Have a terrific day."

After the tone, I left a message. "Tammie, it's Aspen. Adams," I said, adding my surname, as if she wouldn't remember me.

She would. Not even a question. She, like my aunt, had jumped in to be my second mother when Mom died. For six months, I'd let her. I'd needed the support. After my parents' case went cold, Tammie and I had drifted apart, as if communicating with each other would dredge up painful memories. She'd attended my wedding, and we'd exchanged Christmas cards, but that was about it.

"I hope you're well," I said. "Listen, I'm coming to town and need suggestions on where to stay." I hadn't visited the Atherton area in years. It was a strictly residential town, but in nearby Menlo Park or Palo Alto, the business and residential towns that abutted Stanford University, there was plenty of lodging. "A hotel or motel or maybe an Airbnb," I added. "Call me." I left my number.

Within a minute, my phone rang. Tammie's name appeared on the screen. I answered.

"How are you?" she gushed. "What's going on? Why are you coming south? For a reunion at Stanford? You can stay with me."

Her voice was warm and so familiar. I would never forget how she'd encouraged me to return to school after the funeral. *Stick with it,* she'd said. *Your education will take you as far as you can reach.* That first Christmas, when I couldn't remain at the dorm, I'd stayed at my girlfriend Serenity's house, but I'd enjoyed Christmas dinner with Tammie and her daughter. Tammie had regaled me with stories about my parents, in particular my mother.

"I don't want to intrude," I said. "My boyfriend, Nick, will be with me, and—"

"Boyfriend? Oh, Aspen, I'm so happy to hear you've met someone, although I have to say I really did like Damian."

Damian Saint. My ex-husband. Virtuoso conductor. Caught chasing the lead violinist around in her dainties. He had been wearing less.

"I know he screwed up," Tammie went on, "but he was so clever and handsome and talented."

He was talented, all right, at putting me down and making me feel bad about myself. I'd reverted to my maiden name after the divorce.

"You have to tell me about your boyfriend," Tammie said. "I can't wait to hear——"

"Tammie," I cut her off, "let's catch up when I see you."

"Of course. You have my address. What time will you arrive?"

"No," I said firmly. "Nick and I will want our own place."

"Fine. Let me shoot you a few contacts. One of them will be happy to rent to you for a few nights."

• • •

That afternoon, I picked up Candace from school and we returned home, packed up Cinder and his food, and took him to Jewel's house. Her daughter, an enthusiastic young adult, was over the moon that she and her mother could help out.

Then I supervised Candace as she filled her suitcase for a week with my aunt.

"A week," she grumbled. "What am I going to do for a week without you and Cinder?"

"School. And Aunt Max is fully on board if you want the weekend to hang out with Waverly. With limits."

Candace didn't climb into my Jeep kicking and screaming, but she was definitely put out. Arms folded. Mouth a thin line. Before slipping out of the car at my aunt's house, she said, "You'll call me. Text me. Keep me in the loop. And Mom, too. Because maybe . . ." Her voice grew faint.

Maybe the answers I found would save her mother. Maybe.

I promised I would.

23

Chapter 5

At ten past six, Nick knocked on the front door of the cabin and entered. I was in the kitchen, loading a cooler with food.

"You need to keep the door locked," he cautioned from the foyer.

I peeked around the corner. He was smiling, his mouth curved up on one side.

"I unlocked it two minutes ago," I said. "Don't be such a dork."

After he slung his duffel onto the floor, he joined me in the kitchen and pecked me on the cheek. I nuzzled his neck even though it was icy cold from the night air and drank in his aroma—a hint of licorice and lemon. If I weren't packing for a trip, I'd have guided him to the bedroom.

"I like that you worry about me," I whispered.

"I know."

His eyes, his fabulously roguish eyes, drank me in. As always, he looked handsome in his standard black shirt and jeans, a hank of blue-black hair dangling down his forehead. When we'd first met, sparks had flown—not the good kind. After he finalized his divorce, he gave in to the feelings he had for me and I for him.

He caressed my hair. "You okay?"

"I want to help Rosie."

"And yourself."

"It would be nice to have closure."

"Where are we staying?" He helped me put the final items into the cooler.

"A house that my mom's former partner found for us." Tammie had texted me the location within an hour.

"Tammie and your mom teamed up after Tammie quit her job at the law firm, right?"

"Good memory." I smiled. "The house belongs to a Stanford professor who's visiting an overseas campus until the end of the year. He's one of Tammie's clients and willing to rent it out week to week for friends of friends."

At six thirty, we stowed our luggage into my Jeep, leaving Nick's Wrangler parked by the woodpile, and got on the road. I was smart enough to have purchased two deli sandwiches for our dinner. The drive to the Bay Area would take around four hours.

For the first hour and a half, with the heater cranked up to ward off the chill, we listened to a Pandora selection of jazz and ate our sandwiches. As we passed Auburn and the swell of traffic grew thicker, Nick switched off the music, stuffed the remains of our dinner into the cooler, and said, "Do you want to tell me what you remember?"

"Now?"

"Whenever."

My eyes misted over. I wiped them with the sleeve of my *I Love Tahoe* T-shirt. "I was in school. I looked over the incident report, but I didn't ask to see the crime scene or the photos. I was—"

"Distraught."

"To say the least. I remember that first night. Tammie offered to put up Rosie, Candace, and me for a few days, if we wanted. We'd have police protection, in case the killer was someone other than a random robber, but Rosie and I didn't want that. Tammie's place was nice but too small for all of us. I stayed with my girlfriend Serenity. Rosie took Candace to a friend's apartment."

"Do I know Serenity?"

"No. She hasn't come to Tahoe yet." I drew in a deep breath and continued. "That night, we did go to Tammie's to convene, and the detective was there. Evers. Elton Evers. Big guy. Broad shoulders. Whitish gray hair. I remember feeling small standing in front of him, answering his questions."

"What kind of questions?"

"Where was I at the time of the murder? When did I last speak to my father or mother? Evers had extremely pale eyes, but they were warm, not judgmental."

Nick swiveled in the passenger seat. "You liked him."

"I trusted him. At first."

"Not later on."

"He didn't get the job done." I blew out a long breath.

"Were you a suspect?" Nick asked.

"Not really. I was in a psychology class at the time. Lots of witnesses. But the police—Evers and his partner, Foxx—weren't willing

25

to rule anyone out." I ran my fingers along the steering wheel, the movement soothing.

"When had you last spoken to your parents?" Nick asked.

"That day. Mom texted me to say they were safely at the airport."

"Airport?"

"They were supposed to fly to Mexico. They were going to Cabo. I called her to wish them a happy anniversary." The memory of our conversation sliced through me. "Dad got sick at the airport. Something he'd eaten the night before." Even now, I could hear my mother's voice telling me they were headed home and not to worry. She would touch base with me the next day—Sunday. She said the last thing she and Dad wanted to do was to go on a trip and stay in the hotel room. They'd bought trip insurance. They would take the trip another time.

I scrubbed the nape of my neck.

"Are you okay?" Nick caressed my arm.

"Let's leave it alone for tonight, okay?" My stomach was in knots. "How was work?"

He smiled. The dimple in his cheek deepened. "Nothing major going on." For the next hour, he regaled me with his benign week of events. An auto break-in. A false alarm. A suspicious death that proved to be the result of overexertion during a sexual encounter. When he'd exhausted those stories, he started talking about how well his sister, Natalie, was doing. A former alcoholic, she had been sober for quite a while and was working at Safeway in Lake Tahoe. Recently, she'd begun dating an artisan in Tahoe City—he made exquisite pottery, which he displayed in his gift shop—and she was ready to move out on her own. Natalie had been living with Nick for two years to help her deal with sobriety. I told him how happy I was for her. And for him.

By the time we reached our destination, I felt lighter and ready to face the challenge.

"Here we are," I said.

I pulled into the driveway of the place that Tammie had found for us—a three-bedroom ranch-style home in Menlo Park. It was brown with white trim. "The key is in the planter to the right of the door," I told Nick.

Like so many homes in town, the garage was detached from the main house. The interior décor was varied. The living room had a masculine feel, heavy on leather, its walnut bookcase filled with academic journals, but the kitchen was all white and updated. Fresh flowers adorned the kitchen table. A sheet of paper encased in a clear acrylic sleeve on the counter listed where everything was in the house and provided emergency phone numbers. The aroma of Lysol and vinegar lingered in the air, as if a housecleaner had tended to the house earlier.

Nick and I put the groceries away, settled into the master bedroom, which Tammie had redesigned, did our ablutions, and fell into bed.

At seven the next morning, the rude sounds of a lawn mower and leaf blower woke me. I yawned and slipped out of bed. "No time like the present."

Nick growled and rolled over.

"I'll shower first." I padded into the bathroom, the floor cold beneath my toes but not as cold as it would have been at home. The temperature in the Bay Area was a good twenty degrees warmer than in Tahoe.

I dressed in a white silk blouse, black trousers, black blazer, and a pair of sensible heels. For some reason, I'd felt that meeting the man in charge of my parents' cold case required a bit of decorum. I brewed two cups of French roast coffee using the Keurig machine and enticed Nick with a mug to rouse him from sleep.

At five to ten, we drove to the Atherton Police Station.

• • •

The precinct was a simple red-brick building and currently surrounded by construction.

Nick and I entered and stopped at the front counter, which was protected by a bulletproof window. The dispatcher, a chipper young woman, her hair pulled into a ponytail, greeted me. "How may I help you?"

"I have an appointment with Detective Sergeant Quincy. I'm Aspen Adams. This is Detective Sergeant Nick Shaper, Placer County Sheriff's Office."

"I'm off duty," Nick said, although, out of habit, he displayed his badge.

"Right," the woman said. "He's expecting you. Follow me."

She buzzed us in and guided us through the building and out the rear door. We crossed a few feet of yard and climbed the stairs into a modular trailer. "Have a seat." She indicated two chairs we could sit in. "Water cooler's over there if you're thirsty."

As she crossed to a tallish man whose back was to us, presumably to make our presence known, we sat. I perused our surroundings. The Investigative Division shared the huge trailer with other divisions of the Town of Atherton, like Community Services. The noise level was muted but constant. The aroma of coffee hung in the air.

A few minutes later, the tallish man approached. I'd wager that he was a regular visitor at the gym. The muscles of his arms pressed at the seams of his blue-striped shirt. He extended his hand. "Miss Adams, I'm Detective Sergeant Quincy." He looked to be in his fifties. His eyes were keen behind his rimless glasses. "I'm sorry Detective Sergeant Evers is no longer here."

"Detective Sergeant Nick Shaper, Placer County Sheriff's Department." Nick jutted out his hand and they shook. "I'm off duty, so Nick will do."

"Nick, I'm Andrew." Quincy focused his gaze on me. "Miss Adams."

"Aspen, please."

"I spoke with Evers after our conversation, and he would like to see you."

"Really?" I raised an eyebrow. "Are you sure?"

"He said this case has nagged him for far too long. He's more than willing to let you go through his case notes. However"—Quincy's mouth turned up on the right—"let me warn you. I thought I was a note taker? Elton Evers has me beat, hands down." He chuckled.

"You like him."

"Sure do. Admire him, in fact. I reported to him the past few years, until he retired. I didn't work your parents' case. I was still in the military then. Detective John Foxx was second in charge. John has since passed away."

"I'm sorry to hear that," I said.

"Natural causes. Not on the job." Quincy pursed his lips. "If you don't want to go all the way to Napa to see Evers, I'm sure I could walk you through—"

"He lives in Napa Valley? How can he—" I cut myself off.

Quincy said, "Afford to live there?"

Napa was a pricey area. On the other hand, I'd often wondered how a cop or any civil servant could afford to live in the Bay Area. The median price for a home was well over a million dollars.

"Many of us settled here before the Silicon Valley housing bubble," Quincy said. "We were lucky. As for retiring in Napa? Evers's brother is a vintner, and he gave Evers the cottage behind the main house, rent-free. How could he refuse?" Quincy folded his hands in front of him. "As I was saying, if for some reason you don't learn what you need from Evers, feel free to come back and ask me anything."

"I appreciate that."

On the way to my Jeep, Nick said, "Guess we'll get that vacation in Napa earlier than we planned."

I elbowed him. "This is not a vacation. You are not off the hook."

The sound of his laughter helped lessen the tension in my shoulders.

Chapter 6

Two hours later, delayed by dense traffic, we pulled into the Napa Valley area. Nick had offered to drive; I was a jumble of nerves.

During my teens, my mother had done the décor for a number of clients who'd maintained homes in Atherton as well as Napa. Often, I'd joined her on her jaunts to preview their places. Napa, she told me, was one of the original counties in California after it became a state. For a long time, it had been the center for silver and quicksilver mining. Now, it was primarily agricultural. Commercial wineries dated back to the 1850s. Although I'd seen photos of the devastation caused by the 2017 wildfire, thankfully the recent month of rain had made the valley lush and green. Many of the homes were post–World War II structures. Simple. One-story. No bells and whistles.

However, as we drove north into vineyard country, the sun bright in the cloudless sky, Nick couldn't hide his amazement at some of the mansions perched atop the hills. A slow rumbling "Whoa" escaped his lips.

"Don't look so impressed," I joshed. "Incline Village has Billionaire's Row." The road that abutted Tahoe, on the north side of the lake, boasted a wealth of luxurious homes. Each of them whoa-worthy.

"That's about a mile long," he countered. "This goes on and on."

I didn't argue.

The Evers Family Vineyard was situated east of the Silverado Trail and consisted of over four hundred acres. The road to the main building and tasting rooms provided an exquisite view of the valley below.

"Not a bad way to retire," Nick said as he negotiated the sharp turns.

"We'll stay in Tahoe," slipped out of my mouth. I immediately regretted the use of *we*.

Nick threw me a comforting look. "Yes, *we* will."

That was the closest we'd ever come to talking about the future. The thought of spending the rest of my life with him sent a delicious shiver down my spine.

"I already miss Lake Tahoe," I said.

"Picture it in your mind whenever you need a fix."

• • •

Detective Sergeant Evers was sitting in a wicker chair on the porch of his *cottage*—a house twice as large as my cabin, built in a Mediterranean style. He rose when Nick pulled the Jeep to a stop.

I climbed out, then Nick.

Evers shambled toward us looking older than I remembered. Fourteen years had passed, of course, but there was something else. His eyes had lost their luster and his once-ruddy skin was fleshier and pale. His navy jogging suit hung on his slim frame; he'd lost a lot of weight. "My, how you've matured, Miss Adams."

"Aspen, please."

I introduced Nick and offered his title.

"Placer County Sheriff's Department, huh?" Evers pumped Nick's hand. "I knew someone in the Auburn office a long time ago. A tech guy. Helped him solve an identity theft case. Can't remember his name right off the top of my head, but then I can't remember much without consulting notes. This way. Can I pour you a cup of coffee?"

"I'd love some," I said. Neither Nick nor I had eaten before leaving the house. We hadn't had much of an appetite. I'd packed energy bars in the car for later, just in case.

"Let's go to the kitchen." Evers ushered us into his home and down a hall. "It's my favorite room in the house."

The kitchen was elegantly rustic, done in a modern farmhouse style, with dark brown appliances, white marbled counters, and whitewashed cabinetry. The hutch served more as a bookcase than a cupboard. I noticed nonfiction as well as fiction titles on the shelves. A Filipino woman in a white uniform was wiping down the stovetop. The aroma of yeast hung in the air. A loaf of fresh-baked bread sat on a ceramic baking sheet on the countertop.

"My live-in nurse, Blessica," Evers said, introducing her. "Can't live without her. Actually, I won't live much longer, either way. I've got cancer. About two months to go, they tell me, but what do they know?"

"I'm sorry," I said.

He waved off my pity. "I've lived a full life. No complaints. My ex-wife might have a few. My son? He shouldn't. I put him through med school and introduced him to his wife. What a beauty she is. Sit." He gestured to the kitchen table. A newspaper lay folded at the far end. "Cream? Sugar?"

"Black for both of us," I said.

"That's the way I like it, too. Care for a slice of bread? Blessica is a great cook. She makes her own clarified butter."

I shook my head. Nick demurred.

Evers poured coffee into three brown mugs, placed them on the table, and settled into the armchair nearest the newspaper. "Down to business. Quincy says you want to review your parents' homicide case."

"That's right," I said, my voice breathier than I'd wanted. My heart was fluttering like a trapped bird. "Now that I have a little distance."

Evers took a sip of coffee and set the mug down with a clack. "For fourteen years that case has haunted me."

"Haunted how?" Nick asked.

The nurse brought a plate of cheese and fruit and a few cocktail napkins to the table. She also set a pad of paper and a pen next to Evers.

"No cookies in the house," Evers said to us. "Sorry about that. I can't eat sweets. Cancer loves sugar. And I love sugar. If it's here, I'll eat it. Then I could suffer diabetes. Don't want that. Cancer-induced brain fog is enough to deal with."

I'd heard of brain fog. Cancer drugs caused a patient to feel mentally incapable of focusing.

Evers downed a piece of cheese. *"Haunted,"* he said in response to Nick's question, "because I solved all my cases but one. The Adams's case." He thumped the table. "Let's have a look at my primary resource. I never worked a case where the killer's name wasn't in the file. Maybe fresh eyes will give us a new angle." He fetched a worn photo album from the hutch and returned to the table. "Andrew . . . Detective Sergeant Quincy probably told you I like to take notes. What I've really kept are complete case files. I documented all my findings with photos—duplicated for the official records—hence the book. You'll see that my partner, Foxx, and I conducted over one hundred interviews. Suspects. Neighbors. Clients of your father's. Clients of your mother's. Friends. Family. Your older sister, of course."

"Of course," I said.

"She wasn't guilty." Evers ran his finger along the label listing my parents' names and the date of their deaths. "No matter how I tried to spin it, your sister proved out. Yes, she showed up at the crime scene around six p.m., but shots were heard earlier, at four. Mistaken for backfires so the woman didn't call the police. The coroner estimated that your father died when those shots were heard. When your sister was still at her interview. Your mother"—Evers swallowed hard—"held on for quite a while. Her cell phone, sadly, was in her purse, which she'd dropped by the luggage in the foyer."

My heart wrenched as I grasped how long my mother must have suffered. Unable to call for help. Unable to save my father.

"How's your sister doing, by the way?" Evers asked, genuinely interested.

"Rosie is the reason I'm here. She—" I heaved a sigh. "She returned to drugs after all this and hasn't found her way to sobriety."

"Shame. She had a wicked sense of humor."

When, exactly, would Rosie have been able to display her sense of humor to the police? Maybe she'd sparred with them. Used sass as a defense. Put up her emotional armor and challenged them with sarcasm. I supposed many would mistake that for a wicked sense of humor.

"How's her daughter?" Evers asked. "She was a one-year-old at the time."

"She's a teenager now and living with me."

He raised an eyebrow.

"She was sick. I intervened."

"Good for you. We need more people to step up and be advocates." He swiveled the album. "Here we go. Are you sure you're up for this?" He regarded me. "I have something stronger than coffee, if you'd rather."

Under the table, Nick clasped my hand. To steel myself for what I knew was going to be rough waters, I squeezed his hand and broke free.

"I'm ready," I said.

Evers opened the cover. The first page held a copy of a photograph of my parents on their wedding day, one they displayed in a silver frame on the bureau in their bedroom. My father looked handsome in a navy suit, his black wavy hair styled off his face, his eyes gleaming with pride. My mother, light to his dark, was radiant in the floor-length white gown I'd found in the hope chest. Just a hint of cleavage. She wasn't wearing her veil in the photo. Her strawberry blonde hair graced her shoulders and made her look like a movie star. Her easy smile and steady gaze calmed me, as they always could.

"Go on," I said.

The next page held the coroner's report. The third was the incident report.

Nick spent a few minutes reading everything.

When he nodded, Evers proceeded. "The next few pages might be grueling. They're the crime scene photos."

I hadn't gone into my parents' house until a cleaning crew had rid it of any trace of violence.

"From all angles," Evers added.

"Got it. I'll be okay. I'm now a private investigator in Lake Tahoe."

"You've dealt with murders?"

"Yes." Over the past few years, I'd seen plenty of crime scene photos. I'd also found my friend Vikki dead, and not too long ago had attended two crime scenes with Nick to help solve murders committed by a news anchor's adoring fan who, in a demented way, had hoped to win her love. I wasn't inured to death, but I was stalwart. Or at least I thought I was until Evers turned the page.

Seeing my father on the carpet, facedown, his head in the direction of the mahogany hutch in the dining room of our house, a pool of blood spreading from beneath his body, made me want to heave. I covered my mouth with my hand.

"You okay?" Nick asked.

I tamped down the bile crawling up my esophagus and nodded.

According to the report, my father had been shot in the chest. He'd faced his killer. My mother, although she had been shot in the back, lay faceup.

Evers said, "I think she was bending over your father when she was shot."

"Meaning the killer sneaked up on her," I whispered.

"Or she simply ran to your father first."

Rosie said Mom had been alive when she'd arrived. Had our mother waited until the killer left before sliding off of our father so she could position herself faceup next to him? She was clasping his hand.

Tears pressed at the corners of my eyes. "Continue."

Nick's face remained stoic.

"Their suitcases were by the front door, as I mentioned," Evers said, making a note on the pad, as if something new had come to him.

Dad and Mom had taken a cab from the airport to home. Dad would have entered first. Mom would have lagged behind to pay the driver. She'd always handled cash transactions.

"There was no house alarm," Evers said.

My father had been against the idea of installing one. He'd trusted in the goodness of people, a belief instilled in him by Blue Sky.

"My take?" Evers double-tapped the pen on the table. "Your father entered the foyer, and hearing a noise in the dining room, didn't retreat. He advanced. Maybe he thought it was someone he knew, like the housekeeper."

"Not her regular day."

"As we discovered. Plus, we ruled her out because she'd left for a vacation in Guatemala."

"Did my parents call or text anyone about their plans to return?" I asked.

"You and the travel agent were the only two texts or calls that day. Both made from your mother's cell phone." Evers turned a page. "Anyway, we believe your father surprised the robber. The robber fired. Once. Twice. Your mother came running when she heard the shots. The cabbie had already driven off. We questioned him. He didn't see anything. Didn't remember any vehicles on the street, either."

I focused on Evers. "You said someone heard the shots."

"Yes, a neighbor. As I said, she thought a car had backfired."

"When did she come forward?"

"Not until we were canvassing the neighborhood."

Where had the killer parked? Had anyone taken note of a car that hadn't belonged? Because of an incident in a parking garage when a creep had followed me and had tried to force his way into my car—thank heavens for auto-lock doors—I always paid attention to my surroundings, but not everyone did.

"Moving on," Evers said.

The next few pages were filled with evidentiary photographs, each numbered and accompanied by a typed sheet of analysis. Quincy hadn't been kidding when he'd said Evers was a prolific note taker.

"No fingerprints in the dining room," Evers said.

"The killer wiped things down?" I asked.

"Must have. Didn't even find your parents' prints."

Per the findings, there were strands of hair in the foyer, living room, and kitchen—Mom's, Dad's, mine, Rosie's, the housekeeper's, and Tammie's. Like my father, my mother had maintained a home office. Tammie had come over often to discuss their clients' needs. I used to love venturing into the office and going through the books of fabric swatches, feeling the textures and admiring the variety of colors.

"No other hair identified?" Nick asked.

"None," Evers said.

"Did the killer vacuum?" I asked before realizing my idiocy. "Strike that dumb question." If the killer had cleaned up, all of the hair would have been sucked up.

Evers said, "A witness claimed to have seen someone in black with very short hair running through the neighborhood the night before."

"Friday," I said.

"That's right."

"And this matters, why?"

"Because he thought maybe the killer made a trial run," Evers said. "To time things. The guy called the ADT security people Friday, but they had no reason to follow up. There were no break-ins."

"Who was the witness?"

"Viraj Patel," he said, pronouncing it correctly, accent on the second syllable. "Your neighbor."

Chapter 7

"Mr. Patel," I groused and leaned back in the chair.

Evers gazed at me waiting for more. Nick, too.

"Patel lives—or lived—across the street." I deferred to Evers.

"Still lives there, as far as I know."

"He's a programmer who refuses to leave the house," I said. "After his wife died, he became vile and lashed out at neighbors. He doesn't like Native Americans. He doesn't like Irishmen, either. Or Catholics or Muslims. In fact, the only people Patel does like are his own kind, according to sources—programmers or people from Mumbai. Online—not to my father's face—he made rude comments about my father's Washoe heritage." I eyed Evers. "Did you rule him out as a suspect because he's an agoraphobe? Claiming to have seen someone sounds like he was trying to create an alternative story."

Evers said, "Given his history with your father, we questioned him thoroughly."

"What was his alibi?" I asked. "Seeing as he doesn't leave his house. He has all his meals and groceries delivered. He—"

"He was online with a programming buddy. Herman Hoek. Fellow over in Palo Alto." Evers tapped his temple. "Still got the mind for facts. Hoek's interview is here somewhere."

"Hoek confirmed it?" I asked.

"Yep. They chatted for two hours. Hoek described Patel's office to a tee. The aquarium with tetra. The calendar hanging on the wall."

"Things he might have seen before," I said, "if he was a buddy of Patel's."

"True. But there was a TV playing a news station in the background, Hoek said. That fixed the time frame. The sound of the TV, Patel believed, must have drowned out the sound of the shots fired."

"Any reason for Hoek to have lied?" Nick asked.

"None. He's a former Marine. Injured in the line of duty, so he's homebound. A couple of medals to show for his service. He's also a programmer, like Patel. Speaking of facts . . ." Evers flipped a page.

"Your parents were killed around four. It was nearly dark by then, given the time of year. Daylight savings had ended a few days before. However, the exterior lights for the house weren't on, for some reason."

Nick said, "Do you think the killer disabled them?"

Evers fixed his gaze on him. "Possibly, although we discovered the toggle for the light timer was loose. Common problem with that analog-type apparatus."

"I think Dad set the timer for six throughout the year." I flipped the page.

More evidentiary photographs. Carpet fibers. Door key. A minute corner of a foil candy wrapper, probably a remnant dropped by the housekeeper. She was an avid gum chewer. A stub of an airline ticket. A wadded airport restaurant receipt. Fibers from a wool coat that matched my mother's. Each photograph was notated with Evers's legible block letters.

"Did you find footprints anywhere?" I asked.

"Nope," Evers said. "There was no overt dust on the floor to collect anything vital."

"No partial footprints?" I asked. "Not even outside?"

"It was a blustery day, if you'll recall."

I couldn't. All I could remember was being chilled to the bone when I'd entered Tammie's house that night and first met the police.

"Given the direction of the wind," Evers continued, "any exterior evidence had been swept toward the street." He sipped the remainder of his coffee and pushed the mug aside. "Turn the page."

I did.

"The dining room wasn't the only room the killer entered," Evers said. "File drawers hung open in your mother's office. Papers were strewn on her desk and on the floor. Same in your father's office."

"The robber took time to do so after killing two people?" Nick asked.

"We think it was done prior."

"Meaning stealing the silver wasn't the main goal?" I tilted my head.

"Possibly," Evers said. "The bureau drawers in the master bedroom were hanging open, too, as if the robber had been looking for something more. Jewelry, perhaps. The bedcovers were torn free of the bed. Was your mother a messy housekeeper, Miss Adams?"

"Far from it. Everything in its place."

"Now I know where you get it from," Nick joked.

"My mother kept what little jewelry she had locked in a floor safe under the rocking chair."

Evers nodded. "Which you mentioned then, and when we showed you what we'd found, you confirmed all her jewelry was intact."

I remembered tearfully going through it, piece by piece. Her favorite turquoise dangling earrings that she'd bought in Mexico. A pair of arty pineapple earrings she'd purchased in Hawaii.

"Of course, the killer could have rummaged through stuff as a distraction," Evers said.

Nick nudged his coffee mug to the side. "Why waste the time?"

"Yeah, you're right." Evers scratched his ear. "But after all that searching, why not take a watch or a clock or a piece of art?"

"Maybe he found the one thing he was looking for." The *it* my mother had said to Rosie. "And took the silver as a ruse to confuse the authorities."

Nick folded his arms on the table. "Detective, why would you think this was a robbery gone wrong and not a deliberate murder?"

"Because we ran out of viable suspects. All those who knew your parents were out of town had been cleared." Evers went to the next page.

A picture of Rosie was taped to the left side; a photocopy of her witness statement to the right.

"You'll also recall, we believed your sister was the most likely suspect," Evers said. "She knew the house and its contents. She had robbed your parents before. We didn't have that on record, of course. Your parents had never notified the police."

I said to Nick, "My mother wouldn't let Dad call it in. She didn't want Rosie hauled to prison for something they would have willingly given her, had she asked. My mother was, at her core, an enabler."

"But your mother's partner, Mrs. Laplante," Evers said, "gave us a heads-up, as did the housekeeper. They weren't throwing your sister under the bus, mind you. We specifically asked each of the women if they had knowledge of prior thefts."

I studied Rosie's picture, taken in her sophomore year of high school. She'd been pretty before drugs had ravaged her face. There was an impish, defiant glint in her gaze, as if challenging the photographer. The first time she'd robbed our parents, Mom had been devastated. Rosie had taken a gold fob watch that my grandfather had given to my father. "I see you tested my sister for gunshot residue."

Evers said, "We followed all the protocols. There was none on her hands."

"She could have worn gloves," Nick said.

"True, but again, like I said, her alibi proved out."

"And yet you questioned her for nearly a month," I stated, an edge to my tone.

Evers splayed his hands. "We thought a colleague of hers was responsible. We hoped she would break."

"Oh, she broke all right," I said.

Evers cleared his throat. "I'm sorry. We had to do—"

"Your job. Got it." I glanced at Nick. Did all cops talk the same? Did justice always take precedence over compassion?

"Speaking of gunshot residue . . ." I rubbed my neck; the strain of staring at the evidence and trying to conjure up answers where there were none was getting to me. "I see in your notes that you didn't find the murder weapon."

"We think it was tossed in the drink. The bay." Evers took another slice of cheese and downed it in one bite. He wiped his fingers on a napkin. "There were no casings found at the crime scene. The bullet holes suggested the gun was probably a pistol, caliber .45."

I jolted as I realized I hadn't mentioned my grandfather's gun to Nick. "Sweetheart, I meant to have told you about—"

"About what?"

I addressed Evers. "Detective, my mother owned a gun. A Colt .45. It was her father's, passed down to her. I found it in a box in their hope chest."

"We searched your parents' belongings. We didn't find a gun."

"Your people might have overlooked it. The box doesn't look like a gun case, and it's impossible to open without pressing the correct button." It dawned on me that the hope chest might have been straightened by the police, not the killer, which would solve the niggling question that had plagued me yesterday. "My grandmother was a craftsman. All her boxes were artistic and clever."

"Hold on," Nick said. "You don't think the killer used that gun and returned it to its case, do you?"

"I don't know what to think."

Evers hummed. "You should let Atherton P.D. see the gun."

"It's in Lake Tahoe. I own the hope chest now." I didn't tell Evers how I'd discovered the gun. "How about if I have my aunt Max—she owns the detective agency I work for—take it to the Placer County Sheriff's team for analysis? You guys can do that, right? Compare ballistics remotely? A.P.D. still has the bullets, I presume. Or does the San Mateo crime lab keep that stuff?"

"A.P.D. has all the evidentiary materials."

For the next few hours, Evers filled us in on the suspects. There was a page dedicated to each one. Rosie. Viraj Patel. William Fisher, a limo driver and the father of one of my father's clients. Kurt Brandt, a man in his early sixties who, after my grandfather died, had repeatedly dunned my mother for repayment of a loan he claimed to have given my grandfather. Lastly, Antoine Washington, Rosie's former drug buddy, or *colleague*, as Evers had noted, who had a record of shoplifting.

"Fisher and Brandt had credible alibis that held up," Evers said, "which really irked my partner. Foxx was certain Fisher was good for this. The guy was fifty-five at the time and a hothead. He held your dad responsible for his son being in prison."

I tapped the table with a fingertip. "You said my father's office had been tossed. Like my mother's."

"Yep."

"Maybe Fisher was looking for a document. Some kind of proof he thought my father had withheld that would help exonerate his son. What was his alibi?"

"He was on the clock. Driving his boss to and from a four-hour meeting. Now, there was something a little weak about the guy's alibi. See, he wasn't in the meeting, and the limo wasn't spotted in the building's parking garage for about two hours, so we pressed him. He claimed he'd gone to the beach. As luck would have it, a witness verified it . . . a witness with no link to Fisher and no skin in the game. So, we had to cut Fisher loose. Like I said, Foxx was irked. Personally, I"—Evers thumbed his chest—"liked Brandt for the crime. He claimed he was gambling in Vegas, but, see, that didn't hold up. We were getting ready to haul him in when my commander called me and said to let it go. Brandt was innocent." Evers snapped his fingers. "Just like that. Don't know why. I never pressed."

"Is it possible Brandt bribed your commander?"

"Commander Joad?" Evers held up two hands. "Uh-uh. Joad never would have accepted a bribe. He is as honest as they come."

Like my father.

"Someone intervened on Brandt's behalf," Nick said.

"I imagine so. Like I said, I didn't press. The commander was the *man*. I trusted his decision."

Evers turned to the next page. "Here's Fisher's profile."

I studied his picture. He was a proud Native American. Long hair. Chin raised. Intensely brown yet sensitive eyes. "He was a limo driver?"

Evers nodded. "Yep. Drove private for a tech guru in Silicon Valley. He'd be sixty-nine now. He might be working for him still. He wasn't the kind of guy to retire, you know?"

"Tell me about Fisher's son," I said.

"The kid was twenty-five at the time and serving a sentence for murder. Killed a cop. Fisher claimed his boy was framed and blamed your father for not presenting a good enough defense." Evers tattooed the table with the top of his pen. "Fisher kept saying we should focus on Dale Warwick, another of your father's Native American clients, who owned a construction company. He said Warwick thought your father sold him short in a defective design issue, but Warwick was ruled out in nothing flat. He was attending a Patwin council meeting. Four councilmembers vouched for him." Evers spread his hands. "We cut Fisher and Brandt loose and zeroed in on Antoine Washington. He confessed to knowing that your sister had robbed your parents often. He said she'd bragged about it."

I rotated my head to loosen the knots. I'd never heard Rosie admit to robbing our parents, but, at the time, she and I hadn't been friends.

The day she'd entered high school, she'd decided I was a goody-two-shoes and no longer worthy of her confidence. In short order, she became a conundrum to me. Sneaking out of the house at night. Hanging with the wrong people. I'd had no clue how heavily she was into drugs.

"Of all the suspects, Mr. Washington's alibi was the flimsiest," Evers went on. "He claimed he was getting high with friends, and some of them corroborated his story, but none were trustworthy. However, physical and DNA evidence could not convict him, and though he could have fit the possible description of the person Mr. Patel had seen running in the neighborhood the night before, Patel could not identify him in a lineup. When Washington's attorney produced CCTV footage that confirmed Washington was in the vicinity of his supposed alibi at the time of death, we added him to the cleared list and kept looking."

Evers flipped to the end of the book, revealing an extensive list of people questioned, including bankers, creditors, my parents' travel agent, the taxi driver, and the housekeeper.

"Your folks had no outstanding personal debts," Evers added. "They were model citizens."

"Other than the unsubstantiated debt claimed by Kurt Brandt," Nick stated.

"Correct." Evers focused on me. "We questioned many of your parents' friends. They spoke highly of them. Everyone loved them. Ultimately, we had to accept that it was a random robbery. They lived in a high-end neighborhood. Thefts were uncommon in that locale because of the drive-around security guards, but they did occur. Six months into our investigation, our boss said to close up shop. Foxx"—his voice cracked—"quit the force a year later."

"I heard he passed away," I said. "I'm sorry for your loss."

"Foxx was a good man. A good cop. His heart . . . not so good."

Nick said, "Is it possible the CCTV footage that Washington's attorney provided was fake or altered?"

"Doubtful. It was time-stamped and came from a reputable source. But I like the way you think." Evers aimed his forefinger at Nick. "For a long time after we closed the investigation, we put the occasional tail on Washington. To our surprise, the kid actually went straight. It was as if being questioned in a murder investigation scared the spit out of him. He got himself into a drug rehab program, and last I heard, he was holding down a job at a warehouse-type store in San Jose."

Chapter 8

Before leaving Evers's house, I asked if he'd mind if I took photographs of his notes, police reports, and interrogation forms. He was more than happy to oblige, adding that if I discovered anything new, would I keep him in the loop.

"You can call me anytime," he said. "I don't sleep much these days."

Driving to the Atherton area, after each of us downed two energy bars to satisfy our churning stomachs, Nick asked if I'd deliberately forgotten to mention the gun to him. I said it had slipped my mind and apologized.

Then we began to theorize. Brandt or Washington would have wanted my folks gone from the house in order to rob them. Brandt would have had to guess that they were out of town. Maybe he saw them leaving with suitcases. Washington could have learned from Rosie that they were going on vacation. Fisher, on the other hand, would have wanted my father present so he could confront him.

By the time Nick veered off the freeway onto Marsh Road, the exit for Menlo Park, Atherton, and nearby areas, we had come no closer to solving my parents' murders, and the sky had turned gray and foreboding.

"A storm's coming," Nick said.

"Mm-hm." I glanced at my phone, pondering what more we might learn from the photographs I'd taken of Evers's material. I intended to go over every aspect of the crime scene and reread the suspects' statements. Idly, I wondered if I met with each one, in a public place, of course, would I be able to get a read on them. Was there someone the police had missed interviewing? Another of my father's clients or more of my grandfather's creditors? I supposed I could ask Tammie for a list of my mother's clients and friends. I didn't know all of them. Thanks to Tammie, Mom had learned to be meticulous about keeping an up-to-date contact list. Given her bookkeeping background, Tammie had been a stickler for detail.

"Nick!" I grabbed his arm.

He tapped the brakes. "What's wrong? Did you see an animal? Deer? Child?"

"No, sorry. Keep driving."

"What freaked you out?"

"There." I pointed to the left. "Beyond the wooden fence. That's my—" My throat went dry. "My parents' house."

"Holy heck. Why didn't you say so yesterday?"

"I didn't think . . . I didn't realize. I haven't driven through the area for years." Stupid, on the face of it, I told myself, but I'd pushed certain facts from my mind. "Would you . . ." I couldn't form the words.

"Swing by?"

"Yes."

"We won't see much at this time of night."

"I know."

Lindenwood, a pricey area of Atherton, was at one time the Linden Towers estate, the home of James Flood, the son of an Irish immigrant who had hit it big during the silver bonanza of the 1880s. After his death, the property was transferred and transferred again, and ultimately torn down and subdivided into acre estates. Grandpa Gray, who'd made quite a lot of money when he'd first started working at General Motors, had been able to purchase a lot and build a modest one-story house. Homes had sold often since then. Many of them had been torn down and rebuilt as mansions.

As we drove through the original Linden Towers–era gate, a massive stone and iron structure at James Avenue, Nick whistled.

"Yeah." I grinned. "It's impressive. Turn left on Heather Drive."

He spun the steering wheel and whistled again. Each of the two-story houses, with their updated exterior lighting and exquisite landscaping, looked spectacular.

"At the end of Heather, turn left on Irving," I directed. "Our house was the ranch-style one—unless it's been rebuilt—close to the end of the cul-de-sac."

We neared the house and my breath caught in my throat. It hadn't been modernized, although there was now a vast amount of security and exterior lighting. The dark brown L-shaped structure was the same. The century-old oak tree loomed in front of the house like a protective watchman. In the driveway, a petite forty-something blonde in white jacket, jeans, and Giants baseball cap was unloading groceries. There was no direct access to the house from the garage; it was detached.

The woman glanced over her shoulder.

"Stop," I said to Nick. As breathless as I felt, nothing I said could come close to sounding like a command. "Please."

He obeyed.

The woman stood up, hands free of groceries, wary. She held her key fob in her hand, ready to press the panic button, I imagined.

I climbed out of the passenger side and waved. "Sorry, ma'am. I didn't mean to frighten you. I used to live here. In this house. We were driving by, and I—"

"Don't I know you?" She lowered the fob and tented her other hand over the brim of her cap, to block the glare of the evening lights. "Heavens." She clapped a hand to her chest. "You're one of the daughters. Your parents lived here. They—"

"Yes," I said, curious as to why anyone would buy a house where a double homicide had occurred. The price, probably. We had seriously slashed it in order to move the property. Someone eager to live in Lindenwood would have jumped on the deal and figured out later how to handle the sorrowful history. "I'm Aspen Adams."

"Yes, of course. I discovered pictures of you and your sister in one of the drawers in the kitchen as I was relining them. That's how I recognized you. I'm Ilona Isles," she said. "Please come in." She had glowing skin, brilliant blue eyes, and smelled like jasmine. "Would you like a glass of wine? Is someone with you?" She peered past me.

"My boyfriend." I beckoned Nick. He parked the Jeep and clambered out. "We're . . ." I stopped short, not eager to reveal that we were reviewing the cold case. "We're visiting. I'm showing him my old haunts."

"He's quite handsome," she confided and offered her hand to me. "By the way, my husband, Ted, went to Stanford, like you."

The local newspapers had published numerous details about me, including my age and education. All they'd said about Rosie was that

47

she'd worked as a waitress and had a one-year-old daughter. Thankfully, her drug problem had remained a secret. Maybe the police had felt that the information, if leaked, would have hampered the investigation.

Nick helped Ilona with the groceries as she turned off the alarm. I was pleased to see she'd installed one.

"We haven't changed much in the house." Ilona didn't pause to let us take in the view—the living room and hallway leading to the bedrooms on the right, kitchen and dining room straight ahead. She traipsed through the foyer, which was decorated with a variety of orchids, and into the kitchen. "Although we did renovate this room completely."

The kitchen décor was comfortable in an old European kind of way. Soft brown tiles, cream-colored cabinets, granite counters, dark brown faucets, sink, and knobs.

"It's beautiful," I said.

"We also added a new roof." She removed her baseball cap, hung it on a peg on the wall, and fluffed her hair. "I don't think your parents had ever touched the original."

I was sure they hadn't. Not after Dad's business had started to flag.

"We remodeled a wall in the living room so we could install a sixty-inch television, and added a couple of feet to the master bedroom. Plus, we made the swimming pool shallower and got rid of the diving board."

"Diving boards can be hazardous," Nick said like an authority.

Rosie had loved diving. Whenever she dove, she was as courageous as a lioness. Double flips, no problem. Triple summersaults, easy as pie. Me? I panicked if I couldn't see the water at all times. I could do a swan dive and jackknife. That was about it. Swimming was my forte.

Ilona opened a bottle of wine. "My husband will be home in a few minutes. I'd love for you to meet him. In the meantime, I'll give you a tour." She poured sauvignon blanc into three Riedel glasses and handed one to each of us. "I hope white is fine."

We nodded, accepting the glasses. I took a sip to fortify myself, the crisp citrusy liquid sliding down my throat.

"This way." Ilona moved through the living room, its décor white casual chic, its television massive, and headed for the hall. "What are you doing now, Aspen?"

"I'm a private investigator in Lake Tahoe."

"Really? That must be fascinating."

"It can be."

"And you, Nick?"

"I'm a sheriff."

Ilona grinned. "Well, aren't you two made for each other?" Acting like a tour guide, she motioned to the right. "I believe this was your father's office, Aspen."

The room was still wood-paneled, but rather than holding my father's executive desk, file cabinets, books, and photographs, it now contained workout equipment and a big-screen TV. I shivered, remembering the photographs displaying the mess the killer had created.

Nick laid his hand at the small of my back to reassure me. I welcomed the touch. My insides felt like a pinball machine had taken up residence, energy zinging nonstop, up, down, and sideways.

"When we came to look at the house," Ilona went on, not sensing my unease, "I recall having seen many photographs of Native Americans on the walls. Your father and his brothers, I believe?"

"My great-grandfather married a full-blooded Washoe Indian named Blue Sky."

"I don't remember seeing pictures of women," Ilona said.

"My great-grandmother shied away from photographs."

"Your father was an attorney, right?" Ilona asked. "Ted said he championed a lot of causes."

"Yes."

Had the police overlooked a suspect? Had a client other than William Fisher come after my father?

"This was your mother's office," Ilona said and gestured again. All of the rooms along the hall stood to the right. The patio and backyard were out the French doors to the left. "How I loved the cream-and-brown palette she'd chosen," Ilona said. "I kept it exactly as she'd designed, and I've made it mine."

"What do you do?" I asked.

"Like your mother, Aspen, I'm an interior designer. But I do everything online from home."

"Everything?" Nick squinted. "How does that work?"

Ilona grinned. "The customer signs onto my site, Isles Styles dot com, and shares the dimensions of the project and a *before* picture of the particular room. Then they tell me a bit about themselves—their preferred style, their preferred colors—and I get to work. I provide 3-D designs and tweak it until they're happy."

How different Ilona was from my mother. Mom had loved going to a client's home and getting a feel from not only the client but the house too. She believed every house had a spirit. Mom had also enjoyed having her clients come to our house and meet in the kitchen or on the patio while sharing a cup of coffee and going through books of décor. She'd said it was the personal interaction that let her know and understand her clients' needs. I flashed on the few trips I'd gone on with her, searching for the right piece of art for this or that client. Canvases, sculptures, wall hangings. She was very particular. Though I would never be an artist like her or my grandmother, those trips had developed my deep appreciation for art.

"Working remotely has become quite the norm nowadays," Ilona added.

I wouldn't quibble with her business plan. Everything in today's world was changing.

Ilona pressed on, bypassing the door to what used to be Rosie's and my bedroom, and showed us the master. "Isn't it amazing what an extra five feet will do?"

She wanted me to be impressed with her redesign, and I was. The room was much larger, and although it had once been painted forest green with white trim and decorated accordingly, now it was white on white.

"I was going for elegant and airy," Ilona said.

"You nailed it." There were more windows than before, a skylight over the master bed, and French doors leading to the backyard. "It's lovely."

"During escrow, I'd offered to buy that exquisite piece of art that had hung over the fireplace, but your executor said it wasn't for sale.

Do you know the one I'm talking about? The picture of two girls walking toward the beach, hand in hand."

I smiled. "My grandmother painted that. The girls were my sister and me. It's in storage." It was time to go through the rest of what was in the unit and divest.

"Ooh, I skipped a room." Ilona pivoted, swept past me, and opened the door next to the master. "This was your room, wasn't it?" she said, peeking in. "Pink and yellow wasn't a color scheme I could live with." The room, like the master, was white on white, although there were accents of green. Silk plants abounded. And there was a white wicker bookcase filled with leather-bound books. "I hope you don't mind the changes. We don't have children, but we do invite guests."

"Me? No. I don't mind," I said. "I hated that color scheme. I'd wanted to line the walls with knotty pine, but Mom wouldn't let me. She said when I bought my own place, I could decorate any which way I wanted." The memory made me smile. "She could be quite forceful."

"My mother was the same," Ilona said, bonding. "Last but not least, let's return to the living room."

A memory of Grandpa Gray storming into the living room more than twenty-five years ago sprang to mind. He was carrying a gun. Probably the gun from the hope chest. He was drunk and hyped up with rage. My father, mother, and grandmother ordered Rosie and me to go to the dining room and work on a jigsaw puzzle. We left, but we tiptoed to the archway and watched the to-do. Grandpa Gray was waggling the gun. Threatening to use it. On himself. Apologizing for letting everyone down. Saying he'd made a mess of his life. My mother tried to talk sense into him. So did my father. But Grandpa Gray wouldn't hear of it. Ultimately, it was Grandma Patrice who managed to calm him. He set the gun aside and curled into her opened arms. Rosie and I didn't get to hear the aftermath. Our mother caught us watching and spirited us down the hall into our bedroom. She'd stayed with us until our father gave her the all clear.

Standing in the middle of the living room, I gazed at the dining room. Ilona hadn't taken us into it on the guided tour. She must have known that the murders had occurred there. I didn't press. I would learn nothing new from entering it. Besides, the crime photographers had captured every angle of the crime scene.

I stifled a yawn.

Nick, picking up on my fatigue, said, "Ilona, it has been lovely, but we shouldn't take any more of your time."

"I really did want you to meet Ted." She peeked at her iPhone watch. "Aha, he sent a text. He's running late. He's at a board meeting. Goes with the territory." She took our wineglasses to the kitchen and ushered us to the front door. "Oh, I almost forgot. Wait here."

When she returned, she was carrying an envelope. "You'd probably like the photos I found. I kept them. I'm not sure why." She handed the envelope to me. "I believe the one of you is your high school graduation photo."

I removed a photograph and tears welled in my eyes. I'd looked so young and hopeful. No tragedy had struck. The worst heartbreak I'd experienced had been a boyfriend dumping me for a cheerleader. Four months later, all hell broke loose.

"Thank you, Ilona," I said. "I appreciate it."

Chapter 9

Climbing into the Jeep, I spied Mr. Patel, slim, bug-eyed, and silhouetted in ambient light, peering between drapes in his Eichler mid-century-style home, which stood cattycorner from Ilona's house. I shuddered.

"What's wrong?" Nick asked, picking up on my unease.

"Over there. In the window. That's Mr. Patel. Scrawnier and older—he's probably in his fifties, but it's him."

"Pretty garden. His landscaping lighting is exceptional."

"Honestly?" I threw Nick a withering glance. "A well-tended garden doesn't make him a nice person."

Nick held up both hands in surrender.

I continued to stare through the windshield. "He always made my skin crawl. Who carries around that much anger?"

"Lots of people."

"My father tried to say nice things about him, in particular that Patel was mentally gifted, as if that granted him some kind of dispensation for his lack of social graces."

A silver-haired woman appeared over Patel's shoulder, peered out at us, then pulled him away from the window. His mother? His sister? The drapes snapped closed.

Something else seized my attention. Two doors down. "Hold up." I put my hand on Nick's arm. "See that?" A limousine was pulling out of a driveway.

"What about it?"

"Evers said William Fisher drove a limousine."

Nick stared at the retreating vehicle, its brake lights illuminating as the limo veered right. "I can't imagine the guy figured out you were in town, let alone that you were in Lindenwood visiting your former home. The driver is probably taking someone to the airport. In this neighborhood, they can afford those luxuries."

I released his arm. "You're right. I'm on edge."

"You have every right to be." He blew me a kiss and proceeded to drive in the direction of the professor's house.

After a long silence, I said, "I'd like to meet with all of the suspects."

"They've been ruled out."

"Even so, I'd like to speak to them and start fresh, as if I haven't read any of the information Evers collected."

"And say what?" Following the designated GPS route, Nick turned left onto Middlefield Road. Traffic was dense. People were on their way home from work.

I'd forgotten how much traffic there was in the Bay Area. The stop-and-go movement was making me queasy. How I missed Lake Tahoe. Oh, sure, there could be traffic at the lake, but typically it occurred during the day when people were going from point A to point B to have summer or winter fun. Rarely at night.

"I don't know what I'll say, but I'd like to get a fix on them."

Nick snickered. "You're something else. You think you can merely look at someone and know?"

"I'm an investigator. I've honed my skills."

"And I have a crystal ball." Laughing, Nick made a right on Glenwood Avenue. "Let's see if we can figure out a more practical plan, one that doesn't involve getting you killed, okay?"

As Glenwood became Valparaiso, we both grew silent. I kept my eye on the sideview mirror, watching to see if the limo was tailing us. I didn't spot it, although I noticed a nondescript dark sedan. Had Patel followed us? No, he was agoraphobic.

"Nick, let's go to an office supply store," I said. "There's one on El Camino Real, if it's still in operation, not far from here. We'll buy a few things and put together a murder board."

His mouth quirked up. "You want to use my methods?"

"Exactly. You're the expert." I grinned.

He craned his neck and gave me a stink eye. "Flattery will get you everywhere. Tell me where to turn."

"Left at the light and left on Middle Avenue. It'll lead to El Camino. Then left again."

The car behind us continued straight and I breathed easier.

The office supply store was, indeed, in the same place and open for business. In less than a half hour, we were able to print out the photographs we'd taken of Evers's notes, purchase a trifold project board, tape, Post-it notepads, markers, and pens. From there, it was a short drive to the rental house.

In the kitchen, I popped open a Goose Island beer for Nick and poured myself a glass of chardonnay, and we settled at the kitchen table. We would put the board together after we ate.

Nick took a long pull of the beer and set the bottle down. "Ilona Isles was nice."

"Very."

"Attentive."

"I got the feeling she wanted more of the gory details."

"No. She was simply nice."

"Speaking of gory details, did you notice she didn't take us into the dining room?" I asked.

"She didn't want you to relive the event." He caressed my shoulder. "Again, she was a nice woman. Caring."

I caught sight of the pile of printed material on the kitchen counter by the Keurig machine and popped to my feet.

"What's up?" Nick sat straighter.

"Would you mind recreating the crime scene with me in the dining room?"

"I thought we were doing the board after——"

"Dinner. We are. But I want to physically feel myself at the crime scene right now. First."

"How are we going to do that? Nothing's the same. There's no hutch. No dining table."

The professor had turned his dining room into a recreation room, including a caroms game, dartboard, card table, and more.

"We'll use whatever we have." Drawing in a courageous breath, I pulled a photograph of the crime scene from our newly printed collection and held it out to Nick. "Please?"

A half hour later, we'd rearranged the room—the caroms game standing in for my parents' hutch, the card table for their dining table. I set a chair by the archway to represent my mother entering the room. The most direct path from the front door to the dining room was via the foyer. According to Evers's thinking, she finished up outside with the taxi driver, heard shots, and rushed in to save my father.

"Okay." I rubbed my hands together. "Let's say Dad was walking in the front door. He didn't notice anything wrong. No overturned furniture. No busted-in door."

"Right. How did the killer get in?" Nick asked. "Evers didn't say."

"Yes he did. It was on page eight or nine of his notes. He believed the robber used a house key my parents kept in a fake rock in a plant on the porch."

Nick frowned. "How did he know where to look for it?"

I raised an eyebrow. "Lots of people hide keys. Like the one we used to enter this place. Don't you?"

"Nope."

"I do. It's wrapped in foil in a clay pot near the woodpile."

"I'll make a note just in case we ever have an argument and you lock me out," he quipped.

I paced from the stand-in hutch to the stand-in dining table. "My parents kept a house key in the fake rock because my mother was notorious for leaving her purse and keys inside the house and locking the front door on her way out. My father said it was the distracted artist side of her brain." I smiled at the memory.

Nick rubbed my shoulder. "Go on."

"Mom would get halfway to her car when she'd realize what she'd done. U-turn. Let herself in with the spare key. Grab her things and fly out again. Neighbors must have seen her accessing the key numerous times. If the killer was a random robber, he or she could have staked out the house and seen her do it on occasion. Like the stranger Patel claimed to have seen running in the neighborhood the night before."

Nick inclined his head in agreement. "Okay, so your dad rushes in."

"Sees the robber looting the hutch. He calls to him . . ."

"Or her," Nick said.

Her? Tammie and a few of my mother's friends and travel agent had been questioned. Were there other female suspects the police had considered but had ruled out too soon?

"Or her," I acknowledged. "The robber turns and fires."

"Why would your father call out?" Nick asked, playing devil's advocate. "Why not run out of the house, grab your mother, and dial 911?"

"My father never refused a fight. He and his brothers had been bruisers. Tough guys. Dad wrestled on the high school and college wrestling teams. Uncle Jonathan was a boxer. Uncle Matt—he was the one that was married to Aunt Max—played football. Defensive line-backer. Dad grew more genteel after meeting and marrying my mother, but he liked the *fight*. I think that's why he became a defense attorney."

Nick worked his lower lip between his teeth. "Review it again. Your dad hears something. Wouldn't he have come in with some kind of weapon?"

"Like what? A baseball bat? A frying pan?"

"A fireplace poker."

"There's nothing like any of those in the crime scene photos." I sorted through the folder of photographs that I'd set on the card table. "I suppose the killer could have removed a weapon from the scene."

"To come in unarmed seems hasty on your father's part. Naïve."

"Evers said Dad might have thought it was the housekeeper."

Nick rubbed his chin between his forefinger and thumb. "Maybe he thought it was your sister."

I nodded. "Rosie often came to do laundry."

"Your dad peeked around the corner, not anticipating trouble. Instead, he saw the intruder. At the same time, the intruder turned, gun in hand."

"Hold on. Why did the intruder have a gun if he or she wasn't expecting anyone?"

"Good question."

"It makes me wonder, again, whether William Fisher, not knowing my parents had gone on a trip and, therefore, expecting them to come home at some point, had stolen into the house specifically to kill Dad."

Nick considered my theory and said, "Let's move on. Most likely, your father called to your mother. The intruder fired."

"Mom ran in," I said. "She saw Dad lying on the floor. Without thinking of her own safety, she raced to help him." I pictured the scenario. She crouched. Saw the blood. Peered up at the killer. Probably yelled, *How could you?* I said, "The killer, tying up loose ends, shoots her in the back. He or she—" I hesitated. "Let's go with *he*. It's too complicated using both."

Nick motioned to proceed.

"*He* has to cover his tracks," I said. "Get what he came for and get out."

"Except he didn't get in and get out," Nick said. "If your grandfather's gun turns out to be the weapon, the killer took the time to return the gun to the hope chest before rummaging through other things."

"Evers thought he rifled through the offices first."

"Suggesting, as you theorized, that stealing the silver wasn't the main goal."

Why search my parents' bedroom? Why rummage through my mother's and father's offices? Why return the gun to the hope chest?

I flipped to a photograph of my father's office. Drawers hung open. The papers on his desk were usually neat and orderly; in the photograph, they were helter-skelter. Had the killer been searching for a document? A contract of some sort?

Spinning around, I stared at the caroms game, imagining the hutch that had held so many of my family's treasures. Not only silverware and such, but also my mother's *Woman of the Year* trophy from the Atherton Women's Guild, my father's first earned dollar bill, a few of Rosie's medals for diving as well as mine for swimming—the others having found their way into the hope chest—a gold coin for Rosie and me from our grandfather, a few curios that my grandmother had crafted for each of us.

Had the killer taken something other than the silver from the hutch? I recalled Tammie, or perhaps it had been the assistant from the executor's office, offering to pack up the smaller items. Were they in one or more of the boxes in the storage facility?

"What's going on inside your head?" Nick asked, rubbing my shoulders with both hands.

"Nothing. I don't know. I—" I swiveled and hooked my arms around his neck. "Let's rearrange the room and then you order dinner. Chinese, please."

"At your service, ma'am." He saluted.

"I said *please*. Don't get cheeky."

"Never."

An hour later, as we were polishing off our shrimp in lobster sauce,

Nick's cell phone hummed. He stared at the screen and frowned.

"Who is it?" I asked.

"Natalie's boyfriend."

"Answer it."

Nick rose from the kitchen table, pressed Accept, and held the cell phone to his ear. "Hello." He listened and reeled, gripping the counter to steady himself.

I hurried to him. "What's wrong?"

"Natalie was struck by a bicyclist as she was crossing the street," he said over his shoulder. "A racer. Going top speed." Into the phone he said, "Which hospital? What's the prognosis?" His jaw drew tight. "Okay, I'm in the Bay Area. I'll be there in less than four hours." Nick ended the call and turned to me. "I'm so sorry. Nat needs me. She suffered a concussion."

"Her boyfriend is with her."

"Yes, but he has a gift shop trade show in Florida the day after tomorrow. He has to catch a plane in the morning." Nick drew me into a hug and pecked my forehead. He was Natalie's only family. Their parents had died in a car crash six years ago. "Forgive me?"

"Of course."

As Nick threw his clothes and toiletries into the duffel, he said, "The murder board."

"I'll put it together and send you photos."

"After that, what's your plan of action?"

"I'm going to touch base with Tammie tonight. I'll see if she can meet me tomorrow. It's time for me to go through everything we put in storage and figure out what else can be sold and what should be donated. Maybe while I'm there something will trigger a memory."

Nick headed to the front door and stopped, looking sheepish. "The Jeep."

I'd anticipated the moment and dangled the keys to my car on a finger. "Take it. I'll arrange for a rental."

"Are you sure?"

"Positive."

"Be safe."

We kissed passionately and he left.

Chapter 10

I watched Nick drive away, locked the door, and returned to the kitchen. I washed our dishes, made a cup of tea with honey, and texted Tammie. I asked if she was free to go through the storage unit with me in the morning.

She responded quickly: *Absolutely. Will your boyfriend join us?*

I responded: *He had to return to Tahoe. Family issue.*

Tammie wrote: *Too bad. Wanted to meet him. How's 10? Come to my client's house. Want to show you my latest.* She typed in the address.

I replied: *CU at 10.*

I moved into the dining room to contact my aunt. She picked up after one ring. "Hey, sugar, how are you holding up?"

"It's grueling, Max. We met with the detective. He's retired now." I told her about his copious notes and how he'd allowed me to copy everything. "He was more than forthcoming and would love to see this case resolved. Which brings me to my call. My grandfather's gun."

"What about it?"

"Would you please take it to the sheriff's station and have forensic ballistics examiners check it out? See if bullets fired from the gun match the bullets that killed my parents. I think I told you that there are no bullets in the gun or the case, so I'm not sure how that might work. Candace can show you how to open the cedar puzzle box. The key to the hope chest is in my bathroom, lower right drawer."

"I'm on it."

I smiled. What would I do without her? "Is Candace there?"

While I waited for my niece to get on the line, I moved to the archway leading to the dining room and stared at the wealth of material Nick and I had printed at the office supply store. It was, in a word, daunting.

"Aspen, hi," Candace said, her voice high-pitched. "How are you? Where are you? Why haven't you called until now? I've been worried sick. You didn't even text me."

"Did you text me?" I asked calmly.

"Well, no, but I was in school, and—"

"And I was tracking down leads."

"What kind of leads? Have you figured out who did it? Did you—"

"Whoa! Time out. Take a deep breath. I'll fill you in."

Over the course of a half hour, I told her about my meeting with Detective Sergeant Evers. She asked intelligent questions, landing on the same thing that had niggled at the edges of my mind about how the crime scene had been wiped down.

When she'd exhausted her questions, we talked about school and what she wanted to do over the upcoming Thanksgiving holiday.

"Hiking, I think. And maybe some photography," she added. Her BFF Waverly had given up ballet and was seriously into photography. "If I get good at photography," Candace went on, "maybe I can teach you, so you can use it for work, because, let's face it, your cell phone doesn't do the best job."

"Thanks for the compliment."

"Just saying." She giggled. "A P.I. needs a telephoto lens and—"

"Got it, my young tech guru. Go to sleep."

"I'm not young."

I chuckled. "No, you're not." She was getting older by the second. Soon she would be applying to college and taking flight. The thought wrenched my heart. "Good night. Sleep tight."

I ended the call and started in on the murder board, posting suspects' photos on the right side of the trifold project board and the crime scene photos on the left. In the center, I pinned all the photographs pertaining to evidence and the other rooms in the house.

Standing away from my work, I folded my arms. Nothing shouted *Guilty, case solved*. The fact that there had been no foreign hair found at the crime scene nagged at me. I wrote *How is this possible?* on a Post-it and affixed it to one of the photos.

My gaze traveled from the photograph of Antoine Washington to William Fisher to Kurt Brandt to Viraj Patel. I really did want to meet the suspects. How could I do that without putting myself at risk? Go to their places of business? Ask to meet at a diner? Would anyone dare to have a face-to-face with me solely to assure me they were innocent? They'd been cleared.

Each of the suspect's interviews that I'd posted on the board had contact information. I dialed Antoine Washington's number and received an intercept message saying the call could not be completed as dialed. I set up my laptop computer and, using a search engine we used at the office, entered Washington's name with the city of San Jose as his location. Three Antoine Washingtons appeared with accompanying contact numbers. I reached a voicemail for each and left a message saying who I was and that I was in the area and wanted to talk. I added that perhaps he, Antoine, might have insights in regard to a matter related to Lily and James Adams. I didn't say that I was investigating their murders because I didn't want to disturb the two Antoine Washingtons who might not be the real suspect. Or all three, if none was the correct person.

I reached out to William Fisher next, who, according to Evers's notes, lived in Mountain View. I started there. His phone number was still in service, but he didn't answer. An answering machine did. I left a message similar to the one I'd left Antoine and hung up.

Drawing in a deep breath, I did the same for Brandt.

Lastly, I tapped in Viraj Patel's number. On the fourth ring, as I was preparing to end the call seeing as I hadn't connected to voicemail, a man answered. "Who's this?" His tone was waspish and curt.

Still as rude as ever, I noted.

"Mr. Patel," I said, "my name is Aspen Adams. I'm the daughter of—"

"I know who you are." Though he had lived in the United States for most of his life, he had a distinctive Indian accent. "I saw you at Ilona's house snooping around. What do you want?"

Nick and I hadn't been snooping, but I let the comment slide. "Sir, I met with Detective Sergeant Evers, formerly of the Atherton Police Department."

"Yes, yes. Tall guy. Not big on warmth."

Patel was one to talk.

"Sir, I'm reexamining my parents' case. It's a cold case, but—"

"Colder than a politician's promises," he snapped.

I tamped down the frustration rising up my esophagus. "Even though the case is cold, I'm calling a number of witnesses, like yourself."

"I was also a suspect."

"Yes, but that's not why I'm calling." *Liar.* I brushed a stray hair off my face. "I'm reaching out to you because you described seeing someone in the neighborhood on the previous night."

"Yes, I saw someone. Whoever it was looked shifty."

"Shifty," I repeated.

"Out of place. Ducking. Hiding."

A silence fell between us.

I said, "Sir, I wondered if we could meet, and——"

"No."

I nearly laughed. The man clearly had no social skills. Big surprise. "Okay, well, then, would you mind describing the person?"

"Tall and lean. I could not tell the color of the skin. Whoever it was, was wearing all black." He pronounced his consonants deliberately. "I suppose he could have been wearing a mask, and perhaps he had long hair or no hair."

"You told the police he had short hair."

"Yes, but you see, he could have been wearing a cap with no brim. Like a ski cap."

Neither Nick nor I had considered a hat. "You say *he*. Are you sure it was a he?" I asked.

"That was the issue I could not decide," Patel said. "He . . . or she . . . might have been an athlete. Whichever it was, the person took long strides."

As in Lake Tahoe, there were plenty of workout enthusiasts in the Bay Area. Being athletic would not narrow down a description.

I gazed at the picture of Antoine Washington on the board. He was bald.

Rosie had had short-cropped hair at the time, too. Now, she wore it chin-length.

I studied William Fisher's photograph again. My grandfather had told me that many Native Americans viewed their long hair as a symbol of spirituality and strength and, should they cut it, their power might drain away. If Fisher had tied his hair in a ponytail or had tucked it under a ski cap before breaking into my parents' house, he could have been the person Patel had seen.

The picture Evers had included of Kurt Brandt was of Brandt wearing a fedora. I couldn't tell whether he had short or medium-short hair. He had been tall and lean with a hooked nose and receding chin.

"Mr. Patel, did you see this trespasser at any other time?"

"No."

"Were there any robberies in the area previously or later on?" I'd asked Evers the same question. There hadn't been, but neighbors might not have reported them if they were inconsequential or, as in my parents' case, had been carried out by a family member.

"None."

A woman spoke in the background. Her voice was harsh, accusatory. She said something about Patel always being online and inattentive.

"I will be right there," he shouted in clipped tones to the woman. "Miss Adams, before I go, you are going to find out anyway, so I might as well tell you. I lied about my alibi."

My breath caught in my chest. Had I heard him right? I pressed the phone to my ear. "Come again."

"I was not home that Saturday, as I told the police. I had started seeing a woman. My therapist. Thanks to her, I had found the courage to leave my house. If I had told the police about her, it might have cost her career. As you might assume, sleeping with a patient is frowned upon." He blew out a stream of air. "Later on, when I returned home and found out your parents had been murdered, I knew I would be a suspect."

"Because of your feud with my father."

"Yes."

"You told the police you were online with a buddy. A former marine. He verified your whereabouts. Did you ask him to lie for you?"

"No. Let me explain." Patel's voice wavered. "Given my various talents, I was able to compose an alternative narrative. You see, my friend . . ." He cleared his throat. "He loses track of time as a result of his injury. Knowing this, I selected him. I created an online conversation with him the following day, and then I changed the timestamp of the event for the police."

I started to grasp the weight of his statement. "You taped a news program and put it on in the background?"

"Yes."

"To fool the police?"

"It was not my finest accomplishment."

I was pretty sure he meant his *finest hour*, but continued to jot down what he was saying, word for word.

"My friend—"

"Mr. Hoek," I said, cutting him off. "Herman Hoek. Detective Sergeant Evers remembered his name." As detail-oriented as Evers was, I was surprised that he hadn't taken a picture of all of the witnesses, nor had he written down all of their contact information.

"Yes, Herman Hoek. He did not know then and still does not know that I did this."

I believed Mr. Patel because what he was saying was not clearing himself of the crime. "Why are you telling me now?"

"Because the woman—the therapist—has figured it out." He clucked his tongue. "She has retired from her practice and has moved in with me. We are happy. She has taught me courage to try and leave the house. I have taught her to love video games. In fact, she has become quite good at them."

"I'm happy for you both," I said, not knowing what else to say, but hoping he'd continue.

"Seeing you outside the Isleses's home earlier made me panic. I thought what if the police came around again? What if, given how much savvier their tech people have become, they figure out what I did?" Patel's voice picked up pace. "I decided to go through all the old files on my computer and delete the false narrative—it was an oversight not to have done it years ago. My fiancée discovered me in the middle of my deceit. She is not pleased with me. She says truth is vital to a relationship. She is threatening to leave me if I do not come forward and admit my ruse to the police. I love her with all my heart.

"Therefore," Patel inhaled and continued, "I have made her a promise that I will do as she wishes first thing in the morning. So, you see, your phone call is quite fortuitous. For the record, I did not kill your parents, and I am sorry for the horrible things I said about your father. I was not tolerant. I judged people harshly. I was not in my right mind then."

"Mr.—"

He hung up before I could say anything more.

Exhausted and eager to drown out thoughts about my parents' murders, I switched off the lights and ambled to the bedroom to read a book. While plugging the charging cord into my cell phone, a sudden anxiety pricked the nape of my neck. Last night, with Nick in the house, I hadn't experienced a moment of fear. Now? I felt vulnerable.

Quickly, I toured the house. No curtains were wafting. No windows hung open. I peeked out the sidelight by the front door. I saw a sedan drive by, headlights on. It didn't stop.

Seconds later, the heater kicked on, and I breathed easier. At my cabin, an instant before the heater would start, I always felt a chill, as if the intake needed to suck energy out of the room in order to activate itself.

I returned to the bedroom and switched on the electric blanket the professor had placed beneath the comforter. Then I washed my face, threw on my nightshirt, and clambered into bed. I was halfway into chapter one of a new mystery when I thought about Mr. Patel. I wanted to ask him something else, but I couldn't put my finger on what.

My cell phone jangled, ruining my train of thought.

Thinking it was Nick, I pressed Accept without looking at the readout.

"Aspen," a woman said. "It's me. Serenity. Can we bump tomorrow's dinner to seven thirty?"

Serenity Dawson had been my best friend in junior high and high school as well as my postgraduate roommate and my partner in crime at the Bay Area Rehabilitation Clinic, aka BARC. Though we hadn't seen each other in a couple of years, we talked every few months. When I'd texted her last night to say I was coming to the area, she'd responded quickly. She had *so much to tell me*. She still worked at BARC, whereas I'd given up my post as a therapist, no longer able to deliver results after one of my patients had committed suicide. To Serenity's credit, she was now second in command. She loved dissecting the human psyche. Though she was empathetic, she had the wondrous ability, unlike me, to maintain a safe distance from a patient's drama. Her father, a clinical psychologist, had been her role model.

"Sure," I said. "Seven thirty. Same place?"

A long pause. "Yes."

"Are you okay? You sound distant. Distracted."

"I'm fine."

I squinted. Serenity never spoke in one- or two-word sentences. "Don't kid a kidder," I chided.

"Really."

"Okay." I sighed. "Until tomorrow."

"Tomorrow." She ended the call abruptly.

I stared at the readout, disheartened. I'd been hoping that, with Nick gone, I could handle the emotional roller coaster I was about to climb onto with Serenity's help. Now, I wasn't so sure.

Chapter 11

First thing Friday, I contacted a rental car company. By nine, I was driving a new-smelling Prius with twenty-eight miles on it. By nine thirty, I was dining on a Starbucks double-shot latte and gouda-bacon egg bites.

As I pulled out of the parking lot, I spotted a dark green Honda Civic parked between two SUVs. It looked eerily similar to the car that had followed Nick and me down Valparaiso and the car that had passed by the rental house last night. Being slightly paranoid, I memorized the license plate and called my aunt. I asked her to run the plate.

Tamping down the worry—after all, the Honda hadn't torn after me as if we were in a car chase in a movie—I hurried to my appointment with Tammie. As luck would have it, her client was located nearby, on Elena Avenue, not far from the Menlo Circus Club. Started in the 1920s, the Circus Club had a history steeped in charity work, polo events, and gala parties. Much of the area around the club had been rebuilt in the past fifteen years. Many of the homes cost well over ten million dollars, so I had expected to be impressed when I drove onto the street. However, upon seeing the modernized two-story wood-and-stone home that belonged to Tammie's client, my mouth dropped open. I might even have gasped.

Tammie climbed out of a gray Jaguar SUV that was parked in the circular driveway and beckoned me. "This way."

Over the years, my mother had chided Tammie for being too thin. Whenever we would all go out for ice cream at Town and Country Shopping Center or to pizza at the historic Round Table, Tammie would beg off. Admittedly, I hadn't realized how thin she was then, but now, I had to agree with my mother. In a black pencil skirt, feathery flounce jacket, and stiletto heels, Tammie reminded me of an aging ballerina.

I strode up the cobblestone driveway, happy that I'd worn flats, arms outstretched. "It's so good to see you."

"And you." Tammie hugged me and then held me at arms' length.

"You look fabulous. Love the hair. It suits you. And the skinny jeans? You've been working out."

"Always." I'd thrown on a nubby sweater and a leather jacket over the jeans to look professional without screaming *private investigator*.

"You've certainly been in the news the past year." Tammie ran her fingers through her spiky platinum hair. "Ever since joining your aunt's detective agency."

"Those stories have been published here?"

"No. I read my news online. I've kept tabs on you." She petted my shoulder. "Your parents . . ." She inhaled. "They would be so proud."

I blinked away tears. "Speaking of proud, my mother would be in awe of your progress."

Mom had taught Tammie everything she knew, even helped her get her certification. Tammie had minored in interior design in college, but her parents had talked her out of it as a career. Working in finance, they said, would be a more lucrative choice and one that would help Tammie find a husband. And even though Tammie's selfish parents had subsequently checked out of her life after she'd completed her freshman year, and Tammie had had to scrimp and save to make ends meet, she had followed their advice.

I eyed the house. "This place is something else."

"Isn't it? I get to redecorate the guest room, and if the owner, Viola Isles"—she said the name using an upper-crust accent—"likes what I do, she'll hire me to do everything."

"Isles? That's the last name of the woman who bought my parents' house. Do you think she's related to your client?"

"Doubtful. Viola's husband is an only child."

"Small world. Nick and I were driving by yesterday, so we stopped, and Ilona . . ." I halted, recalling the moment. "She was very nice. She's an interior designer, too. Isles Styles."

"I've met Ilona. I didn't realize Isles was her last name."

"She gave us a tour. It was . . ." I paused again.

"Difficult." Tammie dipped her head in understanding. "I'm sorry about Nick having to leave, by the way."

"Thanks. I'm sure it'll be fine." Nick had texted me earlier that Natalie was communicative. "Go on. Tell me about *your* Mrs. Isles."

"Viola is very rich."

"No kidding," I whispered conspiratorially. "How big is this house?"

"Twelve thousand square feet." Tammie gripped my arm and gave a squeeze. "Wouldn't it be something if I could do it all? I could sure use the influx of cash, although I do have another design I'm doing. The Youth Science Institute at Vasona Lake County Park. You know where that is, don't you?"

"Of course. In Los Gatos." During the summer, the park featured weekly concerts. People hiked and played Frisbee or soccer, and there were paddle boats and row boats for rent during the season, although not this late into autumn. My father had enjoyed fishing at the percolation ponds along the nearby multiuse trail that the city had stocked with trout.

"It's a simple assignment, a little one-story place, but if I do well, it could open up all sorts of big-ticket jobs for other cities' parks and recreation departments." Tammie hooked a finger. "Follow me to the guest room. Viola isn't home, so we can talk openly. Unless the housekeeper is around." She sniggered. "Viola swears the woman doesn't speak English, but you and I know she understands every word."

Tammie curled her hand around the crook of my elbow and guided me into the house and up a gorgeous oak-railed staircase.

I glanced left and right. "It doesn't look like anything needs to be redone." Everything was white or tan and decidedly unlived in. Over two dozen white tiger lilies filled an elegant vase in the living room. The pungent scent was perfuming the entire house. "In fact, the place looks staged."

"It does, doesn't it? That's because Viola and her hubby bought the house lock, stock, and barrel. They didn't change a thing. Now, a year later? She wants to put her own touches on it. She came to me on the recommendation of her neighbor, whose guest house I redid." Tammie steered me into a room at the top of the stairs, released me, and spread her arms. "This is it. Seeing as the room has a balcony facing the garden, I'm thinking big bold florals. Viola loves flowers. She spends most of her time in the—" She glanced at me and frowned. "Oh, my,

I'm horrible. Today isn't about me. It's about you and your goal." She pulled me into a hug. "Let's get out of here."

With the propulsion of a steam engine, Tammie guided me out of the house, bid the housekeeper *adios*, and said, "Follow me to the storage unit site." She rattled off the address in Redwood City, although I'd already refreshed my memory. "When we're there, we'll get caught up. You'll tell me everything."

As I followed Tammie, the landscape changed. Atherton was an area of great wealth; Redwood City, less so. Especially close to the freeway. Buildings were run-down. Some of the nearby stores were ramshackle, which was surprising given the cost of living in the Bay Area.

After introducing ourselves to the storage company's manager, a squat man with the thighs of a weight lifter, and after verifying my identity and proprietorship of the storage unit, he invited Tammie and me to climb into a golf cart with him, and he drove us to a ten-by-thirty-foot unit, large enough for the contents of a four-bedroom house. He opened the lock and shoved up the corrugated metal door. The unit was dark and stank of dust and disuse. I steeled myself.

"If you need anything," the manager said, his voice husky from smoking, "you've got to return to the front office. Or call me on your cell phone. There aren't any telephones in the units."

"Thank you," I said.

He handed me the storage unit key and drove off in his golf cart.

The first thing that grabbed my attention after turning on the single fluorescent overhead light was the oil painting of Rosie and me, the one that Ilona Isles had mentioned, propped on an easel by the far wall. The two of us, dressed in short shorts and midriff tops, our hair in ponytails, were walking hand in hand toward the ocean at Half Moon Bay. Rosie had been a good four inches taller than me at the time. The sun had almost set. We had gone in early March. It hadn't been warm enough to go swimming. Instead, we'd spent hours digging for sand crabs and chasing each other through the foamy edge of the surf. We'd come home with sand clinging to every part of us. Rosie and I had enjoyed a few happy moments together growing up. Not as many as we should have.

"It's a beautiful painting," Tammie said, catching me staring. "Your grandmother had such a wonderful talent."

"And yet she never sold anything. I always wondered about that."

"Yes, she did. Well, she didn't *sell* sell them, but she donated her work to charities and they sold them at auction. It filled her heart to do that. She loved her causes."

That was probably the reason my mother had chided my father about being a bleeding heart. Her mother had been one, even though she and Grandpa Gray could have used every penny her art would have earned.

"I have four of her small paintings," I said. After college, I hadn't rented a place large enough to take something as big as the painting on the easel. When I'd married Damian, he'd wanted everything sleek and uncluttered. Now, I would make space.

Spinning in a circle, I said, "Where to start? Which—" I stopped short and stared at the mahogany dining room hutch, simple in design, with two glass shelves and three narrow glass doors. It was empty now. All of the curios were stored in one of the boxes. Or were they? I recalled Evers's comment. Had the killer taken something other than the silver?

Tammie brushed my arm. "Don't start thinking about it. It'll—"

"Where is it?" I whirled on her, my breath trapped in my chest. "The box?"

"Which box?"

"The box holding all the things from the hutch. It should be marked *Dining Room*."

"Calm down. Breathe. I'll find it."

Tammie consulted a list generated by the estate's executor. I hadn't thought to print out a copy. It was on my computer, cached with many of the other documents relating to my parents' deaths. I'd never wanted to review it. Why bother? I'd told myself that I would reread it when the trust needed to be activated for Candace's college fund or something of that magnitude.

"Here it is," Tammie said. "Box seventy. They're all numbered, though I doubt they're in any order. Are you looking for something specific?"

My heart wouldn't stop pounding. *What else might be missing?* "No. I simply want to see everything."

"You said on your voice message to me that you want to divest."

"Not everything. There are a few curios I'd like to keep," I said, sounding more composed than I felt.

For over an hour, Tammie and I sorted boxes by number, trying to establish some semblance of order so they would match the executor's list. One to ten, here. Fifty to sixty, over there. A jigsaw puzzle would have been easier to assemble. It irritated me that my father's and mother's office items were not all located in the same place. We had marked the boxes *Dad's Office, Mom's Office, Kitchen, Bedroom #1,* and so on. But the movers had tagged each with a number, regardless of the box's origin. How hard would it have been for them to have stacked them according to our system?

Tammie tried to talk me down from the ledge every time I grumbled. "We'll get through this. Promise. I'm not leaving until you're satisfied. So, tell me. You arrived yesterday?"

"The night before. Yesterday we met with Detective Sergeant Evers."

"I remember him. Tall and foreboding."

"He's smaller now. He has cancer. Not much longer to live."

"That's a shame." Tammie inspected the number on a box. "Did he have any—" She hooted. "Found number seventy."

Using a Swiss Army knife that my father had encouraged me to carry at all times, I cut through the tape used to seal the box. Tammie popped off the lid and pulled out something oblong, wrapped in plain paper. Another item came out with it, affixed with packing tape. It separated and fell to the ground. I lifted it.

Together Tammie and I unwrapped the items. I was able to reveal mine first—a photo album with the name Lake Tahoe on the cover as well as the year, when I'd turned five. I opened to the first page and saw a picture of Rosie and me sitting on a stand of rocks. Both smiling. Both slathered in sunblock. Happier times. I closed the cover. I couldn't browse through it right now. I didn't have the emotional strength.

"Are you okay?" Tammie asked.

"Pictures. Memories. For another time. What's that?"

"My serving dish." She held it up. Bone china with a delicate red floral trim. "I'd brought it to your mother's for book club night. Two weeks before they . . ." Tears welled in her eyes. "I'd forgotten all about it until now."

"That wasn't in the hutch. Neither was this album." I set it aside. "Are you sure the carton is number seventy?"

Tammie reviewed the label. "Bad me. This is seventy-eight. I need a new prescription for my contacts. Let's keep looking." She set the platter to one side, replaced the lid on the box, and resumed her search. "Did Detective Evers have any new insights? Has anything jogged his memory after all this time?"

"No. We went through his notes." I smiled. "He took copious notes."

Tammie heaved a sigh. "Boy, do I remember how the police grilled me. The questions were endless. What was my relationship like with your mother? How was our business doing? Where was I at the time of the murder? It was harrowing."

"You weren't a suspect."

"No, of course not, but everyone close to them was interrogated. Their clients. Their friends. Even their travel agent. Do you remember her? Lynda Sue Harris."

I'd met her a number of times when she'd dropped off tickets and itineraries for my parents. An image of the Sugar Plum Fairy came to mind. Lynda Sue radiated goodness.

"Sweetest woman in the world." Tammie regarded me thought-fully. "The police left no stone unturned. So, tell me, why do you want to dredge up the memory?"

"Rosie is having a hard time," I said. "Her daughter—"

"Candace."

"Is living with me. She was struggling with bulimia until I took custody."

"I'm so sorry. Your sister is . . . was . . ." Tammie clicked her tongue. "Your mother tried hard to keep Rosie grounded."

"Not hard enough." The words slipped out of my mouth.

Tammie shot a finger at me. "Do not blame your mother. Ever.

Rosie was always troubled. She wasn't diagnosed, but your mother was pretty certain she was bipolar."

"She's not." Over the course of my career as a therapist, I'd done extensive studies. "Rosie got hooked on drugs as a teen and stayed hooked. It didn't matter how many times she got clean. Rosie's problem is that she likes to live on the edge. End of story. No medical imbalance."

"Listen, kiddo"—Tammie clutched my shoulder—"I know how much the two of you would like closure, but it might not be possible."

"Nick said the same thing, but I've got to try. If I can dig up the truth, then maybe Rosie can . . ."

"Maybe Rosie can *what*? Go straight?"

I broke free from her grasp. "She hopes that if I can find the real killer, it will help her get rid of the guilt of not being there for Mom and Dad, and if she can lose the guilt—"

"My sweet girl," Tammie cooed. "You're as much of an enabler as your mother."

"I am not an enabler if Rosie gets clean. Only if she stays hooked."

Tammie threw me the stink eye. "Pollyanna couldn't paint a sunnier picture."

Chapter 12

"Keep organizing." I pointed to the boxes to Tammie's right.

"Yes, ma'am." After a moment, she said, "Tell me more about your plans to investigate."

I told her that I'd called a number of the suspects. She questioned whether that was safe. I reminded her that I was a trained private investigator. She didn't look convinced, but she didn't press.

"How's Mia?" I asked, changing the subject.

"She's good. She has a little girl, Giselle, and her business is thriving."

"Mia's an architect, isn't she?" I remembered reading something about her in the news the last year I'd worked at BARC.

"Not merely an architect," Tammie said, beaming. "She's a full-fledged builder now, eager to design homes like the one we walked through today. Dream Big Associates. That's the name of her company."

"She didn't want to use her surname, you know, for branding?"

"She's going through a divorce. Besides, Smith was too generic." Tammie fanned the air. "You watch. She'll become one of the most famous designers in the Bay Area soon. It may be a man's world, but she will thrive in it." Her cheeks flushed and her eyes gleamed with pride. "Her father had wanted her to become a computer programmer. He'd said that was a job with a future. How she'd hated that route." Tammie rolled her eyes. "When Mia found her true path, it was like someone switched on a light inside her. Your grandmother knew she had talent."

I remembered Mia coming to the house a lot. Not only to hang out with Rosie but also to spend time with my grandmother so she could learn to draw. In high school, she'd stopped coming around. I wasn't sure why. She'd found a new crowd of friends, I'd presumed.

"Tell me about Giselle," I said. "Are you a proud grandma?"

"She's four years old and quite shy, but you should see her color." Tammie mimed furiously drawing. "She's as passionate as her mother. I'm sure I sent you a picture of her."

I was sure she hadn't. I hadn't given Tammie my new contact information when I'd left the Bay Area, hence, the reason she'd had to follow my exploits online.

"Long blonde curls. Pert little nose. Too skinny, if I do say."

Who was calling the kettle black?

"Mia used a surrogate to have her. A gestational surrogate. She couldn't carry to term, so——"

My cell phone trilled. I recognized the wind chimes tone. "Mine," I announced.

By having moved so many boxes, we'd created a blockade to where we'd left our purses. I cut through the mess, rummaged in my tote for the phone, and answered on the third ring. I didn't recognize the telephone number. "Hello."

"Miss Adams?" Viraj Patel said, his intonation distinctive.

"Yes, sir?"

Tammie said, "Who is it?"

I whispered, "My parents' neighbor."

Into the phone, I said, "Go on, Mr. Patel. I'm listening. Are you at the police station?"

"No. I am headed there——"

Reception cut out and returned.

"But first," he went on, "I wanted to tell you that I had a thought about one of the other suspects, so I was doing some research about a——"

The reception cut out again.

"I'm sorry," I said. "Did you say *debt* or *threat?*"

"Being a suspect myself, I kept current with everything the police were doing," Patel went on.

Okay, that threw me for a loop. Had he hacked into the police records? Or had his friend, Hoek, done so? Wasn't that a punishable offense?

"Are you free to talk?" Patel asked.

"Not really. I'm with my mother's business partner. We're cleaning out the family's storage unit."

He cleared his throat. "I am interrupting. I will contact you later. Goodbye."

"Wait. Sir—"

He ended the call as abruptly as he had last night. Odd man. Did I trust him?

"That was brief," Tammie said. "He wanted to discuss a debt?"

I frowned. "Or a threat. The reception was spotty."

"Your mother never liked him." Tammie rubbed a knot out of her neck. "He was always carping about others. Denigrating their religions and such. What a despicable man. How did he get your number?"

"I reached out to him." I told her about our chat last night and how Patel revealed that he'd lied about his alibi, although, according to him, he had a verifiable alternative one.

"He said his fiancée will corroborate his story, and you believed him?" Tammie sniffed.

"You know, I was thinking about him before I went to sleep last night." I noted the number on another carton. "I wanted to ask him something, but I couldn't for the life of me remember what it was. When he said the word *debt*, that triggered something, but again, I'm not sure what."

"Maybe he owes you a debt of gratitude for not contacting the police that very instant."

I smirked. "Thank you. For being snarky. I needed that."

"That's my forte." Sassily, she polished her fingernails on her jacket. "I'd advise you to keep your distance. Want some water?" she asked. "I saw a vending machine near the office."

"Love some."

Minutes after she left, I found a box marked *Master Bedroom*. As I opened the box, I felt as apprehensive as I had when I'd sorted through the hope chest. What would I find? Would the items spark memories? Would I relive the day my parents died? The detective's phone call. The hours of crying. The sleepless night. Slowly, I pawed through the box, recalling all the items my mother had kept on her bureau: tiny silver boxes, her hairbrush and hand mirror. I was surprised not to find the silver frame that had held my parents' wedding photo—the photo Evers had duplicated for his notes—or the cherrywood puzzle box my grandmother had made for my mother. Had Rosie absconded with the items on one of her forays? How I had loved the box and the unique way it opened. Grandma Patrice had laughed at my futile attempts. I pushed the memory aside and continued to search.

When I stumbled upon box seventy, marked *Dining Room Hutch,* I let loose with a whoop. I cut through the tape, unfolded the flaps, and pushed them down so they'd stay open. One by one, I removed the packing paper-wrapped items and set them on the cement floor until the box was empty. Then I sat cross-legged staring at them.

Tammie returned. "Did you find box seventy?"

"Yes."

"What's in it?"

"Not sure yet."

Tammie removed the top on my water bottle and handed it to me. I took a long swig and set the bottle beside me. *Here goes nothing.* I opened the first item. Rosie's diving medals. Three of them, all blue. They were from the second year that she'd been on the team. Months later, she'd started to go downhill. Hanging out with a whole new crowd. Stealing out at night. Getting hooked on drugs. Unwilling to think about her decline, I placed the medals to my left and pressed on.

The next item, which was large and bulky, was my mother's Woman of the Year trophy. Her name was etched into a crystal circle that was fixed on a crystal base. Beneath her name: *For your endless perseverance in social work and service,* and the year—sixteen years ago. I smiled, realizing that she had been, despite her efforts, very much like her mother. A giver.

"I remember going to that luncheon," Tammie said. "Your mother wore that green silk dress, remember? With the cowl collar. She'd looked stunning."

Dad and I had attended the event. Mom had blushed at receiving such high praise. I set the trophy aside and opened more packages: my father's first earned dollar bill, sealed in Plexiglas; the document from the first case he lost, preserved into an alkaline-free album; two boxes Grandma Patrice had made, each holding a tiny gold coin, one for Rosie and one for me, given to us on Christmas—Rosie was six, I was four. Each box was emblazoned with our names. The coins were worth a pittance, our grandmother had said, but she gave them to us to remind us that every cent we earned should make us proud of our achievements. I remembered Rosie hurling the box across the room. She'd wanted our grandmother to make her a doll. My father sent her to her room, and the next day stowed both of the boxes in the hutch to remind us to mind our manners.

A year before their deaths, my mother had wanted to clear out the hutch and display her fine china in it, but my father wouldn't hear of it. The hutch, he'd said, displayed the best and worst in each of us. We needed to be reminded of what we could be and what we shouldn't become.

Rosie had hated the hutch.

"Anything unusual?" Tammie asked. "Anything missing?"

"Not that I can tell."

For another hour, we rummaged through boxes, with me declaring this item a keeper or this item for the trash or Goodwill. I didn't need my parents' bed or my father's cumbersome desk. In addition to the painting Grandma Patrice had done of Rosie and me, I set a few artistic pieces that my mother had painted or sculpted to one side. I'd find space in the cabin for them.

Back aching, I stood and stretched and ran my fingers along my neck to ease out the kinks.

"Something wrong?" Tammie asked.

"I don't see a couple pieces of my grandmother's art."

"Like what?"

"She'd painted a few small portraits on wood blocks, and she'd made other boxes."

Tammie shook her head. "You know, Miss Thaller was in charge of selling off the small, valuable items you had set to one side, things you said you'd never need or wear, like your mother's jewelry." Ulyssa Thaller was the executor for my parents' estate. "Is it possible you mistakenly put those in that pile? You were—"

"Distracted," I said.

"If that's what happened . . ."

"*C'est la vie.*" A saying came to me. I couldn't remember who'd said or written it: *You can't lose what you never had, you can't keep what isn't yours, and you can't hold on to something that doesn't want to stay.*

Tammie rose to her feet and rested a hand on my shoulder. "Miss Thaller will have a full accounting."

"I'll call her later and set an appointment."

"By the way, any income from the sale of those items would have gone into the trust."

"Yes, I know." I peeked at my watch. Four o'clock. I brushed dust off my jeans. "I've kept you long enough."

"Let's finish," she said.

"No." We were half done. "It's okay. I'll go through the rest of this in the next few days. You were a saint. I needed a kick-start. Thank you."

Tammie drew me into a hug. "I wouldn't have wanted to be anywhere else. I've missed seeing you."

"I've missed you, too," I murmured into her shoulder.

Chapter 13

The sun's rays strained to peek through the clouds. The glint stung my eyes as I headed to the rental house. I lowered the visor and, having connected the cell phone to the Prius via Bluetooth, contacted Ulyssa Thaller. She said she could meet with me in the morning. I demurred, reminding her that it would be Saturday. She said she didn't mind. She was an admitted workaholic, which was probably how she'd come to take over her father's business. Years ago, when my parents had first contacted Thaller Estate Planning to draw up their wills, Ulyssa had been a junior partner. She'd sat in on their meetings but had had no oversight.

The moment I turned onto Glenwood Avenue, my cell phone rang. Thinking it was Ulyssa calling back, I accepted the call.

A man cleared his throat. "Miss Adams," he said. Not Thaller. Not Viraj Patel. No accent. The voice was deep, like a soul singer's, but tentative.

"Yes. Who's this?"

"Antoine Washington. You called me."

"Yes, I did." My heart started to flutter. I pulled to the side of the road.

"To discuss what happened to your parents."

"That's right. I'd like to talk to you in person if you have time."

"Why?" He didn't sound upset in the least. In fact, he sounded calm and composed. "I didn't do it. Police cleared me."

"Yes, I know." I hadn't prepared a response. "The case went cold."

"I heard."

"My sister, Rosie, wants me to talk to everyone who was questioned. See if I might learn something the police didn't."

"I don't know anything."

"But you might and not realize it. Please."

There was a long pause. "How is Rosie?"

"Coping," I said. "Barely."

"Still on drugs?"

No sense lying. "Yes."

82

Antoine made a sound like a balloon losing air. "I have a break in thirty minutes. If you can come to me, we can talk."

"Where do you work?" I asked.

"Big Box in Mountain View. On El Camino near San Antonio. You can park beneath the building. Come to the loading dock. I'm a loader."

"I'll be there."

"What do you look like?" he asked.

"I don't look like Rosie. I'm much shorter. Dark hair."

"Got it."

Meeting him at a warehouse-style store meant there would be plenty of people around, I assured myself. No need to be nervous.

Eager to be on time, I didn't return to the house. I didn't freshen up.

Traffic was thick near the Stanford Shopping Center, and dense all the way past the district of Palo Alto. After that, it lightened.

Twenty-five minutes later, I drove down the Big Box ramp into its subterranean parking lot. I parked and asked a woman with a cart packed with bread, meat, and other assorted items for directions to the loading dock. She didn't have a clue. A large delivery truck drove cautiously past us. I followed it on foot.

On the drive over, I'd come up with a few questions I wanted to ask Antoine, but primarily, I wanted to get a read on him. Who was he? Had he, as Evers had claimed, cleaned up his act? The hiss he'd made after hearing that Rosie was still using suggested dismay. Warehouse loaders operated heavy machinery. I'd bet an organization like Big Box tested their drivers with regularity. I couldn't imagine someone on drugs holding down the job.

The loading dock was large enough to handle six large trucks. An African-American man driving a forklift was delivering palletized freight onto the dock leveler, a hydraulically powered platform used as a bridge between the dock and the truck. The man paused the forklift and glanced in my direction. With a toothy grin, he held up a finger and yelled, "Be right with you. Have a seat."

I moved to a bench beyond the trucks in what had to be the designated smoking section, given the overfilled ashtray, and I waited.

Five minutes later, Antoine Washington approached.

I rose to my feet.

Dressed in what appeared to be a uniform of brown shirt, brown trousers, and brown shoes, he looked tall and lean. He sported a flattop Afro hairstyle, and he moved with the grace of an agile running back. "Miss Adams." He jutted out a large manicured hand.

I took hold.

"You lied to me," he said.

"No—"

"You look a lot like Rosie. Same eyes. Same nose. Though you are a might smaller. I'll grant you that." His voice held a gentle twang. His gaze was warm. He released my hand. "Follow me. There's a break room inside the building." He loped ahead and said over his shoulder, "Ever been to a Big Box?"

"No, but I've been to Costco and the like."

"Yeah, they're all the same. My cousin found me the job. Becoming a forklift operator isn't easy. You've got to go to school. Be OSHA-compliant. Get certified. Lots of hoops to jump through." He opened a heavy metal door into the building and veered left. "This way. If you're hungry, the donuts are killer." He balked. "Sorry. That was in bad taste."

"It's okay."

"Coffee's fine, too."

Wanting to be sociable, I said, "Sure." Food sounded horrible. Tammie and I had skipped lunch. I hoped I'd find an appetite by the time I met Serenity for dinner.

Antoine pushed through a swinging door into an employees' lounge. It was beige with no frills. A couple of leather couches. A few tables with metal chairs. Nothing to encourage the staff to linger. Two other employees were in the room.

After filling two disposable paper cups with coffee, Antoine guided me to a table. "So, let's cut to the chase. You wanted to meet me to see if you can tell whether I'm guilty. Am I warm?"

I laughed. "No fooling you."

"My granddaddy made sure I knew the ropes. My mama had her say, too." He grinned and I could see why Rosie had hooked up with him. He had sex appeal. And confidence. "Tell me more about Rosie," he went on. "Where's she living? What's she doing?"

"She's a waitress in Auburn."

"You said she's still hooked."

I blinked at his forthrightness. "Yes."

"That's too bad. How's her little girl?"

"She's a teenager now. Her name's Candace. She's living with me."

He propped his elbows on the table and tented his fingers. "What do you do?"

"I'm a private investigator. In Lake Tahoe."

"Huh. You don't look like one."

I smiled. What should a P.I. look like? Maybe he expected all P.I.'s to be men who wore porkpie hats. I sipped the coffee. It was bitter. I set it aside. "Antoine—may I call you Antoine?"

"Might as well. It's my name."

"Where were you at the time of my parents' deaths?"

"Murders," he said. "Call 'em what they were."

I exhaled. "Where were you at the time?"

He scrubbed his chin. "I already answered all these questions. Haven't you talked to the police?"

"Yes, and I have reviewed case notes, but I'd like to start fresh and pretend I haven't read anything."

"Uh-uh." He tilted his head. "You tell me what you know first. C'mon. Why do a runaround? A dance?"

"Okay, you were hanging out with friends, but none of their accounts about your whereabouts were credible because they were, um, doing drugs."

"We all were. I don't anymore." He took a swig of coffee. "CCTV corroborated I was where I said I was."

"Yes, I know. Detective Sergeant Evers confirmed that."

"Evers." Antoine sniffed. "Mr. Tough Guy. Never cut me any slack. I liked that about him."

I was surprised to hear him say that.

"My old man believed every lie I ever told him. Maybe if he'd cared enough to question me . . ." Antoine let the rest of the sentence hang. "He walked out on me and my twin sister when we were twelve."

"I'm sorry."

"I'm not. Don't want to be like him. Don't want to be like I was. Ever again. I'm in therapy. I'm working on myself. I want to be a better man. Do you believe in therapy?"

I smiled. "I used to be a therapist."

He coughed out a laugh. "Why'd you leave the biz?"

"One of my patients committed suicide."

"Wow, that sucks. Did you feel like a failure for not saving him? Was it a him?"

"Yeah, it was a him. And, yeah, I felt like a failure. For a while. I don't any longer. I've seen a therapist, too." I tamped down the myriad emotions swirling inside me about my patient and my past. I had to stay focused. "Antoine—"

"I never considered suicide," he said. "Ever."

"Good for you."

"A year ago, I had the opportunity to start a pot business with a buddy. All legal and on the up-and-up." He lifted his chin. "I opted not to do that. It would've been a path to the dark side for me. I want a family. Kids. I want to be the father I never had."

Was he telling me this to snow me? Was I buying his lie or believing the truth? Many of my patients professed that they'd wanted to change. Half—maybe less—could stay the course.

I folded my hands on the table. "I'm sure you'll make a great father."

"Thanks." He sipped his coffee, set it aside, and folded his hands like mine. "Go on."

"That day . . . the day my parents were murdered . . . when you were with friends. Is it possible that one of them skipped out?"

"And robbed and killed your folks? No way. FYI, no one ever talked about your folks. Or the robbery. No one ever bragged. Get my drift? There's no honor among thieves." Antoine ran a finger along the rim of his cup. "Know what that expression means?" He gave me a moment to consider the question before continuing. "Thieves aren't trustworthy. If someone had done the deed, someone would have talked about it, you know?"

Rosie had said nearly the same thing.

"By the way, that's a proverb," he added. "People think it's a quote, but it's not."

"Are you sure?"

"Yep." He grinned. His teeth were in good shape. He was definitely taking advantage of whatever medical and dental package Big Box was offering. "I know because I've enrolled in school. Junior college. Nights. I'm studying English."

"Why?"

"I'd like to expand my horizons." His eyes gleamed with hope. "Maybe become a teacher. Or run this place." He chortled. "Who knows? The sky's the limit if you get educated, isn't that right?"

Despite myself, I was liking this guy and what he'd become.

Antoine scratched behind his ear. "By the way, something occurred to me about a year after this all went down. My lawyer told me the police didn't find fingerprints at the crime scene. They said it had been wiped down."

"That's right."

"Seems to me a robber would've been wearing gloves."

"Your point?"

"All I'm saying is whoever it was, if he'd gone in to rob the place, as his primary goal, then he would've been wearing gloves. Ergo, he wouldn't have needed to wipe things down. Feel me?"

I did *feel* him and once again my thoughts flew to my conversation with Evers.

Antoine peeked at his watch. "I got two minutes, max. Anything else?"

"No. I appreciate you meeting with me." I stood.

So did Antoine. He grabbed hold of my arm. "Hey, you tell Rosie I asked about her. Will you do that?"

I hesitated. "Did you and she—"

"Yeah, we did."

He wasn't Candace's father. Couldn't be.

"It was good between us when we were both, you know . . ."

Between highs.

"When we weren't sober, it wasn't so good," he went on. "But I'm clean now."

"So you said."

"Maybe, sometime, I could talk Rosie into doing the same. Wishful thinking?"

"Probably." I started to leave and turned back. "Hey, Antoine, what kind of car do you drive?" It was inconceivable that he had guessed I had come to town and had staked out Ilona's house in the hope that I might show up, but I never ruled out a possibility. Especially if Rosie had mentioned my investigation to someone, and that someone had reached out to Antoine.

"I don't drive one," he said. "Can't afford it. I'm a public transportation guy through and through. Maybe one day I'll own a car, but I want a house first, you know?"

As I was walking to my car rummaging in my jacket pocket for the keys, my cell phone rang. The sound echoed in the cavernous parking lot, which was surprisingly empty of cars, either entering or leaving. I pulled my phone from my purse. *Caller Unknown.* I tapped the Accept button. "Hello?"

"Aspen Adams?" a man growled.

"Yes, who is—"

"William Fisher. Listen good. I'm telling you one time, stay away from me and my family."

"Sir, all I want to do is ask—"

"Do not contact me again. Or else."

He ended the conversation.

I browsed the list of recent calls. His number, one of the three I'd tried last night, was there. I wouldn't reach out to him right now. But I would tomorrow. I would not be put off by a warning.

Climbing into the Prius, I noticed a piece of paper under the windshield wiper. I got out and nabbed it. It read: *GO HOME.* All block letters. The hair at the base of my neck stood on end. I felt eyes on me. Had Fisher put the note there? Was he watching me? Or had someone else?

Antoine was nowhere in sight. A man pushing a cart filled with items was leaving the store. To my right, a woman in a Chevy Suburban casually pulled into a parking spot.

Adrenaline pumping, I pitched into the car, switched on the

ignition, strapped on my seat belt, and sped to my home away from home. On the way, I tried to reach Nick on his cell phone. The call rolled into voicemail. I left a quick message about my two conversations with Viraj Patel and Antoine Washington, but I didn't mention Fisher's call or the note on the car. Why worry him?

A half hour later, safely locked in the house, intent on putting the threatening note from my mind, I poured myself a glass of wine. Maybe it had been a prank. A dare. A teen had taunted a buddy to post it on a windshield. *Any* windshield. Mine simply happened to be the lucky car.

Frustrated, but not despondent, I took a shower, refreshed my makeup and hair, and dressed for dinner with Serenity. I'd brought a black sheath and heels for the occasion. I wasn't a fashion freak, but once in a while it felt good to dress up.

Before leaving the house, I checked voicemail. Nothing from Nick. Nothing from my aunt on the license plate. Nothing from Viraj Patel. What debt . . . or threat . . . or bet . . . had he wanted to talk to me about? A string of Dr. Seuss's rhymes cycled through my head. I stifled a laugh. Whatever Patel had wished to impart would have to wait until morning.

Chapter 14

La Belle de Jour, a French bistro located on the first floor of the Palais Hotel in San Jose, was the new *in* place, according to Serenity. The hotel was beyond ritzy, decked out with Louis XIV furniture and grandiose staircases. When I entered the restaurant, it was more subdued in décor, but I could feel the energy humming. With a maximum seating of sixty, a reservation was hard to come by, but Serenity knew someone who *knew* someone. The candelabra lighting gave the restaurant a warm glow. The array of mirrors provided an intimate view of nearly every table. People were chatting as if their conversations were the most important they'd ever had. The sound washed over me as the hostess guided me to Serenity.

To this day, Serenity made me feel inadequate in the looks department. Tall and lithe, with lustrous blonde hair and intelligent brown eyes, she reminded me of a fashion model. Her voice had the polished tone of a practiced politician or inspirational preacher, which benefited her as a therapist. Patients depended upon her; colleagues respected her. I remembered meeting her on the first day of junior high school. She'd moved from Los Angeles and, even then, had been beautiful though quite shy. Now, she impressed me with her confident calm, as if her parents had known at birth that Serenity would embody her given name.

"Aspen." She took hold of my shoulders and air-kissed me on both cheeks. "You . . . look great."

She was lying. I'd checked myself before leaving the house. Makeup had helped my strained eyes; a dash of hairspray had set my limp hair in place. "Thanks, so do you. How are you?" I sat and placed my napkin on my lap.

"Fine."

Again with the short answers. If I were honest, her eyes looked strained. A waitress appeared with a bottle of chardonnay.

"I ordered wine." Serenity signaled for the waitress to pour two glasses. "Chardonnay okay?"

"My preferred beverage. But I'll stop at one glass. I'm driving."

"Me, too."

I took a sip and sighed. Just what I needed. I hadn't finished the glass I'd poured at the house.

Out of nowhere, I felt eyes on me. No one was staring in our direction. A figure disappeared near the entrance to the lobby. I shook off the unease and focused on my friend.

"The scallops are divine," Serenity said. "Made with a lemon beurre blanc sauce."

"Done." I didn't even open my menu.

She signaled the waitress and ordered. "So, bring me up to date."

"Hold on. You texted that you had so much to tell me."

"It'll wait." Her voice was tight and uneven. She sipped her wine. "You first. How are you? Happy? How's Nick? Tell me all about him. Every last detail. Are you two, you know, going to get engaged?"

"I'm not sure he wants to be married again. His first marriage . . ." Nick's wife had an affair with his boss—the captain. However, during divorce proceedings, she'd claimed that Nick had abused her. He hadn't. The captain had. It had been a sticky situation until Nick was cleared, but tension with his former colleagues had made it difficult for him to remain in San Jose. "We're taking it slow."

"I know how that goes," Serenity said.

Movement outside the restaurant grabbed my attention again. This time, it was someone I recognized. Tammie.

I breathed easier and said to Serenity, "Excuse me. I see a friend in the lobby. I'll be right back." I rushed out of the bistro and called, "Tammie." She appeared to be taking a photograph using her cell phone.

She whirled around while tucking her phone into her large tote. "Hey. Fancy seeing you here."

At the same time, I caught sight of a broad-shouldered man clad in a dark suit and heavy overcoat boarding the elevator. The doors started to close. The man pivoted. He had a thin film of hair and crooked nose. Was he the one who I'd felt was watching me a moment ago? His face looked familiar but I couldn't place him.

"Aspen, are you okay?" Tammie asked.

"Fine." I wasn't. Every nerve fiber was tingling. I focused my attention on her. She looked radiant in a sleek white cocktail dress and strappy heels. "Why are you here? You're sure dressed to the nines for being on a clandestine décor-seeking mission."

"A what?"

"I saw you sneaking pictures. With your cell phone. My mother taught you well." Once, Mom told me that was how she'd dreamed up many of her ideas. Trends came in waves. If she photographed what she encountered, she could remember what had or hadn't worked.

Tammie laughed. "Observe, observe, observe. That was your mother's motto."

"Indeed."

An elderly gentleman passed by us, heading to a second elevator. The doors opened and a young svelte brunette appeared from the restroom and slipped in first. The man followed and pivoted to face us. The woman brushed his shoulder with hers. Accidentally on purpose? The man took in Tammie, head to toe, and frowned.

"Do you know him?" I asked.

"Who?"

The elevator doors closed.

"Never mind. So why are you here?" I asked.

"I had dinner with a client."

"There you are, Tammie." A handsome man appeared over her shoulder and handed her a three-quarter-length coat that matched her dress.

Tammie said, "Bruno Daleo, Aspen Adams."

He and I shook hands.

"My pleasure." He had a slight Italian accent.

"Bruno owns a tech company in Sunnyvale. I'm trying to entice him to let me redo his entire villa in Sonoma."

"If Tammie's taste in décor is like her taste in food," Daleo said, "I might say yes."

Tammie hooked a thumb toward the Italian restaurant on the opposite side of the lobby. "I picked the restaurant. Best pasta Alfredo anywhere. What are you doing here, Aspen?"

Something nagged at the edges of my brain. I couldn't put my finger on it. Did it have to do with the man with the crooked nose or the elderly man and the brunette?

"Aspen," Tammie prompted.

"Oh, sorry. I'm meeting an old friend. You know her. Serenity."

"Of course. That's great. Have a nice time. Tell her hello." Tammie suggested to Daleo that he head to the parking valet, and then she kissed my cheek and said, "Let's talk tomorrow."

I strode into the bistro and drew to a halt when I saw Serenity talking to a man. Not just any man. My ex-husband, Damian Saint. Handsome yet gaunt, long curly hair cupping his neck. Dressed in an elegant Armani suit. He was holding Serenity's hand, as if he'd recently kissed it, and he was gazing at her with those wicked green eyes, the same that had lured me with the promise of adventure.

Heat rose up my neck and bloomed in my cheeks. Drawing in a courageous breath, I strode to the table.

Damian dropped Serenity's hand and stood tall. "Aspen, you look . . . incredible."

"Liar."

Despite his reputation for being a brilliant albeit intense conductor, Damian had always had an easy laugh. "Serenity was telling me about your quest. 'And justice for all,'" he intoned. "Maybe you should have become a lawyer instead of a therapist."

"A patient needs justice, too," I said with a bite.

"Yes, of course. I didn't mean—" He faltered. "I should return to my dinner guest. He manages the New York Philharmonic." He pointed at a massive man with white hair and paunchy jowls sitting alone at a table across the room. "We've ordered dessert. Have fun catching up." He strode away.

Serenity patted the table. "Sit, Aspen. I ordered for both of us. They brought us a baguette and butter." She pushed the breadbasket toward me. Given my dietary restrictions regarding gluten, I abstained. "So, tell me, who were you spying on out there?"

"I wasn't spying. I saw my mother's partner, Tammie. She says hello, by the way."

"That's sweet. I always liked her."

"We went through my parents' storage unit earlier. We hadn't talked about dinner plans. I was surprised to see her here."

"What a coincidence."

"Mm-hm. Almost as coincidental as seeing Damian."

"It's the best restaurant in San Jose," Serenity said. "Lots of local celebrities come here."

"Local celebrities," I muttered, fighting the itch to turn and look at my ex-husband.

"I'm sorry." Serenity clasped my hand. "You look upset. I know Damian wasn't good to you, but—"

I pulled my hand free. "Wasn't good to me? After his fling with what's her name, our marriage became a shouting match. He always made it my fault, of course, and hated how I wouldn't retreat. Hated that I could muster pithy arguments to counter his." I sipped my wine and set the glass down with a thump. "Forgive me. You don't need to hear my drama." I took a deep breath, despising that a moment with Damian could set me off. Heart racing. Anger rising. Memories, both good and bad, flickering inside my mind.

"Let's put it behind us," I said. "Your turn. You texted that you have *so much to tell me*." I used her inflection. "Did you meet someone? Are you in love? Are you leaving your job? Spill." I leaned forward on both elbows.

"I . . ." She hesitated. "Damian."

"Yep, he's over there. Having dinner with the manager of the philharmonic. He had to drop that tidbit. FYI, he wouldn't deign to have dinner with anyone who couldn't help his career." Giving in, I searched the restaurant. Damian was deep in conversation with his dinner companion. I turned to Serenity. "So . . ."

"I've been dating Damian," she blurted out.

My throat went dry. I swallowed hard. "When? Why?" I shook my head. "I mean, I get that you've known each other for years. Heck, you were my bridesmaid. But, Serenity, you know him. You know how he—" I halted.

How he'd broken my heart. Ripped it to shreds. My grousing sounded like a bad romance novel.

I forced a smile. As a therapist, I'd learned to muster composure, even when shocked by a patient's revelations. Tapping into that mental muscle, I said, "When did you start to date? What was the spark?"

Serenity flushed pink. "Three months ago we ran into each other at the grocery store, of all places. We got to talking and set a date to meet. He hasn't been seeing anyone since you two divorced."

I squelched a skeptical snort.

"He's been working on himself. He's in therapy."

Wasn't everyone nowadays? I mused.

Serenity twirled a tress of hair, looking angelic and vulnerable. When had she lost her ability to see through lies? Or had Damian really changed? "We have a lot in common," she said. "I love Mozart. He's an expert on everything Mozart."

I had never liked Mozart. I preferred jazz.

"I enjoy long walks in the woods," she went on. "So does he."

Since when?

"And we both adore poodles."

Okay, that was the last straw. "Poodles?" I asked. "Any poodles, or mixes like goldendoodles and Schnoodles?" When we were married, Damian had ruled out owning anything with fur. Cat, dog, guinea pig.

"Standard poodles," she said, completely missing my snarky tone. "My sweet Tanya adores him. I told you I got a poodle, didn't I?" She swiped her cell phone screen and quickly brought up a picture of a chocolate poodle with ribbons in its hair.

"She's gorgeous."

"Isn't she?" Serenity closed the app. "Like I said, Damian and I have only started dating. It's nothing serious. So, you don't need to be jealous. We—"

"Breathe," I said to reassure her. "I'm not jealous. I'm not anything. We're divorced, and there are no feelings left between us, okay? Just be—" I paused again. Wary? Leery? Alert for the signs that he's straying? "Take it one day at a time."

"Like you and Nick."

Nothing like us, but I said, "Yeah. Like that."

Serenity sipped her water. "I'm going to the ladies' room before they bring our dinner. I'll be right back."

"I'll be enjoying the ambiance."

Moments after she disappeared down a hall near the lobby entrance, I felt a presence behind me. Then hands on my shoulders.

I swiveled in my chair and threw Damian a scathing look. "Cut it out."

"My dinner's over. Care if I join you?"

"Yes." I would not be kind, and I refused to be weak.

"You look great, babe. I wasn't lying before."

That smile. Those eyes. Both were cruel and heartless. Why hadn't I picked up on that all those years ago?

"Better than ever, in fact," he added, a slight slur to his words. He never drank when conducting, but he had a penchant for scotch when he was between gigs. "The lake air must be doing you good."

"Being far away from you is working wonders."

He grinned in the insolent way he had, as if no insult could wound him. He was better than everyone. A god in his own mind.

"I hear you and Serenity are dating," I said.

Damian frowned. He glanced toward the hall. Smoothly, he settled into her chair, uninvited. "It was wrong to start up with her," he said. "We're not right for each other. I did it to hurt you. I knew she'd tell you."

"It doesn't, you know. *Hurt.*" I smoothed the napkin on my lap. "And she thinks you're perfect for each other."

"We're not. I miss you. I want you."

"Stop, Damian." I held up both hands. "You're drunk. Get up. Walk away."

Unsteadily, he rose to his feet and propped both hands on the table. "I screwed up. With you. I'm in therapy now."

"So Serenity said. No time like the present to dig deep. I've gone through therapy, too, and I've learned I'm better off without you. Bye, Damian." I waved to Serenity, who was returning to the table. "Hey, look who stopped by to say good night."

Sweeping his hand through his hair, doing his best to recover from my dismissal, Damian turned to greet her. "Hey, beautiful. My dinner is over, so I'm heading home. I'll call you later."

"I hope you're Ubering," I said snidely.

Damian glowered. "I'm fine."

He didn't mean fine to drive. He simply meant he was *fine*. A catch. Subtext: *You were an idiot to let me walk away, Aspen.*

Damian kissed Serenity on the cheek and swaggered out of the bistro.

Chapter 15

The rest of my dinner with Serenity went well. We talked about BARC and her future as second in command. When I'd exhausted all my questions, staying far away from the topic of Damian, she started in on me. Was my detective work fulfilling? How did I feel being the stand-in mother for a troubled teen? What did Nick look like? I'd never texted her a picture. An hour later, we split the check and promised to keep in touch. I hoped she would. She would need a shoulder to cry on.

Before making the drive home, I checked voicemail messages. There were two. One from Nick saying he was proud that I'd been able to track down Antoine Washington as well as to wheedle the truth out of Patel. He added that he was curious about what Patel might want to tell me. He would check in tomorrow. The second voicemail was from Max. She had news about the license plate but would wait until she spoke to me directly. There was no message from Viraj Patel.

Traffic was light heading north on 101. Even so, the glare of headlights from oncoming cars made me blink repeatedly, and I faced the truth that I was burning the candle at both ends, as my father would say. I needed sleep. I drove down Marsh Road and was nearing Middlefield when I spotted a bright orange flare to the left, followed by a lick of fire. And another. Rising higher. I rolled down my window. The smell of smoke was intense. I heard sirens.

Adrenaline surged through me. I swerved left on Middlefield and sped through the Linden Towers–era gate at James Avenue. I veered onto Heather Drive and spied a fire truck from Menlo Park Fire Protection District at the end of the street.

Don't let it be Ilona's house. Please let her be safe.

A slew of people on foot were racing toward the fire. I parked in front of a contemporary mansion and followed them.

When I reached Irving Avenue, I could see the blaze. It was not consuming Ilona's house—it was destroying the left half of Viraj Patel's home. Firemen sprayed huge arcs of water at the house and the white sedan in the driveway. An Atherton Police Department vehicle stood nearby, overhead light flashing. A uniformed officer was conversing with a fire department official.

A huddle of women stood outside the perimeter that the firemen had established. Ilona, dressed in a raincoat, flannel pajamas, and slippers was among them.

I hurried to her and nudged her elbow. "What happened?"

"I'm not sure."

Near one of the fire trucks, a husky fireman was questioning the silver-haired woman that I'd seen in Patel's window the day before. She was wrapped in a pale yellow bathrobe. Her left arm hugged her body; her right hand protected her throat.

"Who's she?" I asked.

"Mr. Patel's fiancée, Olga," Ilona said. "He's inside. Dead. Isn't that right?" she asked the lean woman standing beside her. The woman bobbed her head. "I think he was in his office," Ilona added.

A third woman, older with jowls, said, "It was arson."

Ilona tilted her head. "I heard it was a gas leak."

"No, no," the lean woman said softly. "Murder."

Rumors could run rampant, but the last comment held a sliver of truth. Had someone killed Viraj Patel? Why? Because he'd wanted to tell me something about a debt or a threat? Had he contacted the killer and revealed his discovery, only to become the next casualty?

I felt eyes on me. I searched the crowd that had gathered. No one was staring at me. I noticed a car parked three doors down, lurking behind a truck, and saw the glow of a cigarette through the windshield. Was the person sitting in the driver's seat watching me? With this many people around, I could approach the car and challenge whoever it was.

Ilona clutched my elbow and drew me close. "I wish Ted was here. He's in the city. Another meeting."

She was trembling. Afraid. She needed a friend. I didn't budge.

An hour later, after police and news reporters had arrived on the scene and the fire was doused, teary-eyed neighbors trudged home, Ilona included. She thanked me for staying with her. I told her I'd be in touch.

Standing alone, I searched the street for the car. It was gone. I turned my gaze to Olga—Patel's fiancée—who was sitting on a camp-style chair beside the fire truck. Earlier, I'd watched the EMTs tending to her, making sure she had enough oxygen and hadn't inhaled smoke. I'd also observed the police questioning her. Now, another woman, very similar in look to Olga, her silver hair pulled into a tight ponytail, was standing beside her, hand on Olga's shoulder. Her sister, I figured.

The Atherton P.D. officer spoke to Olga. She rose to her feet. The woman I believed to be her sister slung an arm around her. Together they shambled to a gold Lexus. The sister guided Olga toward the passenger side.

Although I knew it wasn't the time to intrude, I was eager to learn more. I hurried to the women and said, "I'm sorry for your loss."

Olga regarded me, eyes dull, skin slack. In happier times, she would be considered a striking woman. "I know you."

"Yes, ma'am. You saw me leaving Mrs. Isles's house the other day. Your fiancé reached out to me earlier today about my parents' murders. He was going to talk to the police."

"He went. He confessed." She sucked back a sob. "Look what good that did him."

"He told me he had information to share. About a—"

"My sister is tired," the other woman cut me off, curling her arm protectively around Olga. "Leave her be."

"It's all right," Olga said wearily. "Miss—"

"Adams. Aspen Adams."

"Miss Adams, Viraj was always digging and finding information. It's gone now. His computer is melted. He was in his office when—"

"Was it arson?" I asked.

"He had lit a candle. I'm not sure why. He hated candles. The candle tipped over."

"Ma'am, do you think he was murdered?"

"Enough," her sister hissed at me.

Olga pressed away from her sister and met my gaze. "We don't know yet. The police will have to investigate and do an autop—" She rested her knuckles against her lips. "An autopsy."

"I'm a private detective," I said, pulling a card from my purse. I offered it to her. Her sister made a dismissive sound, but Olga took it. "I'll be glad to look into this for you. Free of charge."

"Thank you, but that won't be necessary. I trust the police to learn the truth." Nonetheless, Olga tucked my card into her bathrobe pocket.

Chapter 16

On Saturday morning, groggy from too little sleep, I put on running clothes and took a two-mile run around the neighborhood. Clouds dotted the sky. The temperature hovered in the high forties. A couple with a Weimaraner and a few other runners were the only people I saw. When I returned to the house, the weekend edition of the *San Francisco Chronicle* lay on the porch. Nice. I enjoyed reading news in print.

As I inserted a pod into the Keurig machine to brew a cup of coffee, my cell phone rang. I pulled it from my jacket pocket and scanned the readout: *Serenity*. I let it go to voicemail and trudged to the master bathroom. I took a hot shower, blew my hair dry, and threw on black slacks, an ecru silk blouse, and a black blazer.

Feeling more human, I slipped into the dining room with a mug of coffee and addressed the murder board. With a shaky hand, I drew a black X over Viraj Patel's face. What had he wanted to share with me? Was his death related to my parents' murders?

I stuck a Post-it note on Antoine Washington's image and wrote: *Innocent*. True, it was my gut reaction, but I did believe him.

Next, I pinned the *GO HOME* note to the board. If I asked the Atherton police for help to identify the author of the note, would they find William Fisher's fingerprints on it? I couldn't see any smudges.

Staring at Fisher's weathered face, it dawned on me that, other than his long black hair, he looked similar to the man I'd seen boarding the elevator at the Palais Hotel. In fact, the resemblance was striking. Had he been following me after warning me to stay away from him?

Setting the marker aside, I moved into the kitchen, microwaved a single egg in a cup, and sat down to eat. I opened the newspaper to search for coverage of the Patel fire. On the front page were articles about the president, who was set to make a visit to the area in December, and the governor, who had new ideas about how to clean up the homeless population. What a never-ending battle that was, but it wasn't limited to big cities. Even in Lake Tahoe, there was a homeless population. How they survived during the freezing cold winters amazed me.

I turned to page two and paused. On the left-hand page was a picture of a distinguished older gentleman who was the district attorney for Palo Alto—the same man I'd seen at the Palais Hotel last night, the one who had ogled Tammie as he'd boarded the elevator with the younger woman. According to the article, he was already facing stiff competition in next year's election. His opponent had made allegations over the D.A.'s lack of ethics and capability.

Synchronicity, the simultaneous occurrence of events that appeared related but had no discernible connection, always astounded me. What were the odds that I would have seen this man last night? Reading on, I learned that he had at one time been a defense attorney in private practice, but he'd given it up to serve his community, which again made me think of Tammie. Had she and the man met when she'd worked as a bookkeeper at the law firm? Was that why he'd gawked at her? Maybe he was married and the younger woman was a paramour and he'd worried that Tammie would rat him out to his wife.

I flipped through the remainder of the first section of the paper but found nothing about the Patel fire. The story was probably too local, or it was too early for a report.

"Get a move on, Aspen," I chided.

I cast the newspaper aside and hurried to the Prius.

On my way to my meeting with Ulyssa Thaller, I phoned Nick. He answered after one ring.

"Hey," he said, his voice gentle and reassuring.

"Hey, yourself."

"How are you?"

"Rattled." I told him about driving down Marsh Road. Seeing the fire. Finding out it was Patel's house and that he'd died in the blaze.

"Why didn't you call me?"

"It was late. I was fine." I told him about the possibility that it could have been arson.

"Arson," he repeated.

"That's one of the rumors. Another was that he was murdered. That got me to thinking about my brief conversation with him yesterday. What if someone—the killer—knew what Patel had discovered and wanted to shut him up before he talked to me again?"

"That's a big *what-if*."

I slowed to a stop at a light. "I'll call Atherton P.D. later this morning following my meeting. See if Detective Sergeant Quincy will loop me in."

"Aspen, maybe you should—"

"No." The light changed. I continued toward Palo Alto. "I'm not backing off." I'd intended to tell Nick about Fisher's warning and the *GO HOME* message—full disclosure—but I wouldn't now. He wasn't here. He couldn't protect me. I had to rely on my own instincts. "I gave my card to Patel's fiancée last night. I'm hoping, after she's had a moment to find her calm, that she'll figure out what he wanted to say and reach out to me." As I spoke, I realized, by questioning her last night, that I might have made her a target. Guilt zipped through me.

"The lake is gorgeous this morning," Nick said, switching subjects. "Not a cloud in the sky. How's it by you?"

"Gray and cloudy and cold." I sighed. "I'm miserable without you."

"Same here, but I'll be on my way to you soon. Natalie is doing much better, and I've found a friend of hers who can stay with her until her boyfriend returns, once she's released from the hospital."

"Don't feel that you have to—"

"Stop." He added a soft, "*Shh*. I want to be with you. I want to support you. However, this friend can't take on the responsibility until Tuesday."

"Tuesday." I sighed. That seemed like an eon away.

"But then I'm coming to you. No arguments."

I loved how much he cared for me. "No arguments."

After we ended the call, I realized that I hadn't told him about seeing Damian and how he'd hit on me. Truthfully, Nick didn't need to know. There was no *there* there. Damian was a nonissue and would always be a nonissue.

I pulled into the lot by the Thaller Building, parked, and hurried to the fourth floor. A receptionist led me into Miss Thaller's chic but sparse walnut-and-leather office. No plants. No photos. All business.

Ulyssa Thaller rose from her desk. "Aspen, how lovely to see you."

Well into her sixties, she reminded me of a formidable warrior goddess. Shimmering silver suit. Gleaming gold jewelry. Hair in a tight French twist. The lines in her face were quite deep. No facial cure-alls for her.

"Miss Thaller," I said, stepping forward.

"Please call me Ulyssa, dear. We're both adults."

As we shook hands, she cupped her other over mine. The warmth of her grip was reassuring.

"Ulyssa, thank you for meeting with me."

"Sit, please." She gestured to a leather chair.

I did and set my purse on the Berber carpet.

"How are you?" Her chair squeaked as she resumed her seat. "My, how you've grown up. You're so pretty, like your mother, with such an easy smile."

Most people thought I resembled my father. I supposed my smile was like my mother's.

"Coffee or tea?" Ulyssa asked.

"No, thank you."

"Let's get to it, then." She removed a file folder from the top of a very neat stack, opened it, and pulled two stapled sets of papers from it. She handed one to me. "As you know, the house itself didn't garner much income as it had been refinanced. What little cash we did recoup, you directed to be put into the trust."

I nodded.

"Page one and two contain the entire list of items recovered from the house."

Page one and two were what Tammie and I had consulted at the storage unit.

"On page three is the list of what we sold. Your initials are noted on these items. Let's go through it, line by line," she said. "If you'll recall, your parents bypassed you and your sister for receiving any of the proceeds, for obvious reasons." Over the years, after Ulyssa became a senior partner, she had gained oversight on more accounts, including my parents' account. Dutifully, she had administered each change as Rosie made bad decisions. If Rosie was still using drugs at their deaths, they hadn't wanted her to run through their wealth.

"It was a good thing you didn't need funds for your education," Ulyssa said.

Because Rosie had been a screwup, I'd dedicated myself to excelling in high school. My social life had suffered because of my commitment.

For the next hour, Ulyssa Thaller and I reviewed the *Sold* list.

My mother's paste jewelry. I didn't wear jewelry, except the locket that had been hers. Rosie had taken a necklace fitted with a gold cross.

A few tabletop statues. None that had been crafted by my mother or my grandmother.

A silver cachepot. Worth four thousand dollars. It had been as ugly as sin. I wasn't sure how my parents obtained it or why they'd kept it. The killer must have overlooked it, thinking it was worthless.

A set of sterling silver jewel boxes. Each worth a thousand dollars. What did Rosie or I need with teensy jewel boxes that could hold no more than a ring? Again, I wondered if the killer had overlooked them or had left them because they were too distinctive to hawk.

A Meissen porcelain tea set. Rosie had complained when I'd let it go, but I reminded her that neither of us liked tea and one chip would ruin the value of it. To pacify her, I'd suggested the estate pay half of the proceeds to her; the other half went into the trust. I didn't take a cent. Miss Thaller hadn't objected.

A collection of silver dollars. It had been my grandfather's. Each coin had been described in complete detail. Photographs of them accompanied the list. Most had sold for fifteen to twenty dollars. My mother had kept them in a cookie tin in the kitchen, which was most likely why the killer hadn't snatched them.

When I finished reading the list, I tilted my head.

"Is something wrong?" Ulyssa asked.

"I don't see any mention of the silver walking elephant that a client gave my mother." Another ugly-as-sin item, but my mother had treasured it because she had adored the client.

Ulyssa made a note on a legal pad. "That's curious. I accompanied the estate appraisers as they took photographs and rated everything, so they couldn't have lifted anything."

"I didn't presume—"

"No worries." She held up her palm. "I'll have my assistant go through the photographs one by one and see if we missed something. Was the elephant worth a lot?"

"Probably not. A couple of hundred dollars." Rosie had admired the elephant. Maybe she'd pinched it. I set the list aside. "Forgive me for asking, I was naïve when this happened and preoccupied with my first quarter of college, so a few things slipped through the cracks, but was my father's business flagging? He suffered so many ups and downs, and a few of his clients were less than satisfied."

"In fact"—Ulyssa folded her hands—"the sale of your father's firm was one of the first things we addressed. We found a small firm that wanted to expand its base and represent defense clients. Plus, due to their goodwill, they wanted to help a lawyer who had died without a succession plan. Being so young, your father hadn't been thinking about selling. You understand?"

"Yes."

"The firm realized the clients would have been ships without a rudder. It hired the legal assistant, purchased all the furniture, ended the lease, and took control of all the files."

Ulyssa unfolded her hands and crossed her arms on the desk. "You might want to know how we put a price on a lawyer's reputation. It's like this. Your father, despite his occasional ups and downs, was a respected attorney. He fought tooth and nail for his clients. That was appreciated by not only his clients—"

"Most of them."

"But, also, by the firm wishing to purchase. However, as to the price," she went on, "each practice is unique. A general rule of thumb for a standardized range is one-half to three times the gross revenues. In your father's case, that was one hundred thousand for each of the three years preceding his death. We were able to obtain an offer for one hundred and fifty thousand and felt that was respectable."

"And that amount went into the trust?"

"Yes."

"And my mother's business, Interior Motives?" Saying the name brought to mind fond memories. My mother had loved reading mysteries. The play on the words *ulterior motives* had struck her fancy. I'd been pleased to learn Tammie had kept the name. "It was doing well," I said. "She had a long roster of repeat clients. How did you put a price tag on that?"

"In much the same way," Ulyssa said. "We compared it to others of its size and scope. Miss Laplante's representative contacted us with an offer. The numbers concurred. We closed the deal. Everything was done on the up-and-up."

"I'm sure it was." I examined my fingertips as a memory wormed its way into my mind. "May I ask . . . did either of my parents have an insurance policy? I mention it because, the night we moved into the house on Irving Avenue, I recall my mother mentioning a policy to me. I was young, so maybe I misheard. When my father and grandfather were arguing about my grandfather's gambling habits, my mother hustled Rosie and me into our bedroom and promised she would always provide for us girls. She said she had an *insurance policy* and not to worry."

Ulyssa set her pen down, folded both hands and sighed. "Alas, no. No policy. Nothing but the trust."

"Might it have been buried in the documents stowed in her business files?"

"We went through every file." Ulyssa did her best to reassure me with a smile. "Every folder. Your mother's business had bills owing. We paid them. Whatever incoming funds were due her went into the trust, with the end date being the day Miss Laplante completed the purchase."

"Yes, that makes sense. I don't need the money," I hastened to add. "I'm doing fine, and Candace's college will be taken care of. I was just—"

"Wondering," Ulyssa cut in. "I understand."

Chapter 17

As I left Palo Alto, I called Detective Sergeant Quincy and asked if he could meet. He told me he had a half hour.

The Atherton Police Department precinct wasn't busy. Parking was a snap. No construction workers were around due to it being the weekend. I strode into the red-brick building, greeted the chipper dispatcher, and told her I had an appointment with Quincy. She led me through the building and out to the modular trailer.

Quincy rose from his desk, shoulders squared, chin raised, attesting to his previous military training. He nudged his rimless glasses higher on his nose. "How can I help you today?"

"I wanted to ask you about the Viraj Patel fire last night."

He regarded me squarely. "How do you know about that?"

"I was driving by. On Marsh Road. I saw the blaze. I went to check it out."

"Check it out? Why?"

"Mr. Patel . . . was a suspect . . . in my parents' case. We spoke." The words came out choppy. "Thanks to Detective Sergeant Evers, I was able to reach out to Mr. Patel by phone. He said he was coming into the precinct to confess that he'd lied about his alibi."

"He did. Sit." Quincy indicated a chair opposite his desk. I sat. He resumed his seat and folded his hands on his desk.

"He contacted me again. Yesterday. He said he had something to tell me." I described the cryptic conversation. "At the time, I was going through a storage unit. He said he wouldn't keep me and we could speak later, but he died before we could." I leaned forward in my chair. "So, I'd like to know, was there anything suspicious about his death? Rumors were flying among the crowd that had gathered. Was it a gas leak or arson? Was he murdered?"

Quincy studied his fingertips for a moment before meeting my gaze. "Yes, it was arson. Yes, he was murdered. He was shot in the back."

"With?"

"A Glock semiautomatic."

My chest tightened. "Do you have any suspects?"

"We've canvassed the neighbors. Most everyone was at work. No one saw anything suspicious. His fiancée"—Quincy glanced to his right.

I followed his gaze. Olga Payne, dressed in a black overcoat, black dress, and heels, was sitting at a desk across the trailer. "What's she doing here?" I asked.

"Filling out forms. A follow-up questionnaire."

"Is she a suspect?"

Quincy leaned back in his chair. "Miss Payne wasn't home at the time. She was having dinner with her sister, who drove to the restaurant. When they arrived at the house, it and her sedan were on fire. Despite her sister's warnings, Miss Payne ran inside the house."

"She was wearing a bathrobe when I saw her," I stated.

"Good observation. By the time she found Mr. Patel—the blaze was consuming his office—she realized she couldn't save him, and it dawned on her that she might need protection to escape. She was wearing a wool dress. One ember and she'd light up like a torch. She flew into her room, grabbed a robe, and threw it over herself. When she got outside, she put it on over her clothes."

I tried to picture last night. I couldn't remember anything peeking from beneath the hem of Olga's robe. It would have hidden a knee-length dress, I supposed. I did recall that she'd been wearing loafers, not slippers.

"I think his death might be related to my parents' murders," I said.

"Miss Adams, it's been fourteen years."

"He had something to tell me. He was silenced."

Quincy rubbed his chin. "I'll give it some consideration."

An officer beckoned Quincy.

"I'll be right back," he said to me.

"Mind if I fetch myself a cup of water?" I hooked a thumb.

"Be my guest."

The water cooler was close to where Olga was filling out forms. She looked better than she had last night. Her skin wasn't as drawn, her shoulders not as slumped. I spritzed water into a paper cup and strolled to her.

"How are you holding up?" I asked.

Olga peered at me. Recognition formed. "You're the lady from last night. The private detective. Adams."

"That's right. Aspen Adams. I'm sorry for your loss."

"I can't believe Viraj was murdered. He never did anything that would cause anyone to—" Olga halted. "That's not entirely true. He was a computer hacker. Maybe he hacked the wrong person or the wrong business this time. He told me he did it for sport. He never took a thing from anyone. He simply liked to prove that he could get inside their computers. He was so sharp. His brain was . . . incredible." She tucked a stray silver hair behind an ear and battled tears. "But this time, who knows? He was such a dear man. He wouldn't hurt a fly. He didn't deserve to be—" A wracking sob escaped her lips.

I yanked a tissue from my purse and handed it to her. "I know what you're going through."

"Of course you do. Your parents."

"It still feels like it were yesterday." It did. I wasn't lying. Especially now that I was opening up memories and exposing old wounds. I sighed.

Olga said, "I'm sorry for your loss. Viraj wanted to make things right. He—"

"I think your fiancé's death might be related to my parents' murders."

"How would that be possible?" she asked.

"As I was saying last night"—before her sister had cut me off—"when Mr. Patel called me yesterday, he said he had a thought about one of the suspects. He was researching something. A debt or a threat." *Or a bet* pealed in my brain. "Did he mention anything about this to you?"

Olga shook her head.

I glanced over my shoulder. Quincy was still talking with the officer, but he drilled his gaze into me. He did not look pleased.

I said, "Miss Payne, Viraj told me that the night before my parents were murdered, he saw someone running in the neighborhood. The person looked shifty."

"Hmm. I don't know about that, but I heard Viraj talking to a friend on the telephone yesterday, before"—her voice snagged—"before

I went to dinner with my sister. Viraj said he'd seen a green car roaming the area."

My shoulders tensed. "A Civic?"

"I wouldn't know what model," Olga said.

Was it the same car I'd seen? The one that had followed Nick and me until we'd made the detour to the office supply store? Or the one that I'd spotted at Starbucks? What had Max learned about the license plate for that car?

"Viraj said to his friend that he wondered whether someone was spying on him because he'd hacked into a financial site."

"Which financial site?"

"I don't know." She shrugged. "He thought a certain someone might be curious to know what he'd discovered."

Who? A financial site definitely suggested that the word *debt* was what he'd said to me. On the other hand, *threat* might suggest that he'd learned someone was doing something illegal within the banking system. If only we'd spoken.

"He also talked about a plant." Olga frowned. "He was involved in a transaction to buy a property. A factory. It was a teardown. In Mountain View. Maybe that was the plant." Her smile was tight but genuine, as if she felt a modicum of pride for coming full circle to an answer. "He intended to start a business. At the factory. He would go there for meetings. Perhaps—"

"I thought he had agoraphobia."

"He used to, but when I came into his life—" She covered her heart with her hand.

Patel had mentioned that Olga had helped him overcome his fear.

"He was very excited about the new business." She lowered her hand. "He intended to create solar cells. Not create them, actually. They've been created. But he wanted to build on that premise. He wanted to change the world." She brightened as she spoke. "Solar cells are vital for the future, he said. He was quite an eco-nut."

That might explain his exceptional garden.

"Did you know Albert Einstein proposed a new quantum theory of light and explained the photoelectric effect in a paper in 1921?" Olga asked. "Viraj loved telling people that." Her cheeks tinged pink, as if she'd revealed too much of her fiancé's private life. She raised a finger. "As to your concern, perhaps Viraj was reviewing financial information about the sellers of the business in Mountain View. Maybe he learned something about them that worried him."

"Why would he need to tell me?"

"I have no idea."

"Who was the friend he was talking to?" I asked.

"Herman."

"Hoek?"

She raised an eyebrow, surprised that I knew his name.

"Do you have his contact number?" Evers hadn't included telephone numbers for all of the witnesses in his notes, but then he'd probably figured he was done with them. An oversight for someone as meticulous as he was.

"No. But I can get it. It was on Viraj's Rolodex. It's charred but not destroyed because it was in the kitchen. Perhaps . . ." She sighed. "If I find it, I will call you. I have your business card."

"Please do. I'd like to speak with Mr. Hoek." I rose to my feet as Detective Sergeant Quincy was returning to me.

He eyed me warily but he didn't press. "Is there anything I can do to help you further, Miss Adams?"

"No. Thank you, sir. I'm following the leads that Detective Sergeant Evers gave me. If I do need your help, I'll reach out."

"Just don't overreach," he cautioned.

Chapter 18

Rain pelted the parking lot as I bolted to my car and climbed inside. I hadn't dressed warmly enough for the weather. A chill slithered up my neck. I flicked on the windshield wipers and cranked on the heat. Headlights strafed the road as I pulled onto the street.

Turning left onto El Camino Real, I felt another chill. Of apprehension. Was someone following me? I peered into the rearview mirror. It was hard to make out shapes in the dank darkness. I didn't see anyone overtly tailing me. I checked the sideview mirrors, too. Nothing.

An image of Damian standing beside me at the table last night flashed in my mind. Had Serenity known he would be dining there and made the reservation so she could break the news to me about the two of them dating with him nearby? Or had Damian found out that Serenity was meeting with me and parlayed a reservation for himself? That would have been just like him, to take control and set the scene.

I craned my head to the right to get a glimpse of the blind spot. No car, and I didn't see one dart behind another to avoid detection.

Another worry struck me. What if, as I suspected, Fisher had written the *GO HOME* note? What if he was tailing me? His threat on the phone, *Or else*, had sounded real. Had he found out where Viraj Patel lived? Had he set the fire? Had he remained in the area and hidden and watched the fire department and police handle the scene?

Get real, Aspen. How would he have found you?

On the other hand, Fisher did work for a tech guy. Maybe there was a digital way to trace my cell phone. I had called him first.

By the time I parked in the driveway, paranoia had planted its roots deeply in my psyche. How I wished Cinder was at the house to greet me. Or Nick. Or better yet, that this case was resolved and behind me and I was back in Lake Tahoe.

I sprinted inside, locked the front door, and switched on the lights. I was trained in self-defense, but that wouldn't protect me if someone broke in with a gun. Given the conversation with Nick the other night, I decided to scout for possible weapons. A fireplace poker in the living room. A fry pan or knife in the kitchen. The decorative bronze statue of a dancing girl in the foyer. Every room had something I could use, should the need arise.

Breathing easier, I shrugged out of my blazer, blouse, and slacks and slipped into a comfortable pair of jeans and Tahoe sweatshirt. In the kitchen, I poured a glass of chardonnay and sliced some cheddar cheese. I set the cheese on a plate with multi-seed crackers, and then sat in a chair, eyes closed, to meditate on Tahoe. I imagined the placid lake, the heavenly scent of the pines, and the chittering of squirrels. Within minutes, I was calm and focused and ready to address the murder board.

I added a note to Patel's section: *Shot with Glock semiautomatic.* If Patel's killer was the same person who'd killed my parents, he had armed himself with a new weapon. Not unheard of given the fourteen-year gap.

By now, my aunt must have taken my grandfather's gun to the Placer County sheriff's forensic division. Had they found anything? Had they contacted Atherton P.D.? Had they determined yet whether the striations on bullets fired by my grandfather's gun proved it was or wasn't the murder weapon used to kill my parents? If it was—

My chest tightened at the notion. I couldn't imagine my mother facing the killer, seeing her own gun being used against her. Had she cowered in fear or steeled herself with righteous indignation? Had she questioned how the killer had found the gun or accepted the discovery as a moot point?

I stared at Rosie's name on the murder board and shook my head. She had not killed our parents, but I had to wonder whether she had instigated the murder. I prayed that she had not sent me to reopen the cold case with the sole intent of finding her guilty.

Tapping the marker against my chin, my gaze traveled to the name *Herman Hoek,* his witness statement among the many in Evers's collection. The detective had interviewed Hoek once. I attached a Post-it note to Hoek's interview: *Ask about the car Patel saw. Ask about Patel's hacking proclivities. Who had he hacked? Might he have created enemies?* I added the cryptic note that Olga had provided: *Where is Patel's new business located? Did he have any partners? Were any of them suspects in my parents' murders?*

I skimmed everything a second and third time. Nothing was gelling. As I opened my laptop to search the White Pages for Hoek's telephone number, I heard a sound outside. The closing of a car door.

Heart jackhammering my rib cage, I flew to a window and peered out. By now, rain was coming down in sheets. Two hooded figures ran up the path to the front door.

I grabbed the bronze statue off the foyer table.

Someone pounded on the door. "Aunt Aspen! Open up."

Candace. My pulse settled down. I replaced the statue, whipped open the door, and let my niece and aunt in. They shimmied like wet dogs and removed their raincoats. Both were wearing sweaters over jeans.

Max grinned. "I hope this place allows dogs. Candace insisted on bringing Cinder."

"Jewel put up a fuss," Candace added.

My aunt clapped her hands and Cinder bounded out of the Land Rover and into the house. He nearly knocked me over with his enthusiasm. All of us hugged.

Snug in a group embrace, I said, "What are you doing here?"

"We missed you," Candace said.

Max nodded. "So we decided you needed company."

"A phone call or text to alert me might have been nice." I freed myself from their grasp.

"Did we scare you?" Candace asked, grinning. "Sorry. We thought you'd like the surprise."

"I like surprises. I don't need a heart attack."

Max eyed me warily. "Are you nervous about something? Or someone?"

I asked Candace to put on her raincoat and fetch their overnight cases.

When she did, I told my aunt about Viraj Patel contacting me, him winding up dead, the note on the car, and the feeling that I was being watched.

"But no one has approached you," Max said. "No one has attacked you."

I hitched a shoulder. "Maybe it's a witness who wants to share information but is shy."

"My sweet girl, you are an eternal optimist." She bussed my cheek. "By the way, I couldn't find the license plate you noted the other night. That's the info I opted not to leave on my voicemail to you. It wasn't a private plate, and it wasn't assigned to a rental car, either."

"I suppose the driver could have altered the plate."

My aunt nodded. "All it takes is a good magic marker or duct tape."

"Or I could be imagining things."

Max winked. "Known to happen to the best of us."

"What about the gun? Are you making headway with that?"

"The sheriff's department is waiting for Atherton P.D. to release the results of the original bullets. Be patient."

Patience was not my forte. It never had been.

Candace bounded into the house with one duffel, a grocery bag, and a box from Chick-fil-A. "Gluten-free chicken nuggets and buns—they're delicious—and a couple of salads. Hungry?"

"Starved," I said.

Max took the bag of groceries and dinner from Candace, carried them into the kitchen, and returned.

Next, I set them up in the two additional bedrooms. Candace chose the one with the white-and-green lace coverlet. Max simply wanted a good pillow.

When the three of us settled at the kitchen table, we chowed down on chicken and got caught up. Waverly had a new boy that she was interested in; Rory did poorly on a test so he's grounded; Yaz and Darcy both said hello. Darcy might be getting engaged. And did I know that Gwen was returning to Lake Tahoe?

"When? Why?" I asked. "Is she still married to Owen?" Gwen Barrows, one of my dearest friends, had owned the Tavern, the restaurant that had become my hangout in the Homewood Area, but when she met Owen Goff, she'd decided to retire.

"The sale fell through. The buyer thought she'd be able to save enough for the lease-option, but she couldn't, and Owen, it turns out, has seasickness. No more cruising for them. It's a good thing he likes Lake Tahoe and adores Gwen. If she wants to go back to running the place, he's okay with that. He'll do whatever will make her happy."

Candace made kissing sounds.

I grinned. "For my own selfish reasons, I'm thrilled to hear this."

Max squeezed my arm. "I knew you would be. By the way, we're only staying the night."

"Aw," Candace whined, even though I was certain Max had spelled out the rules before getting in the car.

"School Monday, young lady," Max said. "And you still have homework to complete."

Candace frowned and folded her arms on the table, elbows and all.

"What's your plan, Aspen, going forward?" Max asked.

"Yeah, what's your plan?" Candace gave up her peeve and sat taller.

"I'd like to reach out to a witness tomorrow."

"Who have you spoken to so far?" she pressed.

"To whom have you spoken?" I corrected.

She moaned. "C'mon. One night without an English lesson, okay? Who have you questioned?"

I did my best to fill them in. Meeting Evers. Going through the storage unit with Tammie. Questioning Antoine Washington. Finding Viraj Patel murdered. I skipped needless details. "Detective Sergeant Quincy, who's in charge of cold cases, doesn't think Patel's murder is related to my parents' case, but he'll give it consideration." I rose to take dishes to the sink. "According to the man's fiancée, Patel was talking to a buddy, Herman Hoek, on the day he died. I need to speak with Hoek. I was getting ready to look up his contact information when you two showed up."

As I washed the dishes and Candace dried, she caught sight of the murder board in the dining room. "Is that what I think it is?"

"Yes."

She tossed the towel on the counter, strode into the dining room, and jammed one hand on her hip.

"Dishes," I said sternly.

"They can wait." She aimed an arm toward the murder board.

"Walk us through it." I had made investigation boards at home. She was seasoned at picking them apart.

"Candace . . ."

"Don't sugarcoat it, Aspen. Please. You know I want to solve this as much as my mother does."

I sighed, realizing how much she hoped, like Rosie did, that I could solve the years-old crime and free Rosie from a guilty conscience. Help her get clean. Help her become a sober, caring mother again to her daughter.

My aunt offered a wry smile and crooked a finger. Dishes would wait.

I grabbed my glass of wine. Max, who had brought a flask of scotch, poured two fingers into a tumbler. We joined Candace in the dining room. Max sat in one of the card table chairs. I hovered beside Candace.

"Is this how Grandpa Jim and Grandma Lily were found?" Candace touched the edge of the photo of them lying together, my father facedown, my mother faceup and holding his hand. Even though Candace had been an infant at the time of their deaths, she had heard so many stories about them from me that she felt she'd known them.

"Yes."

"Where did you get all the photos and details?" my aunt asked.

I explained how Detective Sergeant Evers had allowed me to photograph every aspect of his notes. "He was meticulous. I doubt the cold case file at Atherton P.D. has anything more to offer."

"What is Evers like?" Max asked.

"A decent man. He regrets not having solved this case. He said that all these years later it still haunts him."

Candace perused the material. "It says Grandpa Jim was killed first, but what if Grandma Lily was?"

"No. The notes clearly explain the sequence. The blood—" I halted. I was not going into gross details about the killer's actions. "Trust me. That's the determination. My mother was shot in the back." I described how she had lived long enough to turn herself over and clasp my father's hand.

"How c-cruel," Candace stammered.

"Murder is not kind."

"Did the detective think Grandpa Jim and Grandma Lily knew the killer?" she asked.

I eyed her. "Why would you think that?"

"They weren't killed the moment they came in the door."

"Interesting theory." Max pursed her lips. "Which of the suspects might they have known, Aspen?"

"Kurt Brandt, a man trying to collect on an IOU, was an acquaintance of my grandfather's. William Fisher is the father of one of Dad's clients. And they might have known Antoine Washington, if Rosie had brought him around. The police questioned a ton of other people. Their friends. Neighbors. But those three were the prime suspects. And Rosie, of course."

I stared at the photo of my mother. I couldn't imagine the heartbreak she must have felt at not being able to save my father.

"What are you thinking?" Max asked, rising to her feet and joining us in front of the board.

I brushed a tear off my cheek.

Candace said, "I'll bet you're thinking about what Mom said, that Grandma Lily was still breathing when Mom arrived."

"Still breathing?" Max gasped.

"Uh-huh. Grandma Lily said to her, 'You'll never get it.'" Candace stressed the word *it*.

"It?" Max gazed at me.

"We don't know what *it* was," I said. "Rosie didn't mention the conversation to the police because she thought Mom—Lily—was reminding her that she had cut Rosie out of the will."

"But now"—Candace focused on Max—"Mom's wondering whether Grandma Lily didn't know it was her. She said her eyes were closed, meaning Grandma Lily could have thought she was talking to the killer, which would make a big difference."

Max gazed at me. "Because the killer might have been after something else. Not just the silver."

I nodded.

Chapter 19

Later that night, I made cocoa—Max had thought to bring packets along—and we talked theories for an hour. We couldn't figure out what *it* was. We couldn't come up with new suspects. In truth, we were stymied. All three of us went to bed frustrated.

In the morning, we ate a somber breakfast. Even Cinder picked up on our feeling of defeat. At ten, Max handed me a Post-it with a phone number for Herman Hoek—she'd drummed it up on the Internet before dawn—and then she bustled a reluctant Candace and frisky Cinder into the Land Rover to return to Lake Tahoe.

Tears welled in my eyes as they pulled out of the driveway, but I didn't acknowledge them for fear Candace would force my aunt to turn the Land Rover around. I needed to focus. I couldn't do that with an edgy teenager in tow.

Church bells pealed in the distance as I reentered the house. The rain had stopped and sunshine was straining to skim past bloated clouds. The temperature was warmer than yesterday, but even so, as I closed the door, I shivered. I strode to the bedroom, threw on a down vest over my long-sleeved T-shirt, and returned to the kitchen. At the same time, my cell phone rang. I didn't recognize the number but answered.

"Miss Adams?" a woman said. "It's Olga Payne. I have the number for Mr. Hoek that you asked for."

"Ready," I said, even though I had it.

She relayed Hoek's number and I thanked her.

"How are you doing?" I asked.

"How can anyone whose loved one is murdered be doing? As a therapist, I understand the stages of grief and I know I'm going through the beginning stages, but even so . . ." She drew in a deep breath. "I am coping. I will survive."

• • •

Herman Hoek lived in an ivy-covered duplex in Palo Alto. His unit, the lower level, had a ramp entrance. Hoek answered the door and peered up at me from his wheelchair. "You're pretty," he said matter-of-factly. I'd called before heading over. "Come in."

"Thank you." I'd changed into a thigh-length red sweater, black leggings, and Uggs.

Though he was confined to his chair, nothing about the man said *weak*. He was as solid as a rock. Broad shoulders. Square jaw. Incredibly green eyes that didn't waver. "Follow me." Deftly, he spun his wheelchair around and led me through his living room. "I've got a half hour before the physical therapist comes," he said over his shoulder. When he grinned, his mouth curved up on one side. "Coffee?"

"A glass of water, please."

His apartment was white and gray and everything was in its place. Huge tomes on world history filled the bottom two levels of a gray ladder-style bookshelf. The hefty black flower vase on the level above the books held a lavender bouquet. An acoustic guitar stood in a stand beyond the bookshelf. Instrumental guitar music was playing through a speaker.

"Say hello to Lulu." He hooked his thumb at a blue-gray iguana in a six-foot cage beyond the couch. "She's eight, going on nine. My sister gave her to me. Gave me the flowers, too."

"That's sweet," I said idly. "The music is nice."

"All mine." He ran his hand along the top of his crewcut. "I write country songs."

"I thought you were a programmer."

"Used to be. Actually, I was a hacker. Like Viraj. A white hat hacker, but a hacker nonetheless. I got tired of it."

I glimpsed his bedroom on the way to the kitchen. The bed featured a white sheet and gray blanket, finished with military-style corners.

Hoek trundled into the kitchen and hitched his chin at the small oak table. "Sit." He poured me a glass of water and wheeled into position opposite me.

I sipped the water and set the glass aside. "Mr. Hoek, I'll get right to the point. Viraj Patel—"

"Is dead. I know. Sad. He was looking forward to the next phase of his life. But you don't want to hear about that. You're here to ask me about my witness statement. I now know that he faked his alibi by using me to corroborate his story. I didn't know that at the time. I swear. Viraj called me Friday and confessed to what he'd done." Hoek brushed a finger under his broad nose. "Didn't make me happy, but I understood. He was scared. We've all been scared."

"You're not mad?" I asked, wondering if he had killed Patel.

"Nah. Viraj was trying to do the right thing. Protect his fiancée's virtue. I get it. Now the guy's dead. I won't hold a grudge." He studied a thumbnail and returned his gaze to me. "I may have been a Marine, but I'm no saint, ma'am. I've made mistakes. Given my situation"—he rubbed the arm of his wheelchair—"being confined to this beauty, with only virtual buddies as friends, I can be an easy mark. I'm not in any kind of trouble, Viraj said, though he warned me that the police might want to talk to me."

I took a sip of water. "His fiancée, Olga, said Mr. Patel was digging into some financial site and thought a certain someone might be curious to know what he'd found. Did he mention a debt he'd uncovered to you?"

Hoek rolled his lips forward, his gaze hunting for a memory. "Nope."

"Olga said he was investing in a business. A plant in Mountain View."

"Not investing. Buying. A teardown."

"Was it possible he was investigating the sellers' financial records?" I asked.

"Maybe. Viraj was a digger. Always nosing around in things. For example, I know he found dirt on a couple of the other buyers—his competition—and dissed them to the sellers."

"Do you know any of their names? Maybe Washington or Fisher or Brandt?"

"Washington . . . Fisher . . . Brandt . . ." Hoek furrowed his brow. "I know someone named Gant. Jim Gant."

"Brandt," I repeated. "Kurt Brandt."

Hoek shook his head. "Anyway, as I was saying, finding the dirt is what put Viraj at the front of the queue. Unfortunately, the deal wasn't closed." Hoek drummed the table. "I guess it'll go to the next highest bidder."

I took another sip of water, nearing the bottom of the glass. So much for Patel digging up something about the other suspects in my parents' case. "Olga said she heard him saying to you that he'd seen a green car roaming his neighborhood."

"Green. Ha!" Hoek grinned. "Viraj was color blind. He had tritanopia, meaning blues appear as green and yellows appear gray. My bet? He made an educated guess. My second bet? It was a nothing burger. No car. Nobody watching. We programmers can be a bit paranoid."

"On the other hand, he's dead."

Hoek's eyes widened as if the notion suddenly hit home. "Whoa. Do you think whoever was in the car killed him?"

• • •

On the drive to the house, I missed Nick something awful. Until now, I hadn't realized how often I saw or talked to him. I felt as if my mind wasn't functioning on all cylinders. He was my rock and I was floundering.

Focus, I urged myself.

Being somewhat paranoid, I checked the rearview mirror during the drive to Menlo Park. I didn't notice a tail.

Along Santa Cruz Avenue, I slowed at every crosswalk and repeated the mirror routine. No tail. People in their Sunday best were out in droves and smiling as if nothing in the world could go wrong. A few even waved to me.

At Menlo Church, I was forced to slow again. Churchgoers were streaming out of the massive building. Farther down the street, half as many were leaving St. Raymond's. I gazed over my right shoulder. The motorcyclist behind the Prius was paying no attention to me.

As I slowed deliberately at San Mateo Drive, I checked my mirrors again. The white sedan that had moved behind me veered to the right to avoid colliding with me. A black truck followed suit. A horn honked.

I muttered, "Sue me," and then, confident that I'd lost the tail, if there had been a tail, I veered left.

When I got back to the house, I made a fresh cup of coffee before moving into the dining room to study the murder board. I thought about what Candace had asked last night, whether my mother or father might have known the killer.

I glanced at the Post-it note with the comment that the killer had wiped down the crime scene. Why? Because whoever it was had stolen in, sans gloves, believing he'd had plenty of time to rob the house, suggesting he must have known my parents had gone on vacation.

Reading from left to right, I searched Evers's notes for answers. He'd questioned dozens of people including the travel agent, Lynda Sue Harris. The one note by her name read *Retreat,* whatever that meant. I paced while sipping the coffee, appreciating the bitterness on my tongue. It matched the bitter acid at the pit of my stomach.

My cell phone rang. I pulled it from my pocket. *Serenity.* I let it go to voicemail again and refocused. I would return her call soon. I would even listen to yesterday's voicemail. Just not yet.

Then my phone buzzed. Text message from Tammie: *Dinner tonight?* I responded: *That would be nice. Time?* She wrote: *Six.*

I replied: *Done,* then pocketed my cell phone and narrowed my gaze. My grandfather's gun. If it was the murder weapon, that would prove that one of my parents had known the killer. Otherwise, how would the killer have discovered its whereabouts? I supposed Grandpa Gray could have mentioned it to Kurt Brandt. What about Rosie? Had she shown the gun to anyone? As a teen or later on, during one of her mini robberies? That would have been like her. Bragging, flaunting, proving how clever she was by being able to open the puzzle box.

I polished off the coffee and walked to the kitchen. As I cleaned the mug and set it to dry, I thought again about my grandfather's gun. If the killer had used it, why return it to the hope chest? To protect it because it was an heirloom? That seemed like something Rosie—

My insides knotted. No. Rosie was not a suspect. She had a solid alibi. They'd tested her for gunshot residue. Not to mention that if she had killed our parents, she wouldn't have told me about the gun.

I recalled a note Evers had written about the silverware. It had never shown up at a pawnshop. Being sterling silver, the killer had probably found someone who would melt it down and swap it for cash. Is that what had happened? Had the murderer killed my parents purely to make a buck? Had it been a robbery gone wrong? Was I spinning my wheels trying to solve this case?

Maybe Evers could steer me in the right direction. I sat at the table and dialed his number. He'd said I could contact him at any time.

He answered after one ring. "Hey, how're you doing?" he asked, as if we were old friends. He sounded tired.

"Did I wake you?"

"From a catnap." He yawned. "What's up?"

"I'm not making much headway." I mentioned my thought about the silver.

He hummed. "Yep, in the end, that's what we decided. A pure and simple robbery. All the suspects had alibis; ergo, the killer had no connection to your folks." He cleared his throat. "By the way, Andrew Quincy called me and told me about the Patel murder."

"He's not sure it's related to my parents' case," I said.

"He'll keep an open mind, but honestly, Miss Adams—"

"Call me Aspen."

"Honestly, Aspen, with all these years gone by, it's probably not related. Why wait until now to kill him?"

"Because I came to town. Because I'm asking questions."

Evers let loose with a phlegmy cough. "Sorry."

"Detective—"

"You call me Elton if I call you Aspen."

I smiled, liking the man. "Elton, Mr. Patel phoned me. He wanted to talk to me about a debt or a threat."

"Quincy said as much."

"Before we could speak, Patel died. He was murdered. When I questioned his fiancée, she said he hadn't mentioned anything to her about this debt—or threat—but when I touched base with Herman Hoek—"

"You contacted him?"

"Yes, sir. Everyone so far has been willing to talk to me." Everyone but William Fisher, who'd been rude, and Kurt Brandt, who hadn't responded. "Hoek said Patel was investing in a company, so maybe he was looking into the financials of the other buyers or sellers, and I'm wondering if one of them has a connection to my parents."

Evers whistled softly. "You're thinking that Patel dug up something about the killer that links him to your folks' murders."

"And the killer found out and silenced him."

Chapter 20

Around three, I laid down on the living room couch with thoughts of silverware, Patel, debts, and threats running roughshod through my brain. At five, I awoke with a start. My cell phone was jangling. I hadn't meant to fall asleep, just rest my eyes. Wisely, I'd thought to set an alarm.

I scrambled off the couch and plodded into the bedroom. I slipped out of my leggings and sweater and donned slacks and a plaid blouse, refreshed my makeup and hair, and hurried to a local liquor store. I would not show up at Tammie's empty-handed.

Tammie's condo, tucked at the far end of a cul-de-sac that was lined with redwood trees and located near meticulously manicured rolling hills, looked the same as I remembered. Neat, trim, and understated.

Tammie, dressed in an aqua blue silk blouse and charcoal gray cigarette pants that made her look even thinner than she had the other day, greeted me at the door with a warm hug. "Mia is here with Giselle." She drew me into the foyer and closed the door. "They'll be leaving in a few."

"I can't wait to see them."

"Dinner's in the oven."

The aroma of rosemary chicken wafted to me. "Smells great."

Years ago, the condo had been darker in tone. Now, it was light, redone in tans and whites, with teak furniture and the walls adorned with large abstract paintings or mirrors. As before, the sylvan views from her windows were gorgeous. She had adorned her small patio with twinkling lights.

"Don't worry, sweetie," a woman said down the hall. "We won't be late. Our Uber driver will get us there on time." Mia, in cropped sweater and skinny jeans, walked into the foyer holding the hand of a four-year-old golden-haired beauty dressed in a pink tutu. "Aspen, how lovely to see you. This is my daughter, Giselle."

The girl stole behind her mother's legs.

"Giselle is worried we'll miss the train." Mia peered at her daughter. "Go get your dolly." Like a mini ballerina, the girl tiptoed down the hall and disappeared into a room. Mia, looking leggier than I remembered and blonder, her gorgeous curls matching her daughter's, smiled at me. "Giselle loves taking the train."

I said, "Isn't the station—"

"By the freeway? Yep."

"Don't you drive?"

"Sure, I do, but—"

"They live in Mountain View," Tammie said. "In a townhouse area populated by millennials and a few Gen X'ers, not far from the train station."

Mia clasped my hand. "Aspen, it's good to see you. How long has it—" She stopped short, realizing when we'd last seen each other. At my parents' funeral.

"It's good to see you, too," I said, releasing her hand. "You look fabulous. Your mom tells me you're thriving as a builder."

"Almost thriving. It's a big staircase to climb." She winked. "I wish it were an escalator."

I laughed at the metaphor.

"Come into the kitchen, girls," Tammie said.

The kitchen had been updated with new appliances and granite counters.

"Do you have any photos of your projects you could show me?" I asked Mia.

"I don't. Every night I download photos onto my laptop and clear the phone. It's a storage issue. Mom, do you have photos?"

"Not now, darling. No business." Tammie hitched her chin. "Aspen, I see you brought wine. Want a glass?"

"Sure." I handed her the bottle. "It's a screw top, but the guy at the wine store assured me it was a good sauvignon blanc."

"Mama?" Giselle slipped into the kitchen, sans dolly, and sidled to her mother. She peeked at me.

Mia chuckled. "Aspen doesn't bite."

"Are we going now?"

"Not yet." Mia glanced at the Uber app on her cellphone. "Let's play a little game." She rummaged in her tote and pulled out her wallet. She unzipped it and removed a penny. She cupped it in her hands and shook, and then held out her fisted hands to her daughter. "Okay, which one?"

Giselle tapped Mia's left.

"Wrong." Mia reached behind Giselle's ear and pulled out a penny.

Fondly, I remembered times with my grandfather pulling coins from my ear. He'd say he wished he had a silver dollar for every time I laughed.

"Daddy does the trick better," Giselle said.

"I'm sure he does," Mia replied with a bite. "Where's your dolly?"

"I forgot." Giselle scooted from the room.

Tammie handed me a glass of wine. "I told you that Mia conceived using a gestational surrogate, didn't I? But now the father—"

"He who shall remain nameless for eternity," Mia inserted. "We're divorced."

"Wants full custody, saying it was his sperm that made it happen, not her damaged eggs." Tammie snarled. "The gall. They share custody."

"He takes Giselle every other weekend, Friday night to Sunday night."

"He's always trying to one-up Mia," Tammie added.

"Sharing is never easy," I said and took a sip of wine. It was nice. Flavorful.

"He's giving her all sorts of grief."

"Mom, let's not—"

"Saying she's unfit," Tammie went on, undeterred. "You know Mia. She is the most reliable person in the world. Ever since her con artist father walked out on us and left us without two dimes to rub together, Mia has been a rules follower. Mommy's best girl."

I glanced at Mia, who rolled her eyes.

Tammie's ex hadn't been a con artist. He'd been an attorney and probably still was. Because he'd foreseen a faithfulness problem in his future—his faithfulness, not Tammie's—he'd made her sign a prenuptial agreement. When they divorced short of their tenth anniversary, he dealt a mighty death blow to any kind of financial package for Tammie, California alimony law notwithstanding. I recalled my mother and Tammie discussing the issue in hushed voices.

Mia said, "Do you have children, Aspen?"

"Not my own," I said. "I took custody of my niece, though. She's a teenager."

"You're not married?"

"No. I was, but it didn't work out." Damian flashed in my mind. The fluke of him being at the restaurant. His touch on my shoulder. An image of Serenity and him in a passionate embrace. I pushed it aside.

"I'm sorry." Mia combed her hair with her fingers.

Tammie petted my arm. "You have to tell me more about Candace over dinner."

"I will. She's—"

"Nana?" Giselle tiptoed into the room carrying a box. "Can I have this?"

"Giselle, no. Give that to me." Mia held out her hand. "I told you to get your dolly."

Tammie beat Mia to Giselle and slipped the box from the girl's hands, but not before I'd recognized it. It wasn't just any box. It was the four-inch cherrywood puzzle box that should have been included with my parents' master bedroom items.

"Tammie, that's—" My voice snagged. "I thought my sister had stolen it. My grandmother made that box. When my mother was a little girl."

Tammie blushed hot pink. "Aspen, I'm so embarrassed. I was sure that I'd told you. Maybe I didn't. It was such a daunting time. As I was putting all the things in storage, I took it as a keepsake. I know how much your mother had prized the box. I wanted one little thing to remember her by."

"Can you open it?" Giselle asked me, wide-eyed. "Show me the treasure."

"What treasure?" I asked.

"There's something inside."

Tammie said, "She asks me every time she's here to open it, but for the life of me I can't figure out how to do so. There's no lid. No lock. I think your grandmother built the box around whatever is inside."

"Giselle," Mia said, "do you have to use the bathroom? We're going in one minute."

"Aspen," the girl said in barely a whisper. "Please?"

A profusion of emotions welled within me. My mother had cherished that box, often reminding me how much my grandmother had loved secrets. Was there something—a *treasure*—inside? My mouth went dry. Was the thing, the *it*, that my mother hadn't wanted Rosie or the killer to get inside?

I held out my hand. Tammie gave me the box.

"Watch carefully," I said. My mother had revealed the secret of the box to me. "You have to spin the box." I set the box on the table and spun it. Hard. It twirled and twirled and finally, thanks to centrifugal force, the lid opened.

"Magic!" Giselle cried.

Mia crept closer. "What's the treasure?"

Tammie flanked her.

Inside, lying on the felt lining, was a silver dollar. It clacked whenever the box was shaken because the box was not lined. Recognizing what it was instantly, I lifted it out. "My grandfather gave this to my mother. It's engraved with the year she was born. She was so proud of this coin." I handed it to Mia's daughter, who inspected it like a minter. "That's why she stashed it in the box."

"I doubt that it's worth much," Tammie said.

"It's not," I said. "None of the silver dollars Grandpa Gray collected were. The estate sold each for about fifteen to twenty dollars. For some reason, silver dollars were the few things of value that he could hold on to."

"Your mother talked often about your grandfather and his—" Tammie balked.

"Gambling?" I asked, filling in the silence. "It's okay. I knew he was a gambler. He racked up a ton of debt."

Saying the word *debt* stopped me cold. Had Patel learned about my grandfather's debt? Had he been trying to warn me about Kurt Brandt, the creditor who had dunned my mother after Grandpa Gray died?

"Gray was quite a rogue," Tammie said to Mia. "Everyone loved him."

"Especially my grandmother," I said, "despite his flaws."

Giselle handed the silver dollar to me. "For you," she said politely.

"Thank you, sweetheart. For being so generous, I'll give you this." I offered her the box. "Now that you know the secret, you can surprise your friends."

Tammie demurred. "No, Aspen, it's yours."

"And now it's your granddaughter's. Put something precious in there for her. A memory. Okay?"

Tammie threw her arms around me. "I will."

Chapter 21

When Mia's Uber ride arrived ten minutes later, she and Giselle, with her dolly, left for the train station.

"More wine?" Tammie asked, holding up the wine bottle. "Dinner will be ready in about fifteen minutes."

"Sure."

Tammie poured some into both of our wineglasses.

I took a sip. "It was so odd running into you at the Palais Hotel Friday night."

"What a coincidence, huh?" She placed the wine bottle on the counter.

"What was even more of a coincidence was when I was going through the newspaper looking for the story of the fire—"

"What fire?"

"Oh, my gosh, I haven't told you." I pressed a hand to my chest. "On my way to the rental house that night . . ." I filled her in. The fire at Patel's. Following up with the police. Meeting with Herman Hoek to see if he knew what Patel had wanted to tell me. "Hoek didn't," I said.

"Aspen"—Tammie put a hand on my arm—"Patel was murdered. Is his death linked to your investigation? To your parents' case? If so, this isn't safe. Do you think you should continue to pursue—"

"I'm fine. Promise." I slipped from her grasp.

"This Herman Hoek. Do you think he's trustworthy?"

"I do. What I was going to say before about the newspaper is—"

She hooted. "You're as good as your mother at diversion."

"I learned from a pro." My mother may have been an enabler for Rosie, but she was quite a master at dodge and deflect, and making people—customers, mainly—come around to her point of view. "What I was going to say is, while I was flipping through the newspaper, I saw a photograph of the elderly man who passed by you at the hotel. When he entered the elevator, he pivoted and gave you a curious look. I pointed him out, but you missed seeing him."

She tilted her head. "Go on. Who was it?"

"The D.A. for Palo Alto, a former defense attorney." I said his name. "Do you know him from your prior work? At the law firm?"

Tammie's gaze narrowed as she searched her memory. "No." She moved her head left and right. "Don't think I do. Was he handsome?"

"Sort of."

"Too bad I missed him." She winked.

"Isn't that a coincidence, though? To see him ogle you and the next day to see his photograph in the newspaper?"

Tammie smiled. "The more life you live, the more you'll notice there are coincidences that can't be explained."

My aunt hated coincidences. They piqued her interest and made her delve deeper. This one, however, was banal. Tammie was attractive. Men stared.

I shook off my unease and appraised her condo. "By the way, I love what you've done with the place."

"It could use a face-lift. It's been a few years since I redid it. I'm like the cobbler's daughter who has no shoes." She brandished a hand. "Want to see the rest?"

"Sure."

Along the hallway were framed pictures. Giselle in a tutu. Mia on the running team. Giselle holding up a finger painting. Tammie with Giselle and Mia attending *The Nutcracker Suite*.

I paused by a picture of six women with virtually no hair, each wearing a cropped T-shirt emblazoned with the words *Let Freedom Reign*, and gestured with my thumb. "Is that Mia in the middle?"

Tammie groaned. "Yes. They all shaved their heads to protest for a woman's right to choose. Mia hadn't even had sex yet, but she was quite vocal. Thanks to October Fest courage, she and her pals had fortified themselves for their act of defiance."

"With the short hair—"

"Nonexistent hair."

"She looks so much like you."

"Yes, I noticed that, too."

Tammie led the way down the hall and strolled into her office, which reminded me of my mother's with all the file cabinets and books of fabric swatches. Tammie had installed a corkboard wall above her desk. On it she'd pinned numerous order sheets.

"You're sure racking up business," I said.

"Those are all prospective clients, not done deals. It's a never-ending challenge, trying to expand the business. Luckily, Vasona Lake and the Isles job will carry me for quite a while."

I paused inside the door. "Proud Mama?" I hooked a thumb at Mia's college diploma hanging by the light switch.

"Mia didn't want to hang it in her office. She said it was prideful. She felt only doctors and lawyers should do that." Tammie stopped outside a pink room that she'd decorated with white furniture. Ballerina silhouettes adorned the walls. A rocking chair beside the twin bed was filled with pretty dolls. "I have updated this room for Giselle. If you hadn't noticed, she loves ballet."

"Sweet."

After showing me the master bedroom, done in the same tones as the living room and boasting the same kind of artwork, Tammie headed to the kitchen. "So, tell me how you're doing so far on solving your parents' case. If you're going to continue with this, despite my warnings, I want all the sordid details."

I thumped her on the shoulder. "You're not being very supportive."

"Nope, I'm not. I'm being protective. What do you think you can do that the police couldn't?"

"I'll search under every rock. They've let the moss grow."

"Okay, fill me in." She assembled table mats, napkins, and silverware to the left of the stove.

"I met with one of the suspects, Antoine Washington. He used to be a friend of Rosie's."

"The drug addict."

"Good memory. The police dismissed him as a possibility. He had a verifiable alibi. He was captured on closed-circuit TV near the location he claimed to have been."

"Lucky him."

"He's gone straight." I told her about his job at Big Box and his hope to become a better father than his own had been. "He seemed like a regular guy who really wants to get it right this time around."

Tammie asked me to set the table while she plated dinner.

I started with the table mats. "I forgot to mention that my aunt and

Candace showed up last night, unexpectedly. They've already returned to Lake Tahoe."

"That must have been nice to see them. Especially since Nick had to leave."

"You have no idea." The ache of being away from Lake Tahoe this long was taking its toll on me. My jaw was tight, my stomach sour. I missed Nick and my family. I missed a cool, brisk walk in the forest. Simply imagining the beautiful lake and its ring of magnificent mountains made me breathe easier. Soon, I told myself. I'd return home soon.

Using mitts, Tammie removed a baking dish from the oven and pulled off the glass lid. Steam wafted out. She spooned rice from a rice cooker onto two white plates and topped the rice with strips of rosemary chicken and the accompanying sauce. "Gluten-free," she said.

"You remembered."

"An elephant never forgets." She tapped her temple. "So, do you love living in Tahoe?" she asked, as if reading my mind.

"I do. I feel such a sense of peace when I'm there, and I miss being there more than I can possibly explain."

Tammie glanced over her shoulder, tenderness in her gaze. "The loss of your parents will always color your feelings about the Bay Area. That and your broken marriage and failed career."

"I didn't fail. I . . . ." I hesitated. I did not want to talk about my time at BARC.

"Have you visited your parents' graves?" Tammie said, switching gears.

"Tomorrow." Until I'd moved to Tahoe, I'd gone yearly to the cemetery.

In companionable silence, I arranged forks, knives, and spoons. As I was folding the napkins, a notion returned to me. "You know, after reviewing the notes I've made about the case, I had a thought."

Tammie brought the plates to the table, nabbed her glass of wine, and sat opposite me. *"Bon appetit."*

I toasted her. "Thank you for making this."

"A girl has to eat. Go on. What was your thought?"

"There were no fingerprints at the crime scene. The robber . . ." I toyed with the napkin on my lap. "The *killer* wiped the area clean. Why?"

"Wouldn't you?"

"Antoine said that if he'd come to rob the place, he would have come in wearing gloves, which made me wonder . . ." I propped my elbows on the table. "If the killer had come in, sans gloves, then maybe he hadn't come in to steal anything. On the other hand, if he knew my parents were out of town and thought he had plenty of time to get whatever he was after, he would've had the luxury of time and wouldn't be sloppy and leave fingerprints."

"So, which is it?"

"The latter. The killer *knew* my parents were out of town."

"How?" Tammie placed a hand on her chest. "I didn't tell anyone."

"How about Lynda Sue Harris? Do you think she shared private information? Did she have an alibi?"

Tammie coughed out a laugh and wagged a stern finger. "Uh-uh, rule her out. She is not a murderess. She is the most religious person I've ever met. She goes to church every week without fail, attends weekly Bible studies, and serves food to the homeless at Thanksgiving."

"Okay." I held up a hand. "She's off the list. For now. But I believe someone who knew my parents killed them. Not an unknown. Not a robber. A friend or a client."

"Or that Antoine Washington, who knew your sister and could have had the inside track."

I took a bite of the chicken. "This is incredible."

"My nana's recipe." Tammie cut her meat. "Wasn't one of your dad's clients a suspect?"

"The father of a client. William Fisher. A limo driver." I told her how Fisher believed my father hadn't presented a good enough defense for his son, and the son ended up in prison. "I called Fisher. He returned the call and was quite caustic. He warned me to stay away from him and his family. He might have put a note on my car saying *Go Home.*"

"What? He's following you?" Tammie blanched. "How would he know where you are? Aspen—"

"Relax. I'm being cautious." And I was. I hadn't seen anybody following me on the way to Tammie's place. "Fisher had an alibi, too."

"Who else was on the suspect list?"

"A guy named Kurt Brandt, who wanted my mother to make good on Grandpa Gray's outstanding debt. He hasn't returned my call." I made a mental note to try him again in the morning.

Tammie jutted her fork at me. "Hey, hold on. That guy Patel wanted to talk to you about a debt."

I motioned between the two of us. "We're in sync. Brandt heads my list. He repeatedly dunned Mom for payment."

Tammie set her fork aside and took a sip of wine. "How your grandmother resented your grandfather for putting the family in such a bind. All the gambling. All the IOUs."

"No, she didn't."

"Yes, she did. You were too young to be privy to the conversations between your grandmother and your mother, the year before your grandfather passed away."

I was eleven when he died. I'd heard plenty.

"Patrice was so afraid for the family, which made your mother scared that someone would come after you girls, like this Brandt guy. For years, she went to a shooting range to practice."

My mouth went dry. "I didn't know that."

"Between you and me, I was glad she didn't own a gun. Otherwise—"

"She did own one," I rasped.

"What?"

"I mean, it belonged to Grandpa Gray, but Mom had it. After he died."

Tammie inhaled sharply.

"She kept it in her hope chest. It's still there. Or it was—"

"What do you mean *was*?"

"I had my aunt take the gun to the sheriff, to compare ballistics."

"Why?"

"Because Rosie wondered—" I batted the air. "You see, if bullets from that gun match the bullets found at the crime scene, then . . ." I rolled my upper lip between my teeth. "Placer County Sheriff techs are doing the comparison."

"Hold on. Time out." Tammie formed a *T* with her hands. "I don't recall a gun being mentioned in the list of items from the estate."

"It wasn't listed because it was hidden. In a box that my grandmother made. Another puzzle box. Stored at the bottom of Mom's hope chest. It was a much bigger box. Large enough to hold the gun, a Colt .45, as well as ammunition."

"You can't possibly think the killer found the gun, used it on your parents, and returned it to the hope chest? How would he have known about it? How would he have figured out how to open the box?"

I tapped the table. "Look, if it proves to be the murder weapon, then it would suggest that the killer knew one of my parents. Probably my mother, as she would have had to reveal how to open the box—"

"Or the killer was a magician," Tammie retorted.

I acknowledged her attempt at humor with a smile. "But to have personal knowledge of the location of the gun—"

"If that's what happened."

I nodded. "If."

"Why would the killer have put it back?" Tammie asked.

"Put it back *neatly*," I stressed. "Everything in the hope chest was orderly. I suppose the police could have repacked the chest after their search."

"Wouldn't they have known the box held a gun?"

"No. It looks like a decorative piece of art, and nothing clacked inside, like the silver dollar in the cherrywood puzzle box."

"Wow," Tammie murmured.

"Yeah, wow." I fingered the base of my wineglass.

Silence fell over us. Tammie stared at her unfinished meal.

After a long moment, she met my gaze. Tears leaked from her eyes. "I can't tell you how much I regret not knowing your parents were coming home. Your mother sent me an email. She wrote that your dad was ill. I didn't put two and two together. If I'd been there to greet them—"

"You couldn't have done anything."

"If only Mia and I hadn't gone college hunting that day."

"She wasn't attending college by then?"

"She took a gap year. Two, actually."

Until I'd heard about Mia becoming an architect, I'd lost track of her after she'd broken ties with Rosie. We hadn't talked at the funeral.

Tammie dabbed her eyes with her napkin. "I keep thinking if I'd stopped by your parents' house while they were away, then my car would have been in the driveway and that would have been a deterrent. Something. Anything." She pushed her plate aside. "Want some tea? We'll sit on the patio."

"Sure."

The night air was cool. I was glad I'd thought to bring my parka.

Minutes later, Tammie set two cups of tea on the table as well as a plate of green grapes and cheese.

"In case you get hungry," she said. "You practically skipped dinner."

"So did you." I held the cup with both hands but didn't drink. Honestly, my stomach felt so raw, I didn't think it would be wise. "Look, Rosie's the reason why I'm here. She told me about the gun."

"When?"

"Last week."

"How did she know about it?"

"She'd seen it. Years ago."

Tammie set her mug on the glass table. "If she knew about it . . ."

"No, she did not kill our parents." I spat the words. "I told you she had an alibi."

"Maybe she paid someone to lie for her."

"Tammie, I know in my gut she didn't do it."

"But Rosie kept the gun a secret," Tammie said quietly, driving the point home. "Why reveal that now?"

Chapter 22

As I returned to the rental house, thoughts of Rosie scudded through my mind. Why hadn't she mentioned the gun before? Why hadn't she told me about her conversation with Mom until now? Because she'd felt angry at being cut out of the will? Honestly? I hadn't been included, either. But then I wasn't Rosie. I'd made a future for myself. My career as a therapist had paid me well. Rosie, because of her addiction, had suffered.

Lost in thought, I'd forgotten to look in the rearview mirror. The moment I veered into the driveway, a car screeched to a halt behind me. Sideways. Trapping me. My purse was on the floor by my feet. I kept mace in it. I bent to retrieve it. Too late.

My pursuer smacked the window with his palm. "Sit up, Miss Adams!" he bellowed through the glass. "Now."

I bolted upright.

He aimed a gun at my face. "Hands up."

I obeyed.

"Get out. Slowly." His voice sounded like ice cracking.

The security light by the garage illuminated the man from the side. He was tall. Mid-seventies. Rumpled shirt and aging leather jacket. No fedora, but I was certain he was Kurt Brandt. His thinning hair clung to his head. His hook nose flared.

"I need to lower a hand to open the door," I yelled through the glass, doing my best to maintain my calm. Was my voice shaking? I couldn't tell. My pulse was pounding too loudly in my ears. Though I'd faced a number of on-the-edge patients during my tenure at BARC, most had wielded knives or handmade shanks. None had come at me with a gun.

"Yeah, okay," he said.

I stepped out of the car, ruing the fact that my cell phone was in the cupholder. "You're Kurt Brandt," I said. Yep. My voice was definitely tight, betraying my fear. "I called you. You didn't return the call."

"How do you know who I am?"

"How do you know who *I* am?" I retorted.

"Answer me," he hissed.

"Detective Sergeant Evers, the man who investigated my parents' murders, had photographs of you and your contact information. He said—"

"Enough. Inside. March."

Breathe, Aspen. Get control of the situation. I eyed Brandt's ride. A black RAV4. Not the sedan tailing me—if someone was really tailing me. Or Brandt owned two vehicles. I glimpsed to my right. The neighbor I'd noticed watering her roses on previous evenings wasn't there. Lights were off in her house. Swell.

"I need the house key. It's in the car." I jutted a thumb. "On the floor. In my purse."

"Get it. Only the key. No funny stuff. And leave the cell phone."

Dang. He'd seen it. I did as told and inched out of the car with the key, a single key on a wire ring. Not much of a weapon.

Brandt pulled me clear of the door, shut it, and shoved me forward. "Let's go." He smelled rancid, as if he had smoked two packs of cigarettes a day for years. He let loose with a raucous cough, confirming my assessment.

I opened the front door of the house and stepped inside. I switched on the foyer light.

Brandt crowded in behind me, slammed the door, and locked it. Without taking the gun off me, he peeked into the living room. "Your boyfriend left the other day," he said. "The older woman and girl? Where are they?"

To take control, I had to exert control. I didn't answer his question and instead said, "Your SUV is black. Do you also own a—"

"Hush," he commanded and thrust the nose of the gun at me. "The older woman and girl."

"My aunt and niece drove to Lake Tahoe this morning."

"I need water," he said.

"This way to the kitchen." I moved ahead of him, feeling the heat of his anger on my back.

"Evers was a tough nut," Brandt said.

"I heard you're no slouch."

"I'm innocent of your parents' murders."

At the sink, I reassessed him. He came across as a bit of a sad sack. Fleshy jowls, hangdog eyes, slumped shoulders. Did that make me any less frightened of him? Not really. I drew in a deep calming breath, poured him a glass of water, and set it on the kitchen table.

He inched to the archway facing the dining room and quickly spied my handiwork on the murder board. "I told you I'm not guilty."

Coolly, I said, "If I took everybody at their word, sir, I'd get nowhere."

"I'm not guilty."

I raised my chin in the direction of the gun. "Would you mind putting that down and telling me what you want?"

"Sit." He used the gun as a pointer—a Glock semiautomatic, upon closer inspection. Quincy said a Glock had been used in the Patel murder. Had Brandt killed him? "Sit," he repeated.

The putrid odor of nicotine oozed out of his pores. He was nervous. Not a good time to test him. I did as told.

"I want the treasure," he stated.

I shook my head. "I don't know what you're talking about." I flashed on my mother's last words to Rosie: *You'll never get it*. Was *it* a treasure? My parents didn't have any that I knew of. I thought of the treasure that had been trapped within the cherrywood puzzle box—a silver dollar worth nothing more than a memory.

"Sure you do," he said, his voice taunting. "The treasure. Your grandfather went on and on about it."

"My grandfather was a gambler and quite a drinker. He told tall tales."

How I wished that the silver dollars my grandfather had collected had had value, but they hadn't.

"This one was real." Brandt jabbed the gun toward me to make a point. *"Real."*

"You were his creditor, is that correct?"

Brandt growled. "I was more than a creditor. I was a friend. A longtime friend."

"You weren't contemporaries."

"No, he was older than me, but we were kindred spirits. We saw the world through the same lens."

I narrowed my gaze. Was he telling the truth? I didn't remember him ever coming around to the house, but then I couldn't recall any of my grandfather's friends having visited us.

"I lent Gray money all the time," Brandt continued. "He always repaid what he owed until—"

"Until he couldn't any longer." I sighed. "At the end, he'd sucked all the cash from the house that he could. He was bankrupt."

Tammie said I was too young to remember the arguments, but I'd heard plenty of them. When my mother and father took over the house, they inherited a huge mortgage. All they could do was make payments. If they'd lived until the ripe old age of seventy, they might have been able to pay it off, but when their lives ended prematurely . . .

"Gray said he had a way out," Brandt said. "A magic pill."

"The railings of a befogged mind."

"I'm telling you, your grandfather waxed on and on about it. It was untouchable, he said. His ace in the hole."

"Mr. Brandt, my grandfather didn't have an ace in the hole. If he had, I would have known about it." And if Rosie had found it, she sure as heck would have flaunted it at me before spending every last penny without sharing. "My parents discussed investments openly in front of me." The day they told me they had to sell the vacation home in Lake Tahoe, I'd been heartbroken. "More water?" I rose from the table.

Brandt bellowed, "Sit down!"

I slumped into my chair. "Okay. Okay." I put both palms on the table. "I'd like to help you, sir, but I don't know any more about this treasure than you do." Briefly, I told him about my meeting with Ulyssa Thaller. "Weeks after my parents' deaths, we went through all of the estate items. There was nothing of great value. We sold off some jewelry boxes and fine china and such. There were also a few paintings and statues that we sold. Nothing was worth more than a few thousand dollars."

"Did you check the backsides of the paintings?" Brandt snarled. "Maybe Gray taped this ace in the hole, whatever it was—a key to a safe-deposit box or the combination to a hidden safe—to something you wouldn't part with."

I'd never thought of inspecting the art. "Yes, sir, we did," I lied.

"And we examined the bases of and insides any of the statues." I'd read *The Maltese Falcon*. "We inspected my mother's jewelry box, too. She only wore paste jewelry."

Brandt narrowed his gaze. "I kept an eye on your mother. From the day Gray died, I followed her. I waited for her to cash in the treasure. Change her lifestyle. She didn't."

I reassessed his claim of innocence. Had he gone to my parents' house that day to rob them? Had he done so previously and come up dry? Had he anticipated my parents' comings and goings, except this time my parents had changed plans?

"My parents lived a modest life," I said. "So do I."

"But you're here. Snooping around. You're on to something." Brandt's voice grew bitter. Beads of sweat dripped down his face. "I can feel it."

"I don't know—"

"After Gray died, I approached your grandmother, but Patrice said she wouldn't pay me. She called me a usurer. That was the furthest thing from what I was. I'd been a devoted friend. A gambling buddy. I . . ." He frowned, recalling a bitter memory, I guessed. "I felt bad for Gray whenever he lost, but I was also a sap for lending him a dime that last time. I should've known he'd die before he could repay me." He leaned close. "I deserved to get paid, don't you agree?"

I kept mum.

He moved behind me again. Pressed the nose of the gun into my neck. "Your grandmother said without an IOU, I deserved squat. When she died, I reached out to your mother. I asked her about the ace in the hole. I said maybe Gray had buried something in the backyard. She assured me I was wrong and warned me, like Patrice, to stay away. I watched. I waited." He stretched to his full height. "And now you're here. You're investigating. Why? Someone else owns the house you grew up in now, so maybe she hasn't given you permission to dig. Yet."

"I didn't ask for—"

"Why are you here?" Brandt asked. "Why?"

"I want to know who killed my parents."

"Not me."

I gazed over my shoulder. He lowered his arm to his side.

Feeling less frightened with the gun not poised to blow my head off, I said, "Why should I believe you? I read your statement to the police. You said you were gambling in Las Vegas. Evers said you couldn't prove that, not definitively, and yet the police let you go. The commander interceded on your behalf. Why did he give you a pass? Did you bribe him?"

Brandt barked out a laugh and moved to face me again. "Bribe Commander Joad? As if that were possible. I'll tell you where I was. I can say it aloud now. Couldn't then. I was in the Bay Area at Graton Resort, an Indian casino. I couldn't let my wife find out because I was with a socialite who was married to a guy who donated big-time to the police fund. The woman vouched for me to the commander, but she said she would have his head if a hint of our affair came out. Joad kept his word to her and cut me loose. She and her husband are both dead now, so I can come clean."

"You're married?"

"My wife is. To another man. She has sixteen grandchildren. She divorced me and took me for everything I had."

Which explained why he wanted the treasure.

"She left you because of your affair?" I asked.

"To this day, she doesn't know about that."

"Do you own a green car?" I asked, trying again to get control of the conversation.

"My SUV is black. You saw it."

"Did you kill Viraj Patel?"

"Don't know anyone named Patel." He pronounced it *paddle*. "Who's that?"

"Mr. Patel was a witness in my parents' murder case. He came up with new information. About a suspect with a debt. You want to settle a debt. Did you set his house on fire?"

"No, no, and no," Brandt said acidly. "Not me." He swiped a hand over his face to mop up the perspiration. "I would never set fire to anything. My house went up in flames when I was a boy. I've been afraid of fire ever since."

I heaved a sigh. "Look, Mr. Brandt, we're at a stalemate. I don't have what you want. I don't have extra cash to give you, either, or I would. I'm raising my sister's teenage daughter, and I'm strapped. I'm sorry."

He pursed his lips, thinking. "Okay, listen up. I'm walking out tonight, but I'm watching you." He trained two fingers at his eyes and then my eyes. "You're going to slip up, and when you do, I'll pounce. Got me?" He hovered beside me and ran the butt of the Glock along my jaw.

"Got you." I shuddered.

The moment I heard the front door close, I dashed to the sink and washed my face to get the stink of his gun off my skin. As I did so, tears streamed down my cheeks. How I hated the feeling of helplessness.

Moments later, determined to find my center, I raced to my car, fetched my cell phone and purse, returned to the house, checked to make sure all the doors were locked, and dialed Nick.

He answered after one ring, his voice muted. "Hey."

"Hey," I echoed. "Where are you? Why are you whispering?"

"I'm at Natalie's. She's asleep." He sounded like he was walking to another room. A door closed. "What's up?"

"I . . ." I inhaled and let out a sharp breath.

"Sweetheart, talk to me."

More tears. "Kurt Brandt. He was . . . here." I told Nick about the encounter. The nonexistent treasure. "My grandparents didn't have anything of value. Neither did my parents."

"Calm down. You did great."

No, I hadn't. Okay, maybe I had. I was alive.

"Do you want me to come down?" he asked. "I'll find a way."

"No, stay with Natalie. I'm okay." I wasn't. My body was cold. My hands were shaking. I had to get a grip.

"You need to call the police. What he did was kidnapping."

"In my own home? I mean, rental home?"

"Yes." Quickly, Nick explained that someone entering a residence with force, with the intent to commit a crime, was a terrorist threat.

"Terrorist?"

"It's a general term. But yes. And the fact that he, a former suspect in your parents' murders, kept you from leaving the residence makes it kidnapping. You need protection."

"I don't know how the police will find him," I said. "I didn't get the license on his SUV."

"They'll go door to door, check surveillance cameras, Ring cameras, et cetera. They'll get a bead on his car and license plate and find him. After which, they can get a search warrant and bring him in."

"He'll deny he was here."

Nick said, "Authorities can now use geo-fencing; it's like triangulation. Google keeps the information from all those camera doodads."

"Is that the official term, *doodads?*" I asked, willing the tension to ease from my shoulders.

"It's in the handbook," he teased. "The data will show, on this date at this time, which cell phone devices were physically near this location. It can put Brandt within ten centimeters of where his phone was."

"If he was carrying a phone." I sighed. "If they charge him, can't he get out on bail?"

"If he's wealthy, maybe, but the average guy might not be able to come up with money for a million-dollar warrant."

My breathing steadied. "I don't think Brandt will hurt me. He wants me to find whatever it is he believes I have not yet *found*. He craves the treasure. He needs me alive."

"I still want you to call Quincy," Nick said.

"Yes, sir." A nervous laugh burbled out of me. "I suppose I should look on the backsides of pictures and inside statutes for this treasure."

Nick chuckled. "That's my girl. Find the humor."

A long silence fell between us.

"Have you locked all the doors?" he asked.

"Yes, and I have the fireplace poker at the ready."

He let loose with a full-throated laugh. "Go get 'em, tiger."

"Sleep well," I said.

"You do the same."

After I ended the call, I phoned Evers again. I wanted his take on Brandt.

His nurse answered. "Hello?"

"Blessica, it's Aspen Adams. We met the other day. Is Detective Sergeant Evers available? I know it's late, but he said I could call—"

"I am sorry. He is no longer with us."

"What?"

"Mr. Evers"—she sucked back a sob—"died an hour ago."

My insides snagged. He'd sounded fine when I'd spoken to him. Tired, but fine. I asked the unthinkable. "Was he murdered?"

"No, miss. He went peacefully. His brother was with him. I am sorry, but I must hang up. He, the brother, needs me. You understand." She didn't wait for a reply.

My heart heavy with sadness, I called the Atherton police station. Quincy wasn't in, so the dispatcher directed me to a female officer for my statement. I explained to her that Brandt had been a suspect in my parents' murder case years ago and went on to spell out how Brandt had threatened me. I mentioned my conversation with Nick, providing his credentials for weight. The officer said that, given my location, the Menlo Park Police Department ought to handle the matter and said she would contact them and have an officer swing by to take my statement.

The Menlo Park P.D. officer arrived within minutes. Tall and burly with day-old stubble, he had an easy way about him. I told him what had happened as we roamed the house together, checking doors and windows to make sure they were secure. After assuring me I was safe, he bid me good night, adding that I shouldn't worry. He'd have a patrol car drive by often until morning.

Although I was pretty certain Brandt would not be returning during the night, I slept with one eye open.

Chapter 23

When I awoke Monday morning, my eyes were puffy and my hair tangled. I showered, fixed my hair and makeup, and dressed in a black sweater and jeans. I grabbed an energy bar—I wasn't sure my stomach could handle anything more—and before heading to the cemetery, swung by the grocery store for a spray of calla lilies and roses.

Astra Green Memorial Park, named after a young woman who had died in the 1800s, featured acres of grassy plots and myriad columbarium niches, all located within a grove of century-old oaks. My grandparents had been buried in the cemetery, but until my parents died, I had no idea that we'd owned a family plot. Ulyssa Thaller informed me that the week after my parents married, they had invested in the grassy expanse—for my mother's parents, my parents, and their descendants. I didn't want to be buried there, but I didn't want to think about that now. This visit was to celebrate the memory of them.

The weather, as if anticipating my visit, had turned drearily cold and foggy, but thanks to the recent rain, the scent of grass was fragrant. As I strolled past the bank of niches, I saw a few hazy figures crossing in front of me. They were so shapeless, I could barely make out whether they were male or female. They spoke in whispers as if raising their voices might wake the dead.

A lawn mower powered up, disturbing the quiet. So much for reverence.

I approached the family plot. All of the headstones' designs were simple, created by my mother. I set the flowers in the copper container between the headstones for my mother and father and stepped away. I wanted to believe in heaven. If it existed, were my parents watching over me, following my foibles?

I moved to Grandpa Gray's gravestone and peered at it. Was there really a treasure? His ace in the hole? Was that the *it* my mother had vowed to protect? Had someone other than Brandt known about it? I willed my grandfather to tell me where the treasure was. To tell me who had killed my parents. All I heard? Crickets.

As I had the other day, I felt eyes on me. I whipped around. No one ducked out of sight. Even so, I wondered if Brandt was doing what he'd promised, watching me, waiting to pounce. He couldn't possibly believe the treasure was buried at the cemetery. I certainly hadn't come with a shovel. I moved right and left, adjusting my angle, looking for an intruder behind the trees, but saw no one.

No one, Aspen. You are alone. So very alone.

For an hour I stood at the site, tears trickling down my cheeks. I promised my parents that I would solve this case. I vowed that I would take care of Candace. I swore that I would do my best to ease my sister's broken soul.

When a couple appeared at a nearby gravesite, I whispered a quick prayer that my great-grandmother, Blue Sky, had taught me.

> *I give you this, for you to keep.*
> *I am with you still, I do not sleep.*
> *I am a thousand winds that blow.*
> *I am the diamond glints on snow.*
> *I am the sunlight on ripened grain.*
> *I am the gentle autumn rain.*
> *Do not think of me as gone.*
> *I am with you still, in each new dawn.*

"Goodbye, Mom. Goodbye, Dad."

I wouldn't visit again. I could commune with my family's spirits in Lake Tahoe as easily as I could here.

• • •

My cell phone rang as I veered right on Middlefield Road. Rosie was on the line. I answered. "Hi."

Typical Rosie, she barged ahead. "What have you learned? Why haven't you kept me in the loop? Did you meet that detective? Evers was his name."

"Slow down." I told her I'd just left the cemetery.

She let out a little moan. "I haven't been there since . . ." Another moan. "I suck."

"It's okay. They're not there. Their souls—"

"I know. I know." She clicked her tongue. "But I really suck. I—"

"Look, I'm doing all I can to pin this down, Rosie. Yes, I met with Evers. He died yesterday of cancer. But I got all his notes. I've met with a couple of the suspects." I didn't tell her about Patel and the fire. "I plan to meet more."

"Did you see . . ." She hesitated. I imagined her twirling hair around her index finger, a habit she'd had all her life.

"Antoine?" I asked.

"Mm-hm."

"I did. He's straight. And clean. He works at Big Box."

"Clean." She hummed. "Good for him."

"Tammie says hello. I had dinner with her and saw Mia and Mia's little girl yesterday."

"How are they?"

"Doing well. Mia's working hard. By the way, Tammie had Mom's cherrywood puzzle box."

"Wait, hold on." Rosie clicked her tongue. "Why did she have it?"

I told her about Tammie taking a keepsake and how embarrassed she'd been, not having informed me. "A silver dollar with Mom's year of birth was inside."

Rosie sighed. "I remember Grandpa Gray saying he wished he had a silver dollar for every time I laughed."

I smiled, happy that we shared the same memory. "Listen, I'll call you if I find anything that will help solve this. When I know more, you'll know more. Promise."

"I'm two days clean," she whispered and ended the call.

Chapter 24

At a quarter to noon, while downing a container of Greek yogurt and a glass of water, I touched base with my aunt. I asked her if she'd heard anything from the Placer County Sheriff's forensic people about the ballistic match to my grandfather's gun. She hadn't. She would reach out to them after we ended the call. Then I asked her to do me a favor. Go to my cabin and inspect the four paintings done by my grandmother that were hanging on the walls. I couldn't imagine my mother or grandmother having affixed a treasure to any of them, but it was worth a look. Maybe, as Brandt had suggested, one of my grandparents had a safe-deposit box that I wasn't aware of and the number was written on a piece of paper taped to a piece of art. But if Brandt had stolen into my parents' house on previous occasions, wouldn't he have already checked that? Maybe not. Maybe he'd recently come up with the notion.

I noticed a text message from Detective Sergeant Quincy. *Call me re: Brandt.* Pulse elevated, I stabbed in the precinct number and was transferred to the detective.

"Menlo Park Police Department has located Brandt and has booked him on kidnapping charges," he said. "You're safe."

For now, but I breathed easier. "Thank you. By the way, is Commander Joad still active? I'd like to follow up with him about Mr. Brandt's alibi in my parents' case."

"Evers didn't tell you? The commander is in a retirement facility, suffering from early-onset Alzheimer's. Happened about three years ago. His memory isn't reliable."

Had Brandt been aware of the commander's condition when he'd given me his alternate alibi last night? Had he known Joad wouldn't have been able to refute it?

"About Detective Sergeant Evers," I started. "Have you heard—"

"That he passed? Yes. It's all over the precinct. His are big shoes to fill."

I murmured that I was sorry and ended the call.

After lunch, I contacted Tammie and Ulyssa Thaller. Not only did

I want to inspect the backside of the painting of Rosie and me, but I was ready to tag everything in the storage unit and divest of what I didn't want. Tammie had offered to help. So had Ulyssa. I hoped doing something mindless yet orderly would help me sort through my thoughts.

Was I ruling out suspects too soon? Was I too trusting when I should be delving deeper? Was Antoine's *new man* act purely that—an act? Kurt Brandt's claim to be looking for a treasure had certainly made him look guilty. And he'd held a gun to my head. Would he hurt me—kill me—if I didn't come up with the goods? And what about William Fisher? I needed to meet him in person. Just because he'd forbid me to come near him didn't mean I had to obey. I texted Max and asked for help locating him.

She responded: *You're pretty bossy today.*

I laughed and replied: *Taking my cues from you.*

• • •

An hour later, I opened the storage unit with the key I'd received the other day and pushed up the corrugated metal door. I switched on the light and stared, hands on hips, at the task ahead.

Tammie, who stood with Ulyssa behind me, said, "I know it looks daunting, but you can do it. *We* . . . can do it." Cold breath billowed from her mouth.

Ulyssa agreed. I'd told her she didn't need to join us—it was last-minute, after all—but she'd insisted. She handed me the checklist. "Ready when you are."

Tammie had dressed casually for the occasion in stretch jeans, turtleneck, and pullover. In contrast, Ulyssa, in a blue suit, overcoat, and stiletto boots, looked as though she had come from a meeting with a powerful client.

"You can sit in that chair, if you want," I said to Ulyssa, indicating one from the dining room set. "Take a load off."

She took me up on the offer.

Prior to coming to the facility, I'd stopped by the office supply store and had purchased four rolls of stick-on tags: one each of red, blue, green, and yellow. I would put red on the things I wanted to keep, blue for items I thought Rosie might want, green on items to be sold, and yellow for all the things that should go to charities.

"First things first," I said and crossed to the painting of Rosie and me. I examined the back. It had been professionally mounted. The hanging wire was medium-grade. The edges of the framing paper were sealed and plastic buttons attached to each corner. There was nothing else. No code or key taped to the paper. No handwritten notations. Nothing. It was a dead end.

"What are you looking for?" Tammie asked.

"A man—Brandt, I told you about him—thought my grandfather might have had a safe-deposit box and might have taped its whereabouts to another of my grandmother's pieces of art. The man said my grandfather told him there was something of value in it." I heaved a sigh. "It was wishful thinking."

Tammie rested a hand on my shoulder. "We've gone through nearly everything. There's nothing of real value here. Everything remaining is purely sentimental."

"You're right. Moving on." I clapped my hands.

For an hour, I rummaged through the items, checking each on the list, with Tammie and Ulyssa weighing in occasionally. The living room furniture: *sell.* The bedroom furniture: *sell.* The dining set—my insides lurched as I pictured the photograph of my parents lying dead on the floor beside it—*sell.*

In the end, for myself I'd tagged the standing Tiffany lamp from my mother's office, the mementoes from the hutch, two of my mother's scarves—she'd had a penchant for colorful chiffon scarves—and a few needlepoint pillows. For Rosie, I'd set aside all items pertaining to her, like medals and ribbons, plus a blanket Blue Sky had woven, and my mother's vanity. As a little girl, Rosie had loved sitting at the vanity and donning makeup and jewelry.

When I'd reviewed every item on the first two pages, I flipped to the third page and paused, my breath snagging in my chest. Bittersweet memories of my mother in the master bedroom, showing off an arty new necklace or ring to my father, washed over me.

"Are you okay?" Tammie asked.

"Remember Mom's teensy silver jewelry boxes?" I formed little *O*s with my fingers. "We sold them in the first go-around."

Tammie smiled sadly. "They weren't even big enough for a pair of earrings."

"Exactly."

"And remember that horrible cachepot?" I asked.

"Ugh." Tammie laughed. "You sold that, too."

"Hey, you don't recall seeing the silver walking elephant that the world-traveling client gave Mom, do you?" I motioned. "In the boxes?"

"It's not on the list."

Ulyssa said, "My assistant didn't find a photograph of that, by the way."

Tammie said, "Rosie might have—" She bit her lip. "I'm sorry. I blurted that out."

"You're probably right," I acknowledged. "Over the years, my sister certainly took more than her due."

My gaze landed on another line item. "Hold on."

"What's wrong?" Ulyssa asked.

"This says ninety-nine silver dollars." I showed her the page.

"That's what we sold." Her lips turned up at the corners. "It always made me think of that old song, '99 Bottles of Beer on the Wall.'"

"Grandpa Gray had collected one hundred."

"Add the one in the puzzle box," Tammie said. "That makes one hundred."

"Not including that one."

A recollection of my grandfather and me counting the silver dollars in the living room of their house—when they had owned it, not my parents—coursed through me. He had been teaching me to sort by year. We were sitting on the carpet and he was making me turn each coin heads-up so I could see the date—1970 before 1971; 1960 after 1950. When Grandma Patrice found us, she got so angry with him. She snatched a silver dollar from the carpet and shook it in front of his face. Grandpa Gray had cowered. I stiffened as my grandmother's words rang out in my mind: *What are you doing, you fool? This is our insurance policy,* she'd shouted and then pocketed the coin and stormed out of the room.

Was the coin the insurance policy my mother had been talking about when she'd hustled us out of the living room the day my father and Grandpa Gray had argued? Was a silver dollar the *it* my mother had sworn the killer would never get? Was the coin the treasure Kurt Brandt was seeking?

"Aspen, sweetheart," Tammie said. "Yoo-hoo."

I lifted my chin. Tammie and Ulyssa were staring at me, waiting. I explained my theory and went silent again, digging through my memories, trying to dredge up where my grandmother—or my mother—might have hidden the coin. Had my grandfather gotten his hands on it when my grandmother hadn't been looking? Had he squandered it at a poker game?

Gazing at the sea of boxes and furniture, I said, "Maybe we missed it."

For two solid hours, the three of us searched for the coin, browsing under, behind, and in everything.

We came up empty.

Chapter 25

Tammie and I met Mia at Tea for Two, a charming restaurant in a cluster of shops near the train tracks in Mountain View. Mia had come from a meeting with a prospective client. The nanny was watching her daughter. After we ordered tea and scones, Tammie told Mia about our discovery.

At the word *treasure*, Mia smirked. "Like the one in the puzzle box?"

Tammie said, "Not exactly. It's—"

A train pulled into the nearby station. At the same time, my cell phone hummed. I glanced at the readout. Max had sent a text that included William Fisher's address in Santa Clara, adding that he was home right now.

I apologized for my hasty departure, promised I'd stay in touch, and hurried to the Prius.

On the drive to Fisher's house, I texted Max a reply: *How did you find him? Maybe he's at work. Is this a fruitless venture?*

She responded: *Yaz tracked him down. Fisher is independent now. No longer working for tech guru. Yaz acted like prospective client. Fisher home sick. Good luck.*

William Fisher lived in a pale green house off of Los Padres Boulevard, a residential neighborhood near a school. I didn't see a car in the driveway, but that didn't mean anything. The house had a two-car garage. Ample space for a limo. The yard featured succulents and drought-tolerant flowers. There was no lawn.

I parked on the street and, drawing in a deep breath, walked along the brick path to the front door. I paused to pick up the newspaper that lay on the path and continued on. I rang the doorbell, which buzzed like a horde of bees.

A ropy elderly man with a weathered face and long salt-and-pepper hair that hung in curtains around his face peered through the left etched-glass sidelight. His dark eyes peered at me with suspicion. He yanked up the zipper on his jogging suit jacket and yelled, "What do you want?"

"Mr. Fisher, I'm—"

"How do you know my name? Are you a realtor? I don't talk to realtors."

"No, sir. I'm . . ." I hoisted the newspaper. "I was walking and figured you must be sick since you didn't pick up your paper."

"Are you one of those nosy neighbors?"

"No, sir. Not nosy." *Not a neighbor, either.* "Want it?" I blazed a hundred-watt smile.

He grunted, opened the door, and stuck out his hand. Not to shake. He wanted the paper.

I didn't comply. "Sir, I'm Aspen Adams."

He tried to close the door.

I thrust the newspaper forward to block the action. In the nick of time. The door wouldn't close completely. Through the inch of space, I said, "Please, sir, talk to me. Five minutes."

"I warned you to stay away. What didn't you understand?"

I stared at the inch of face I could see and flashed on the man who'd boarded the elevator at the Palais Hotel. Fisher looked leaner, but the man had been wearing a heavy coat. Was he the person I'd seen? Was he the one following me in the sedan, if, indeed, someone other than Brandt was following me?

How paranoid are you, Aspen? At BARC, our doctors were rarely fazed by where the mistrustful mind might take a person. I, on the other hand, wanted to remain sane for at least a few more years.

"Sir, what kind of car do you drive?" I asked.

"A limo."

"How about when you're off work?"

"A Chevy Impala." He screwed up his mouth. "Leave."

"Green?"

"Dark blue."

Blue could look green in certain light. "Have you been following me?"

"Why would I and how could I? I don't know where you live. Which raises another point." Fisher whipped the door open and crossed his arms, as if looking like a big tough guy might scare me. It didn't. He had no weapon. He didn't make a move toward me. "How do you know where I live?"

"I'm a private detective." I stood taller, doing my best to look as intimidating as he. "Look, sir, I merely want to hear your account of your relationship to my father."

"I had no relationship with him."

"You were not happy with his defense of your son."

Fisher glowered at me. "I did not kill your parents. Police found me not guilty. You want a suspect? Follow up on Dale Warwick." He poked a bony finger toward the street. "Now, get. I've got a cold."

"The fresh air could be good for you." The sky was cloudy, but the temperature had warmed up to at least the mid-fifties. "How about we sit on the porch and chat?" Where the rest of humanity could keep an eye on us. I motioned to the two wicker chairs fitted with striped cushions. "Tell me your side of things. Tell me why I should believe you."

Begrudgingly, as if he realized I would stick to him like cement until he complied, he lumbered outside. He eased into a chair but kept his focus on me, like a panther ready to attack at the slightest provocation.

"Would your wife like to join us?" I asked.

"Divorced. Left me a year to the day after our Johnny went to prison. A year after that she died of a broken heart." The misery he suffered oozed out of him.

"Tell me about Johnny." I kept my body language open, my arms resting comfortably on the arms of the chair. "You thought my father did a lousy job of representing him."

Fisher pulled a tissue from the pocket of his jacket, blotted his eyes, wiped his nose, and returned it to his pocket. "Johnny is still in prison."

"What did he do?"

"He was a member of AIM, the American Indian Movement. Do you know what that is?"

I nodded. It was an organization initially formed in urban areas to address systemic issues of poverty and police brutality against Native Americans, but now it addressed even more things, like tribal rights and high rates of unemployment.

"Of course you do. Because of your father's work." Fisher leaned forward, elbows braced on his thighs. "Johnny was a good boy and dedicated to reducing violence on reservations, but one day, two policemen trespassed on the reservation searching for a Native American who was wanted in regard to a robbery. The policemen were shot, and Johnny became the main suspect."

I listened intently, searching for a lie.

"Johnny's alibi was flimsy," Fisher continued. "He said he was walking the perimeter. The police didn't believe him because it was raining. They asked why he would walk the perimeter in the rain. He said he needed fresh air. To meditate. I believed him."

"He wasn't on patrol? Keeping a lookout?"

"No." Fisher blinked rapidly and fingered his eye. "Darn xeriscape. Dust kicks up all the time. Where was I?"

"You said you believed your son, but . . ."

"But the police didn't. Plus, a gun was found in Johnny's truck and his girlfriend, also a Native American, said she *saw* him do the killings."

I opened my hands. "If there was a witness—"

"The woman framed him. She planted the gun. They'd recently broken up. She held a grudge."

"Where'd she get the gun?"

"That's just it. I don't know. Maybe it was hers. Maybe she offed them." Fisher spanked his leg. "Johnny had no motive. None. If the police had pressed that woman harder, she might have confessed. But they didn't and your father didn't make them."

Fisher sat back abruptly and drummed his fingers on the arm of the chair. His gaze grew ominous. After a long moment, he exhaled slowly. Evers had mentioned that, years ago, Fisher had been a hothead. Apparently, he'd learned how to temper his outbursts.

I said, "No one saw your son walking the perimeter?"

"No, but my boy doesn't lie. Never did. That woman. That—" A moan escaped Fisher's lips. "Johnny maintains he is innocent, even after being in the pen fifteen years."

So did half the other cons in jail.

"Does he have new representation?" I asked.

"Can't afford it." Fisher heaved a sigh as if he were bearing the weight of the world. "I lost my boy and my wife because of your father's ineffective defense."

And therein was his motive to kill my parents. But why rob them? To muddy the theory that it had been a revenge killing? Maybe he'd stolen the silver to pay for his son's defense. Except he hadn't retained another lawyer. Did that make him innocent?

"Tell me about your alibi for my parents' murders, sir."

He huffed. "It's all in the report I signed."

"Yes, I've read it, but sometimes people taking notes don't catch all the facts. I'd like to hear you tell it."

His nose flared but he proceeded. "I had a steady ride then. Mr. Thomas. He owns TT Technology. I was driving him that day, as I had nearly every day for two years."

"You were seen in the vicinity of my parents' house earlier in the week."

"Mr. Thomas had meetings all over the Bay Area. At buildings. At private homes. But not that day. His meeting was in Sunnyvale. He was investing in another tech company. The meeting lasted for about four hours."

According to the police report, for nearly two hours, nobody remembered seeing the limousine in the building's garage or on the street. I said, "You drove somewhere."

"Not to murder your parents. I . . ." Fisher tapped the armrest. "I know this is in the police report. I drove to the beach. I was upset about my wife walking out on me. I needed a dose of fresh air. Good clean ocean air."

"Sounds a lot like your son's alibi."

He glowered at me. "I'm not lying. I drove to Santa Cruz, kicked off my shoes, and walked barefoot in the sand. A beachcomber saw me and provided testimony. Plus, there was sand in the limo."

The memory of Rosie and me coming home from the beach coated with sand gave truth to his story. On the other hand, Fisher could have put the sand in the limo and paid the beachcomber to cover for him.

"And that took you two hours?" I asked.

"I told you I'm not lying. My son and I don't lie."

"Why did you toss my father's office?" I blurted out. "What were you looking for?"

"What the heck are you talking about? I didn't toss nothing. I didn't break into your folks' house. I'm clean," he growled and splayed his hands. "Like I said before, you need to look at Dale Warwick. He was a client of your father's. A big-time builder. Wealthy as all get-out. He did a lot of work in the Bay Area. I know about him because one day we had back-to-back appointments. Warwick looks like me. Native American. Tall. Dark. About my age. Maybe a witness in your folks' murders described someone like us and that's why the police went after me. It's called profiling."

I exhaled. "The police followed up with Mr. Warwick. He was at a Patwin council meeting. Four men vouched for him."

"He could've paid them to lie," Fisher said, employing the same theory I'd attributed to him for his witness.

"Why would he have killed my father?" I asked. "What was his motive?"

"Warwick thought your father didn't represent him well in a defective design issue. I know because I heard him ranting at your father the day I had an appointment to discuss Johnny's defense. Warwick was Mr. Cool on the outside, but behind closed doors? Bad news." Fisher ran a finger across the top of his knuckles. "You know, after the murders, I followed Warwick for a few days, thinking I could get the cops off my case if I could prove he killed your folks. Guess what I caught him doing? Bribing a lender. Warwick made the guy turn down loans for the competition so he could seize the deal."

Was this the debt Patel had been researching?

"And did I mention Dale's a gambler?" Fisher continued. "Private games. Big money. He hangs with the wrong crowd. I'm telling you, bad news."

Did Warwick know Brandt? Were the two in cahoots?

"Did you report all of this to the police?" I asked.

"Didn't have time to because a week after your folks' murders the police were hauling Warwick's sorry butt into prison for beating his wife. He went to jail for a year. Did Evers tell you that?" Fisher demanded. "Did he even know?"

I was pretty certain Evers didn't, or he would've mentioned it. He had believed Warwick's alibi and had let the thread unravel.

• • •

On the drive home, I contacted Max and brought her up to date. While on the call, she did a quick check on Dale Warwick.

"Sugar," she said, "I hate to tell you this, but Dale Warwick is deceased."

"What?" I squawked. Was the universe conspiring to prevent me from solving this case?

"He died Saturday."

I jolted. "How?"

"Car accident. Run off the road at night. Accident report says the other driver was not identified."

How portentous if he'd killed my parents, but then I reflected on Warwick's alibi. Four council members had vouched for him. I could see him paying off one, but four? No way. Despite Fisher's belief that Warwick was a viable suspect, like Evers, I had to let him go.

Another call was coming in. *Serenity*. I thanked my aunt, ended our call, and tapped Accept. "Hey, what's up?"

"You haven't returned my calls."

"I've been—"

"Can we have drinks?" she begged. "Now. Or in an hour? At our old haunt. Please. I really need to see you."

She sounded rattled and in desperate need of a friend. I said, "Yes."

Chapter 26

The Grapevine, a wine and appetizers bar on El Camino Real, featured an etched cement floor, exposed beams, and brick walls. There were ten hardwood booths for intimate conversations and a number of cushioned corners with throw pillows for larger parties. The chalkboard hanging on the wall to the right displayed tonight's selections.

Serenity was perched on a high-backed swivel stool at the horseshoe-shaped oak bar. Her purse sat on the stool beside hers, to reserve it for me, I presumed. She moved it the moment she spotted me and set it on her lap.

I kissed her cheek, slid onto my seat, and offered a soft whistle. "That's some look you're sporting. Did you have a big donor meeting?"

"No."

The red silk suit complimented her skin tone. The ice-white blouse enhanced her femininity. The diamond drop earrings were either fake or had cost her half a year's salary. Had Damian bought them for her? In our three years of marriage, he'd never bought me more than a bouquet of flowers. I tamped down any ill feelings. I had no right.

Serenity said, "I just felt the need to give my confidence a boost." Her lower lip quivered ever so slightly.

So much for the boost.

"Because you don't feel powerful?" I asked.

"Let's order wine first."

The bartender, an elegant young man with an easy smile and engaging eyes, laid two cocktail napkins on the bar. "What'll it be, ladies?"

"What do you recommend in red?" I asked.

"Luca Old Vine Malbec is nice. Red ripe fruit. Vanilla oaky tones. Or if you prefer daring, try the Enfer d'Arvier, which has a compelling rusticity with a wild berry impression."

"I'll go with that."

Serenity said, "I'll have the Malbec. And would you bring an appetizer of the three hard cheeses with the seed crackers? Thanks."

He nodded and moved away.

I swiveled on the stool, propping one elbow on the bar. "So, what's up, Serenity?"

She grimaced. "I know you're angry about Damian and me, and you have every right to be."

"I'm not." Okay, I was, but only a tad. I didn't want him in my life, and if she could find happiness with him—

"You don't have to worry any longer because we broke up. Not that we were a couple, but he ended it. So . . ." She whisked her hand through the air as if swatting away bad energy. *"C'est la vie."* Tears leaked from her eyes. She swiped them with a knuckle. "I'm sorry. I should've known he'd break my heart. You warned me. We had so much in common. I thought we . . ." She worked her chin up to a semi-confident level. "Moving on."

The bartender set our drinks down. We raised our glasses and clinked.

"To new beginnings." I took a sip.

Serenity did the same and set the glass down, but she didn't release the stem. "How's the search for the killer going?"

I filled her in on my meeting with Fisher and the encounter with Brandt.

"For heaven's sakes, Aspen, why didn't you call me?"

Her distress made me realize that because I'd been avoiding her calls I hadn't told her about the fire or the meeting with Hoek or—

"You can't take risks like this," she said. "You're not bulletproof."

"Once Brandt left the house, I felt safe," I lied, unwilling to reveal that I'd gone to bed with a fireplace poker as my bedmate. "And now that he's been arrested . . ." I explained about the kidnapping charge.

"What is the treasure he wants?" Serenity asked.

"My grandfather told him it was his ace in the hole. Until earlier today, I had no clue what he could have been talking about."

"Had?" she echoed. "Meaning you know now?"

I told her about my grandfather's silver dollar collection.

"One coin could be considered a treasure?" Her eyes widened.

"It depends on how rare it is." I remembered my grandfather expounding, in childlike terms, about why coin collecting mattered. For a week, he'd tried to teach me to say the word *numismatist*. When I finally got it right, he'd clapped me on the shoulder and hooted with glee.

"How could he have afforded the coin?" Serenity swirled her wine in the glass and inspected its legs. "Didn't you say he was bankrupt?"

"I think"—I nudged my wine aside and propped an elbow on the bar—"he must have stumbled upon it. Maybe at a pawnshop." He had loved browsing them. "Or he'd won it in a poker game." I told her how my grandmother had burst into the den, furious, and had snatched the coin off the floor. "I think she knew its value and hid it."

"But you don't know where?"

"Nope. For all I know, my grandfather found it, used it to ante into another poker game, and lost it. Poof. Like the wind." I pressed my lips together and released them with a click. "But I think whoever killed my parents believed my parents had it."

"Brandt."

"Or someone else. My grandfather was a talker. He could've mentioned it to anyone. A friend. A neighbor. Dad's and Mom's clients both came to the house." I shook a finger. "That's the big question. Who?"

"Did you ask any of the suspects point-blank?"

"I didn't know about it then."

"You have to do so. Listen to me"—she leaned closer—"you're trained to see holes in patients' stories. You'll know if one of the suspects is lying."

"I feel like everyone has told me the truth."

"But you haven't mentioned this treasure to them. Are there any suspects you haven't questioned?" Serenity asked.

"Not that the police had in their sights."

The waiter set the platter of cheese accompanied by seed crackers as well as tiny bowls of apricot jam, nuts, and olives on the bar. Serenity prepared a morsel for each of us. My insides were raw, but one bite wouldn't hurt and might help absorb the wine.

"Who knew your parents were on a trip?" Serenity asked.

"Tammie, Rosie, their travel agent, Lynda Sue Harris." I downed the snack and blotted my fingers on a napkin. "She would have known their exact schedule, but Tammie ruled her out, saying Lynda Sue was as good as they come."

"You should question her, all the same. Since she was booking their trips, I'll bet she knew their net worth," Serenity said. "Maybe your mother even mentioned the coin could be collateral, should they ever need it." She sipped her wine. "How is Tammie, by the way? My mom said she's fallen on hard times."

"What? No. That was years ago when Tammie's jerk of a husband divorced her and left her high and dry with a child to feed."

Serenity's forehead puckered. "No, this was more recently. You know, Tammie redecorated the spare bedroom for Mom, right?"

I didn't.

"Mom thinks she's low on cash. She thinks it's because Tammie overextended when she helped Mia split up with her husband." Serenity's mother was a loan officer at U.S. Bank, one of the many lenders that had turned Tammie down, causing her to ask my mother for help. "Whatever the reason, Mom said Tammie was reaching out to anyone she knew for referrals. She'd take any small job to make ends meet." Serenity nibbled an olive and set the pit on a cocktail napkin. "Speaking of Mia, wasn't she one of the sweetest people?"

As preteens, Serenity and I had looked up to Mia and Rosie until Rosie took a wrong turn and Mia stopped coming around.

I said, "She's an architect now. Actually, a builder. Dream Big Associates."

"I've heard of that company. I've seen signs. Gee, I have to admit, I didn't see that kind of success in her future."

"Why not?"

"C'mon, Mia liked to excel at a lot of things, but she wasn't a student. She was an artist. How did she get through that many years of math and science?"

"She was calculating," I joked.

"And how could Tammie have afforded it?"

"Maybe that's what put her in the hole," I murmured, as thoughts ran headlong through my mind. Tammie had known my mother better than anyone else. She'd known that my mother went to the shooting range. Mom must have told her about the gun. Had Tammie pretended not to know that Mom kept it in the hope chest? Plus, she'd known my parents' travel schedule.

No, no, no. I would not go there. Tammie did not kill my parents. Tammie, like Lynda Sue Harris, was one of the most caring people on earth. Besides, she had been on a college tour with Mia.

Chapter 27

For the next hour, I pushed thoughts of the murders aside and concentrated on Serenity. No matter how much she claimed she was fine with Damian calling it quits, I could tell her confidence was shattered. Despite her beauty, she'd never had good luck with men. She believed she was either too clingy or too demanding. Now, she doubted she'd ever meet the right guy. If only her mother wouldn't press her to settle down and have children, she joked. Tick-tock.

I listened. I counselled. Two hours later, feeling as if I'd done a good deed simply by being present, I headed to the house. I'd restricted myself to two glasses of wine. I was fine to drive. Learning from my experience with Brandt, I checked the rearview mirror repeatedly on the drive, and I didn't get out of the Prius before scanning the surrounding area for lurkers. None.

Even so, I hurried into the house and locked the doors. I switched on a bunch of lights and fetched a glass of water from the kitchen. On my way to the bedroom, I peered into the dining room at the murder board.

Yes, it needed updating. I strode to it and added notes to Fisher's profile. *Beaten-down man. Alibi sounded real.* I added an additional Post-it with Warwick's name on it and a question mark. Then, reluctantly, I wrote a Post-it with Tammie's name on it and added: *In debt? Knew Mom's secrets. Alibi confirmed?*

Moving away two steps, I peered at the overall picture.

I had no idea who had killed my parents, but I was pretty sure that the missing silver coin was what the killer had been after. Brandt didn't have it. Had the killer found it? If not, where was it? In the morning, I would—

My cell phone trilled. I didn't recognize the number and let it roll into voicemail. It rang again. At the same time, the doorbell chimed.

Every fiber of my body tensed. I grabbed the statue of the dancing girl and peeked through the sidelight. "No way," I groused.

Damian stood outside in a pin-striped suit and sloppy tie, hair disheveled. How did he know where I was staying? I hadn't even told

Serenity the location. Had he followed me the other night from the Palais Hotel?

"Hey, babe. Open up." Cheekily, he hoisted a bottle of champagne. "I want to celebrate," he announced loudly enough to wake the neighbors.

He couldn't have meant he wanted to celebrate breaking it off with Serenity, could he? He wasn't that crass.

"C'mon. Open up. I'm going to become the new conductor for the New York Philharmonic. Woot!" He kicked the door. It rattled.

Not eager to pay for damages should he continue, I drew in a deep, calming breath and opened the door. My ex stumbled in, reeking of alcohol. A Ford Explorer reversed out of the driveway.

"I Uber'd," he slurred and waved goodbye to the driver.

"How did you discover where I was staying?" I asked, not allowing him to move farther into the house.

"I ran into Tammie Laplante, of all people. At the liquor store. What a coincidence, right?" He did his best to straighten his tie but failed. The knot remained lopsided. "She revealed that she'd found this place for you. I had to bribe her with tickets to the San Francisco ballet to wheedle it from her. They're hard to come by."

Dang it. How could Tammie have done that to me? Did she hope Damian and I would reunite? Dream on.

"Nice digs." Damian squeezed past me to take in the front of the house. "Where're the glasses?"

"It's too late for champagne. I'll make you some coffee."

"No caffeine. I don't want to lose the buzz." He grinned his wickedly enchanting smile. "Didn't you hear me? I'm going to be the conductor for the frickin' New York Philharmonic. My life's dream."

"I'm happy for you." I moved into the kitchen.

He followed, his free hand brushing my shoulder. I shimmied away and ordered him to sit. "Don't touch me," I sniped.

He snickered low and slow and slumped into a chair. He set the bottle of champagne on the table. "Tammie said you're not happy."

"No, she didn't."

"She said P.I. work isn't for you."

Tammie and I would have to have a chat. Boundaries.

"I'm very happy, I'll have you know." I jammed a pod of coffee into the Keurig machine, poured in the requisite water, and begged it to brew fast. I'd give Damian one cup and send him packing. "I love my work. I adore Tahoe." How I wished I was there right now instead of here. How I wished I was sitting on the patio with Nick, inhaling his cologne, not Damian's.

My ex-husband's gaze grew gentle. "Yeah, you always had a soft spot for anyplace with water." He rose to his feet and crowded me by the coffee machine. He fingered the foil on the champagne bottle seductively. "But, c'mon, at least admit that you miss being with me."

"No."

"Not even a little bit?"

"Not a whit, Damian." I eased away from him and opened the refrigerator. I pulled out the carton of half-and-half. Before I could turn around, he was behind me. He traced the top of the neck of the champagne bottle along the back of my neck.

"Cut it out!" I whirled around.

He held his ground. His breath was rancid.

Through gritted teeth, I said, "Move away from me and listen up. Your philandering erased all possible feelings I ever had for you. You betrayed me and cut out my heart in the process. It's been a long road for me to heal, but I've healed. I'm in love with another man."

"In love," he scoffed, moving even closer as he finger-combed his hair.

"It's time for you to leave, Damian."

His eyes hooded. "Not yet. Not until you promise to go to New York with me."

"Are you nuts?" I screamed, all civility gone.

"You're my wife."

"We're divorced."

"Marry me again." He dropped to one knee and pressed his forehead against my abdomen.

I gripped a hank of his hair and tugged hard. "Get real. Get up. And get out." I released him and stomped to the foyer.

He struggled to his feet, teetered, and stumbled after me. He grabbed my arm. I wrenched free and shoved him. He reeled into the wall. The impact made him lose his hold on the champagne bottle. It crashed on the parquet floor. The explosion made the cork fly out with a *pop!*

He scowled. "Now look what you made me——"

The front door of the house burst open. Nick, gun drawn, bore down on Damian. "Hands where I can see them."

Damian scuttled backward like a crab. He stopped when he hit the wall and raised his hands. "It's okay, man. I'm cool. Who are you? There's no need for a gun." His words ran together.

"Nick," I said, my cheeks flaming hot, "holster your weapon. Meet Damian Saint, my ex-husband. Damian stopped by to celebrate his new post in New York."

"Why's he on the floor?" Nick asked.

"The floor's slippery," Damian said.

I did my best not to hurt his pride by disputing his claim.

The corners of Nick's mouth twitched; an amused expression crinkled his eyes. An excellent detective, he'd quickly gleaned what had happened; the broken bottle, Damian's mussed hair. He stuck out a hand to help Damian to his feet.

"Damian was just leaving," I said. "I'm going to arrange an Uber for him, and then I'll mop up the mess."

"I'll clean the mess." Nick strode into the kitchen. "You two finish things."

I pulled up the Uber app on my telephone. As it so happened, the Uber driver who'd dropped off Damian was still in the area. He returned in less than two minutes.

Damian and I waited for him on the path in front of the house.

"I'm sorry, Aspen," Damian said somberly. "I'm a jerk."

"Yes, you are."

"A loser."

"You'll get no argument from me."

"I didn't know what I had when we were married."

"No, you didn't."

"I really want this gig in New York."

"Then don't screw it up." I brushed the lapels of his jacket and straightened his tie. "If I were you, I'd cut out the booze. It doesn't suit you."

He lowered his chin and peered at me from beneath his long lashes. "It would mean the world to me if you would forgive me."

"I'll do my best." I escorted him to the Explorer and waited until it pulled away. I didn't wave goodbye.

When I returned inside, Nick was sitting at the kitchen table enjoying a beer. "Want to tell me what really happened?" He patted his thighs.

I nestled on his lap and threw my arms around his neck. Tears started to flow. When I had no more tears to shed, I kissed his cheek and thanked him for rescuing me.

He brushed the moisture off my cheek and kissed me tenderly. "Mmm, salty," he murmured. "My favorite. By the way, I didn't rescue you. You had the situation handled."

I swatted his shoulder. "Why are you here? How did you know I needed you?"

"Fate," he said. "Actually, Natalie's friend was able to cut loose a day early. I didn't call. I wanted to surprise you."

"Mission accomplished." I kissed him again. "I miss Tahoe. And Candace. And Max. I need to wrap this up and go home." The words *go home* made me sit taller.

"What?" Nick asked.

"Nothing. I'm . . ." I swallowed hard. "What if I fail?"

"Then life will be no different than it was last week."

"But Rosie . . ." I gazed into his eyes, searching for an answer.

"Rosie will survive."

"Yes, I suppose she will." I stifled a yawn. "I'm exhausted."

He ran a finger along my jawline and cupped my chin. His eyes twinkled with mischief. "How exhausted?"

Chapter 28

When I woke the next morning, birds were chirping and daylight was peeking through the drapes. The lull wouldn't last for long. Another storm was rolling in.

I spied Nick lying on his side, gazing at me with pure lust, and felt a sudden rash of self-consciousness. I pulled the sheet up to my neck. "How long have you been staring at me?"

"About an hour." He caressed my hair, his fingers snagging in the ends. Gently, he disentangled them and ran the tip of his forefinger along my jaw.

"I need to brush my teeth." I felt like I'd eaten cotton balls.

"Not yet." He pulled me to him. "I have something I need to ask you."

He sounded so serious. Intense.

Cautiously, I said, "What?"

"Do you have bacon?"

I swatted him. "Eggs and bacon in a half hour."

I swooped out of bed, took a shower, and brushed my teeth. Then I threw on a sweater and jeans and padded barefoot into the kitchen.

As the bacon was sizzling, Nick sauntered in looking as handsome as I'd ever seen him. Blue plaid shirt and jeans. Cheeks ruddy. Eyes gleaming. And an aura sizzling with passion.

"Beverage of choice?" I asked.

"It'll wait. I have something I want to ask you."

"I already told you I've got bacon. Are your olfactory senses dulled?" I swatted him with a kitchen towel.

He grabbed hold of the towel and tugged me to the kitchen table. He made me sit in a chair and signaled for me to stay, as if I were Cinder and might bolt. He pulled a small box from his jeans pocket and knelt on one knee.

My heart leapt into my throat.

"I wanted to do this in Tahoe," he said, his voice thick with emotion. "On the beach, with the waves crashing on the shore. I wanted blue skies overhead and seagulls squawking. I wanted it to be you and me and nature and the knowledge that the whole world was ours for the taking. But I also didn't want another second to go by without you knowing how much I love you and need you in my life. Aspen Adams, will you marry me?"

He opened the box. Tucked into velvet was a princess-cut, diamond-and-sapphire-studded engagement ring I'd admired in the window of a Tahoe City jewelry store on one of our Sunday morning window shopping romps.

My eyes brimmed with tears. "Yes. Yes. Yes."

Grinning, he removed the ring from its case and placed it on my finger. "You have made me the happiest man alive."

"I'm the happiest and luckiest woman alive."

We hugged and kissed. Then, realizing the bacon might burn, I leaped to my feet to attend to it.

While I was plating breakfast, Nick's cell phone rang.

He swore mightily. He rarely swore. He glanced over his shoulder at me. "A ski resort owner is dead. Murdered. I knew the guy, plus we're shorthanded. I have to go."

I threw my arms around him. "This will be a moment we'll never forget. Propose and run."

He held me at arms' length. "Are you going to be okay?"

I flashed my ring at him. "I have this mighty shield as my defense. Nothing can harm me. Go."

I tucked the bacon and eggs into a toasted English muffin, handed it to him along with a paper towel and bottle of water, and sent him on his way.

A short while later, while gazing at my engagement ring and nibbling bites of egg, I pondered all the things Nick and I hadn't discussed. Things we would have to talk about in the days to come. Whose house would we live in? Was he okay with Candace being part of our lives? Did he want children? Did I?

To distract myself, I made a fresh mug of coffee, added creamer and sugar—I needed pampering—and moved into the dining room to study the murder board. I felt like I was missing something. How I yearned to know what Viraj Patel had intended to tell me.

While stirring my coffee, I stared at the three main suspects' photographs. Kurt Brandt, Antoine Washington, and William Fisher. I set the coffee aside and grabbed a red pen. On each of the men's interrogation sheets, I jotted notes about them. On Antoine's, his aspirations. On Brandt's, his deep desire to find a treasure. On Fisher's, his anger at my father's failure.

Rereading their testimonies, I put a star by anything I'd missed before. Antoine had been working for a body shop at the time. Now he didn't own a car. I wrote: *Truth or lie?* Brandt had dealt cards at a casino years ago. I'd missed that tidbit the first time around. Had he lent money to my grandfather out of the goodness of his heart or to get him hooked on gambling? Fisher had taken on Dale Warwick in a parking lot. That was the last note Evers had added to his sheet. Why hadn't Fisher mentioned that to me?

Suspicion wormed its way into my psyche. Had Fisher, after hearing my initial voicemail message to him, tracked down Dale Warwick and forced him off the road to ensure Warwick couldn't defend himself against Fisher's baseless accusations?

Rather than call Fisher, I drove to his house. I parked on the street, hustled out of the Prius, and assessed my surroundings. Children, supervised by a woman in her thirties, were playing tag in front of the house to the left. I waved to the woman. She waved back.

Bolstered by her presence, I marched to Fisher's front door and knocked on it while ringing the annoying bell.

Fisher, dressed in a Giants' warm-up suit and high-top Adidas, peered through the sidelight. "What d'you want?" he rasped.

"I have a question."

"Lady—"

"Why didn't you tell me that you and Dale Warwick had an altercation in a parking lot?"

"Big deal. Two guys fight. He's a real hothead."

"You're one to talk."

Fisher opened the door and stepped onto the porch, an inscribed baseball bat in his hand. A keepsake. He whirled it upward and slapped it against the palm of his other hand. *Smack.*

I flinched and took a step backward. I teetered on the edge of the porch but maintained my balance. Fisher's tight-lipped grin was vile.

Intimidating. I glanced at the woman and her children—she was watching me—but I didn't call out. I would not show my fear to Fisher.

Raising my chin, I pressed on. "Did you know Mr. Warwick was dead? Run off the road Saturday night?"

"Too bad."

"After you got my voicemail message."

"What're you implying?" He jogged past me to the grassless garden and swung the bat hard. It whooshed through the air. He wielded it again. And again. To show his power, like a teenage boy flexing his muscles.

"Sir." I trod down the steps, pursuing him, keeping wide of the swings. "Did you run Mr. Warwick off the road? May I take a look at your cars?"

"Get a warrant." He snickered. "Oh, that's right. You're not an official policeman. You're a gumshoe." He stopped swinging and leaned in close enough for me to know he'd had something spicy for breakfast. "Listen up and listen good. There's not a scratch on any of my cars. I had nothing to do with your parents' murders or any other accident, past, present, or future. I am a law-abiding citizen. And I resent your insinuation. Dale Warwick's dead? A fluke. Not my problem. Listen up"—he thrust the baseball bat at me—"keep off my property, or next time I will come out swinging with intent to harm. I'm allowed to protect myself. Got me?" He took one more swipe at the air, twirled the bat, and caught it in one hand. "Goodbye, Miss Adams."

Questions roiling in my head, not to mention nerves jangling from head to toe, I returned to the Prius, waved to my guardian angel and her kids, and sped to the house. I reread the statements of other people that Evers and his partner had interviewed. An older woman who'd lived down the street had mentioned hearing a car engine backfire, although, she said, it could have been a gunshot. A gardener who took care of ten properties in the area had seen a dog off its leash. When he'd tried to capture it, the dog had growled. He'd felt that was an omen. An omen for what? Murder? I rolled my eyes.

A woman in my mother's garden club mentioned that Mom had been quite concerned about my father's health for weeks before their trip. Dad had suffered a mild heart attack in September. I stared harder at her statement. Had my mother known her well enough to have told her the details of their trip? Would the woman have stolen in to rob them while they were away? Evers had written the word *Sister* at the end of the woman's statement. What did that mean?

Lynda Sue Harris, the travel agent, had been surprised that my parents had ended the trip, in spite of the sickness. She said the two of them had created a bucket list of destinations and hadn't wanted to miss any opportunity to visit them. Evers had written the single word *Retreat* at the end of her testimony. If only he were alive to clarify.

Reading on, Tammie had wondered whether Rosie's best friend Yvette from high school might have reentered Rosie's life. That girl had always been bad news. Tammie suggested that perhaps Yvette had concocted the idea to rob our parents and had promised to cut Rosie in on the take. Yvette was one of the reasons Rosie had taken the road less traveled in her freshman year of high school. Yvette had goaded Rosie into using drugs, and she was always hitting her up for money. As Evers had for the others, he had written something at the end of his assessment of Yvette: *JC.* Did the initials stand for Jesus Christ? Had he ruled her out because she had turned religious?

I searched the board for other mentions of Yvette. In a small note at the bottom of a sheet Evers had titled *More Friends of Family*, he wrote that he'd questioned Yvette's mother and had confirmed that Yvette had moved to Los Angeles to live with her father two months before the murder. To her credit, she had abandoned her old ways and had enrolled in junior college. Was that the meaning of the *JC* notation Evers had written?

My cell phone rang in the kitchen. I abandoned my analysis and hurried to answer. *Candace.* "Hey, sweetheart," I said. "You're supposed to be at school. Are you sick?"

"Sort of. I mean, no." She slurped tears. "I mean, Mom called and she's antsy and, like, not cool and—"

"Slow down. Breathe." Needing something to keep my mind going full speed, I fetched my coffee. "Is Aunt Max with you?"

"She had to deliver a subpoena. I was heading out the door to catch my ride to school. Waverly's mother was right on time, like always. But my cell phone rang. When I saw Mom's name, I told Waverly and her mom to go on without me. Waverly was *not* happy, as you can imagine."

I tamped down a smile. Waverly could be prickly about doing things the right way. It was what made her a good student and beautiful ballerina and now an ace photographer. Her mother, who I adored, was much more flexible than her daughter.

"What did your mother say?" I asked.

"She said if you, meaning *you*, don't get answers, she's always going to feel like a loser. She said she felt like . . . like—" Candace inhaled sharply.

"Like what?"

"Like hurting herself. Can you help? Please, Aspen. Call her."

"I talked to her yesterday."

"Talk to her again." She sputtered with despair. "Give her some hope."

Calmly, I said, "Yes. I'll call her. Relax. She's not going to hurt herself."

"How can you be sure?" Candace cried. "She sounded strung out. Wired. Like she was on uppers."

"How do you know about—" I stopped myself. Candace had seen her mother get high too many times to count. A couple of years with me would not erase those memories. "I'll text you after I talk to her. Now, call Aunt Max and tell her you need a ride to school. Maybe she can get Darcy or Rowena to help out. You'll need a note for the office, too."

"I can forge a note."

"Don't even think about it!" I snapped.

"Psych," she said. Her brittle laughter was music to my ears.

I dialed Rosie. She answered after two rings.

"S'up, little sis?" she asked, slurring the words.

So much for being two days clean. "I hear you're worried," I said. "I thought I'd put your fears to rest yesterday."

"I want answers."

"There's a lot of material to go through," I said. "Chill."

"Like I could chill," she growled.

"Rosie, you've lived with this for years. You can—"

"I'm having more nightmares."

"Cut out the drugs."

She snarled. "Dang it, Aspen, you can be such a—"

"Don't say it. Just. Don't. Say. It. I want resolution as much as you do," I hissed. "You know that."

She gave me a muddled, "Yeah."

"Are you working?" I asked. "You've got to distract yourself."

"I'm working. But my hours were cut."

Not good. She needed to be busy. "Maybe you could pick up a shift at another diner," I suggested. She was a good waitress. A people person. She could listen to others share stories for hours. And stay relatively sober in the process.

"I'll try. About Antoine . . ." Rosie lit up a cigarette and inhaled then exhaled.

I moved into the dining room, my gaze landing on Antoine's picture. "What about him?"

"Is he still handsome?"

"Very."

Rosie hummed.

"Question for you," I said.

"Yeah?"

"Did Antoine ever go with you when you robbed Mom and Dad's house? Did he know how to get in? Like, did he know where the secret key was?"

She was quiet for a long time.

"Yes or no?" I pressed.

"Yes."

"Did he know about the gun in the hope chest?"

"Lots of people did. I told—"

"I'm talking about Antoine. Specifically."

"He never would have touched it," Rosie said.

"Why not?"

"Because a buddy of his . . . died . . . and he . . . just wouldn't." She huffed. "Was it the murder weapon? Have you found out yet?"

"Not yet."

"You know what? You're useless." She huffed again, louder. "Call me when you have more."

My head begin to throb. She could huff and she could puff, but she would not blow me down. "Rosie, contact me from now on. Not your daughter."

"Don't tell me what to do—"

"I mean it. She's fragile. You call me, not her. Got it?"

I didn't wait for a reply.

Chapter 29

As much as I wanted to believe Rosie about Antoine, I needed to see him again and ask him, face-to-face, about what he did and did not know. Serenity was right. I could read people. This was my chance. I called him. He said he was working and couldn't talk to me now. His shift would end around eleven a.m. We set a date.

My gaze landed on Lynda Sue Harris's name. Serenity said I should talk to her. I wasn't sure what Lynda Sue could add to the conversation, but maybe, just maybe, Evers had missed something. So I reached out to her.

• • •

A line of customers stood outside Le Café waiting for an inside table. I approached the hostess, who said I could sit at any of the empty tables on the street patio. All along Santa Cruz Avenue, restaurants spilled onto the sidewalks. There was a nip in the air, but I'd dressed for the occasion, so I took one of the bistro-style tables by the railing. I hoped Lynda Sue had dressed warmly, too.

When she approached, I recognized her instantly. She hadn't changed in fourteen years. Cherub cheeks, cheery smile.

"Aren't you as pretty as your mother, bless her soul." Lynda Sue reached over and patted my hand before taking her seat. She was forty-something but looked thirty. Her pink coat over pink blouse and trousers, as well as the sparkly clips in her blonde bob, once again conjured up the image of the Sugar Plum Fairy. She set her purse and a pink New Testament on the table and took her seat. I picked up a whiff of Shalimar, which absolutely suited her. Soft and warm.

"I'm coming from a Bible study," she said, "and we prayed for your mother and father."

"Thank you." I hoped she didn't intend to proselytize. I didn't need saving today. I needed answers.

I ordered a sparkling water from the waitress. Lynda Sue ordered coffee black.

Then she tucked a strand of hair behind her ear and leaned

forward on her elbows, giving me her rapt attention. "Why did you want to meet, Aspen?"

"You might not know it, but I'm a private investigator now. In Lake Tahoe."

"I'd heard you'd given up being a therapist. That must have been a challenging profession." Lynda Sue nodded, agreeing with herself. "Dealing with the insane every day."

"Not everyone was insane," I said. "Some were simply troubled, but I gave it up because . . . I needed a fresh start."

"Fresh starts are what faith is all about. Taking a leap. Not knowing what could be around the corner."

The waitress set our beverages on the table. Lynda Sue loaded her mug with cream and sugar. I squeezed a wedge of lime into my water.

"Let me get right to the point, Miss Harris."

"Honey, you call me Lynda Sue. Like your parents did." She didn't have an accent, but her cadence suggested she'd originally come from somewhere in the south.

"Lynda Sue, you booked that last trip for my parents. To Mexico."

"Of course I did. I booked all their trips. They had such dreams. They didn't need to travel first class or stay at the finest hotels or resorts—their budget was limited—but they wanted to see everything." She threw an arm wide, almost hitting the person at the table behind us. "Oops." She snickered. "My husband says I need to watch my elaborate gestures."

I imagined her in church, throwing her arms wide to receive the holy spirit. Lynda Sue was all about embracing life. I couldn't see her as a murderer. "My parents called you when they were on their way home, isn't that right? When they needed to cancel the trip?"

She licked her lips. "Not exactly. I mean, yes, they called the office, but I wasn't there. My assistant handled the details."

"Where were you?" I sipped the sparkling water.

"On a retreat."

Aha. The note Evers had written on her account, *Retreat*, made sense now. Perhaps Evers's note for the neighbor meant she had been with her sister . . . or a nun. Either way, I'd deciphered how Evers had coded alibis.

"Where was the retreat?" I asked.

"The female pastor of our church and ten of us ladies went to Mount Hermon. It's a lovely place for us to get away from it all and reflect on God's love and purposes in our lives. Have you ever been?"

"No."

"You could come with me sometime."

I shook my head. "I reflect on God's love and purpose in Lake Tahoe. It's the ideal spot for me." Moving on, I said, "So, your assistant handled the details of my parents' cancelation."

"Yes, she contacted the cruise line and the airlines and they weren't charged a cent. They'd bought travel insurance, just in case. Your father had been ill in September, and—" She blanched. "Listen to me drone on." She placed a hand to her chest. "If only I'd been the one to take the call. I have to wonder whether I would have, you know, dissuaded them. Made them turn around, go on the trip, and ride out the illness. That would have saved their lives."

"Don't blame yourself."

But I could tell she would. She would carry the burden for years to come. She gazed at her coffee, battling tears while dragging her tongue across her lower lip.

"Did your assistant tell anyone that my parents had canceled?" I asked.

Lynda Sue lifted her chin and gazed at me blankly, as if scanning her memory bank for a conversation about it. "I can't imagine why she would have. On the other hand, she is a bit of a flibbertigibbet. She could chatter all day if I let her, so who knows what she might have said to another client?"

The assistant hadn't been questioned by the police. Did I need to contact her? Would the woman remember revealing my parents' plans to someone?

"About my parents' finances, did they—"

"They always paid cash," Lynda Sue said matter-of-factly. "They never charged a thing."

Cash. Yes, I could see my mother insisting on that. *One should live within one's means,* she would say. Given her father's gambling pro-clivities, she had learned to be frugal. "Did they ever mention their savings to you? Possibly a nest egg or a treasure or even a safe-deposit box?"

"Your mother often said she treasured your father." Lynda Sue winked. "That's about the extent of my knowledge of their funds. They booked. They paid." She leveled her stirring spoon at me. "I have to say, you've asked a lot of questions those detectives never asked. You're good at this."

I accepted the compliment, and for the next half hour, realizing I'd learn no more from her, allowed the conversation to turn to small talk—about her next retreat, the weather, and the darling antics of her high school–aged girls.

As she parted, she bussed my cheek and said, "Godspeed."

I wished her the same and peeked at my watch. I had barely enough time to get to Mountain View to meet Antoine Washington.

Traffic was thick, and the sky was turning ominous. Another storm was brewing. In Tahoe, whenever the weather acted up, I welcomed it. I loved the rumble of thunder and the snap-crackle of lightning bolts. Here, in the Bay Area, the weather seemed to match my gloominess.

When I arrived at Big Box, I headed to the employee break room, as Antoine had instructed. I knocked on the break room door and opened it. There were two employees milling about. A third occupied the beige couch.

Antoine, clad in his brown uniform, was slouched in a chair at one of the tables, a cup of something between his hands. He frowned, clearly not happy to see me. After running a hand along his flattop hairstyle, he rose to his full height and offered me the chair opposite him. "To what do I owe the pleasure?"

"I was talking with Rosie earlier."

"Get you something to drink?" he asked.

"I'm fine." I folded my hands on the table, hoping the noncombative gesture would help him trust me.

He lowered himself into his chair and pushed his cup aside. Mirroring my folded hands, he tilted his head to one side. "What did Rosie have to say for herself?"

I jumped right in, sharing that Rosie said she'd taken him to our parents' house and she'd used the spare key to enter. "You saw where they stashed it."

"Doesn't make me a killer." He sat taller.

"No, it doesn't. However, Rosie also said that she showed you where my parents kept a loaded gun."

Antoine thumped the table. "Uh-uh, no way. I did not touch that gun."

That gun, confirming that he knew which gun I was talking about.

"I don't touch any guns. Guns and me . . . Guns and *I*," he revised, "don't mix."

"Why is that?"

He shoved away from the table and crossed his arms. The screech of the chair's legs against the flooring made me wince. The others in the room glanced in our direction. The two by the water cooler tiptoed out. The third hopped off the couch, grabbed a packet of chips, and followed the others.

"I had a buddy. We was . . ." Antoine paused. "We *were* fourteen." He heaved a sigh. "He died in a drive-by shooting. A spray of bullets. Right into his chest. I was down the street, fetching a football he'd thrown. He fell like a sack of potatoes." Antoine's face contorted. "Guns kill. That's not my thing. Killing. Never was. Yeah, I robbed people. Yeah, I stole drugs. Yeah, I used a knife to threaten people. But I never killed nobody . . . *anybody*. Not your folks. Not anybody. Ever."

Switching tactics, I said, "You used to work at a body shop."

"That's right. So?"

"Yet you don't own a car now?"

"Cars don't grow on trees. I can't afford one. Plus, I wasn't a grease monkey. It's not like I could fix up a heap. I worked the register. Set up appointments. That kind of thing." He rose to his feet and shoved in his chair. "We done?" He scowled and nodded. "Yeah, we're done. You tell Rosie I'm on the right path, okay? I paid my debt to society."

I felt Antoine's eyes on me as I walked to my car in the underground parking lot. He had his cell phone out and was talking rapid-fire to someone. Was it a partner in crime? Or was he touching base with his lawyer to slap an injunction against me?

Curious, I slid into the Prius, started the car as if to leave, and idled, watching him. He ended the call, made another, and then clocked out of his shift and strolled to the street. I lagged behind and watched as he caught a local bus heading south toward San Jose. I trailed it, stopping whenever it did, to see if and when Antoine exited. He got off in front of a high-tech-looking medical facility.

Parking on a side street, I trailed him into the facility and watched as the elevator he boarded went to the fifth floor. Catching the next elevator, I mirrored his movement. I exited the elevator and peeked down the hall. Antoine headed for the last office on the right. A pretty and lean African-American woman, who looked remarkably like Antoine, was waiting by the door, cell phone out. They hugged and then she knuckled him on the shoulder. I recalled him mentioning that he had a twin sister. She stuffed her cell phone in her pocket. The door opened and a professional older woman, eyeglasses hanging on a chain around her neck, greeted them. After they entered and the door closed, I stole to the office to read the placard: *Nancy Shane, Therapist. LCMFT.* Antoine was meeting a licensed clinical marriage and family therapist. He'd said he was in therapy to work out issues. Perhaps his sister was making sure he followed through.

Realizing that I needed to get over my paranoia, sooner rather than later, I made a mental note to see my own therapist.

On the way to the rental house, I thought again of Antoine. His last comment about paying his debt to society triggered a memory. Not about him or Rosie. About Tammie. And her debt to my mother. When they had first become partners, Tammie had been flush with cash. Her husband, a well-to-do attorney, had fronted her the buy-in for the partnership; however, when they divorced, he'd demanded she repay him. I remembered Tammie tearfully explaining the situation to my mother. Mom, who was enjoying having Tammie as a partner, had readily given Tammie the loan. A few years later, Tammie, barely making ends meet, asked for another loan. And then another.

When I was nearly thirteen, I recalled a conversation between Tammie and my mother. They thought I was doing algebra homework in my bedroom. I wasn't. I was daydreaming. Rosie was off gallivanting. My father was meeting a client for coffee. Tammie and my mother were in the office across the hall. Tammie asked for another loan and my mother denied her. *Four is too many,* she said and added that she needed to draw the line. Tammie argued and begged and, out of nowhere, began to accuse my mother of treating her like Rosie, acting as if she thought Tammie might let her down. The words *I'm nothing like your loser daughter* resonated with me. Tammie went on to say she didn't have the blessing of a husband like James. A good man. A steady man. She needed her friend—her *best* friend—to help her out one last time. Mom repeated the word *No*. Tammie used some colorful language. The force of the quarrel cut through me as it replayed in my mind. Ultimately, my mother had relented, but on the condition that Tammie would sign a promissory note. I couldn't remember seeing anything of the kind in the estate documents. Tammie might have paid it off, I supposed. I made a mental note to check with Ulyssa Thaller. Not that I wanted to dun Tammie for payment. But if there was an outstanding debt—

I drew up short as the word rang out in my head. *Debt*. Could Viraj Patel's cryptic message about debt or threat have been in regard to Tammie?

No, Aspen, don't be ridiculous. Tammie did not kill your parents.

The argument between Tammie and my mother had occurred five years before my parents were murdered. They had remained partners. And, to my knowledge, Tammie had never asked for another loan. So how had she afforded purchasing my mother's portion of the business? I couldn't see her ex-husband assisting her. Maybe someone from her previous work had come to her aid. Or maybe she'd hit upon another source of income.

The word *debt* tolled again in my brain. When I'd mentioned the job notes pinned to the corkboard in Tammie's office, she'd said they were for *prospective* clients, not actual clients. In addition, she'd admitted to not being able to update her condo as of late. Was Serenity's mother correct? Was Tammie struggling? How tight were funds? Did she need help? She drove a new-model Jaguar, but perhaps she leased it and made minimum payments. I chided myself for knowing so little about her. My mother would have been upset to learn that I'd let our relationship slide.

A truck filled with crates pulled to a sharp halt. I slammed on the brakes.

Staring at the crates, I flashed on the puzzle box Tammie had kept as a memento, and unease started to churn inside me. Had my mother mentioned to Tammie, years ago, that one of my grandfather's silver dollars was worth a lot of money? Had Tammie hoped that particular silver dollar—a *treasure*, as her granddaughter had called it—had been inside the box? Had she hoped the treasure would bail her out of financial debt?

Chapter 30

As I swung into the driveway, the skies opened up. Rain sloshed onto the windshield. Staying in the car, doors locked, I called Ulyssa Thaller. I asked her whether there had been a promissory note executed between my mother and Tammie Laplante. Ulyssa couldn't recall having seen one. Eager to learn more, I decided to drop in on Tammie. I didn't want to speak on the phone, I wanted to hear her answers in person.

Window wipers flapping, I reversed out of the driveway and drove to Sharon Heights. I turned onto Tammie's street and proceeded toward the end of the cul-de-sac. Tammie was standing on the stoop, chatting with a toned woman in a tennis outfit who was holding an umbrella over her head. Rather than intrude on their conversation, I pulled to one side and idled. After a moment, Tammie bussed the woman's cheek and waved goodbye. As the woman trotted down the stairs, ponytail bouncing, Tammie returned inside.

I waited until the woman had driven off in her Mercedes before turning off the Prius. As I reached for the door handle, I froze. Tammie was already exiting her condo. She'd thrown on an overcoat tied at the waist, a brimmed hat, and black-rimmed sunglasses. Her outfit, including the sizeable tote bag, reminded me of the getup Audrey Hepburn had worn in the movie *Charade* when she'd tailed Cary Grant. My mother had loved that movie. Every time she watched it, she would pat the couch and ask me to join her.

Tammie hurried to her Jaguar, roared it into gear, and tore down the street, never looking in my direction.

Intrigued, I followed her. Why the stealthy getup? Why the hurry?

I maintained a discreet distance behind her. Luckily, a number of people on the road were driving Priuses. Mine could blend in. The rain helped, too. Tammie drove down Sand Hill Road, past the Stanford Shopping Center, right onto El Camino Real, left onto University Avenue in Palo Alto, and stopped in a parking spot in front of Bartlett Law on Bryant Street. Bartlett Law was the firm where she'd worked as a bookkeeper. She didn't get out of her car. What was she waiting for?

An SUV on the opposite side of the street pulled out of its parking spot. I made a U-turn, swooped into the spot, and slinked down in my seat.

After a long moment, a man in his late forties with shoulder-length hair, strong jaw, and Roman nose exited the building. Looking powerful in a sharp black suit, he opened an umbrella and strolled leisurely toward Hamilton Avenue. Tammie raised what appeared to be a telephoto lens. Was she taking photographs of him? I flashed on the other night at the Palais Hotel when I'd hurried to the lobby to say hello to her. Deftly, she'd stuffed her cell phone into her tote. Moments later, the elderly Palo Alto D.A. had passed by and joined the younger woman on the elevator. Had Tammie been taking pictures of him and not the décor, as I'd theorized?

Deciding two could play the game, I raised my cell phone and snapped photos of Tammie.

The man neared the corner. Tammie slipped out of her car, fed a coin into the meter, and stole after him on foot, no umbrella.

I followed in my car, driving slowly.

At University Avenue, the man veered left. Tammie stayed put. I couldn't. I drove past her and turned in the direction the man had. I pulled into a loading zone spot, peered over my shoulder, and took a picture of the man from the front. He stopped under the awning of a tony restaurant, collapsed his umbrella, and consulted his watch and then his cell phone. Soon, a leggy brunette in a body-hugging raincoat appeared. She walked past him into the restaurant as if she didn't know him, but I sensed she did because, as she passed by, she plumped her lips seductively, miming a kiss. The man glanced over his shoulder. Checking for observers? After a long, tenaciously casual moment, he slipped into the restaurant.

I searched for Tammie. She had hidden behind a lamppost, but she was still aiming her telephoto lens in the man's direction.

A parking enforcement officer stopped by the front of my car and hooked his thumb. I saluted and cranked the Prius into gear.

With questions about Tammie's purpose cycling through my mind, I drove back to the rental house. I parked in the driveway, hurried into the house, and phoned my aunt. She assured me Candace had made it safely to school, and I thanked her.

"Listen," I said, "I—"

"Me, first. When are you coming home?"

Home. Lake Tahoe. The Bay Area would never be home again. My lungs felt heavy, like I'd been holding my breath for days. "Soon. I feel like I'm close to something."

"We don't have anything on the gun comparatives yet. I've left messages for Nick and his colleagues at the sheriff's department, but—"

"Stop by the precinct," I suggested. "See if you can light a fire." I didn't tell her about our engagement. I wanted to do that in person. With Candace present. "I've got something else you can help me with in the meantime. I'm sending you a photograph of a guy. I hope you can identify him."

I selected the photograph I'd taken of the man from the front, sent it via text, and waited.

"Not much to go on from this photo." Max clicked her tongue. "Do you think he killed your parents?"

"No. This has nothing to do with that. I'm trying to figure out why my mother's best friend is tailing this guy."

"Lover? Ex-lover?"

"Too young."

Max chortled. "As if age has anything to do with matters of the heart," she said. Growing serious, she added, "Okay, I'll work on it."

As I was fixing myself a snack, my cell phone trilled. I checked the screen. *Lynda Sue.* I stabbed Accept. "Hi, there. What's up?"

"I talked to my assistant. She said she didn't tell anyone, not a soul, about your parents' canceled plans."

"Okay, thank you."

"However, when she tried to call your mother to tell her she'd spoken to the airlines already and refunds were handled"—she inhaled sharply, the words racing out of her—"your mother didn't answer her cell phone, so she left a message on her work line. She hopes you're not mad."

"Tell her that sounds perfectly reasonable."

"Bless you. By the way, it was so good to see you this morning," Lynda Sue added, "given the circumstances. If you ever want to attend a Bible study—"

"I won't be staying in the area. I'll be going home to Tahoe the moment I've resolved things here."

"Of course. Well, I'm available, day or night."

The moment I ended the call, the cell phone vibrated in my hand. *Tammie.* My scalp prickled with apprehension. Had she spotted me tailing her earlier?

I answered. "Hey, what's up?"

"I was thinking about you. I thought you might like a friendly ear. How is your investigation going?"

"With all the rain, I've been hunkering down, reviewing notes."

"Care to run anything past me?"

"It'd be futile. I'm coming up empty. What have you been up to today?" I asked breezily.

"I worked from home all morning. There was so much to do on the Vasona project. Window treatments. Flooring." Her light tone matched mine. "Then I picked up Giselle at school and treated her to lunch."

Oho. Lying to me. Apparently, whatever she'd been up to was not share-worthy.

"How nice," I said. "Where'd you two go?"

"A sushi place at the shopping center. My granddaughter adores sushi."

"Isn't sushi a little pricey for a child?"

"She eats one California roll. Any nana worth her salt can afford that." Tammie chuckled. "Have you spoken to Nick?"

"He was in town for a split second and had to return to Lake Tahoe for business."

"That's too bad. How about dinner tonight, then? Nothing fancy. Burgers and a salad."

"I've got a killer headache. How about coffee tomorrow morning? Ten?"

"Sounds good," she said. "Love you. Don't stay up too late."

"I won't."

Desperate for a run to relieve the killer headache, a.k.a. tension, I shrugged into leggings and a long-sleeved shirt, slipped on my tennis shoes and baseball cap, and headed outside. On foot, despite the rain, I could admire the oak-lined neighborhood and the houses.

On the way, I saw two children playing in manicured yards. Both wore slickers and rain hats. Me? I was adoring the refreshing rain dripping off the brim of my cap onto my face. I was also feeling relieved that Kurt Brandt was in custody. I wouldn't have to check over my shoulder to see if he was tailing me. On the other hand, why would he tail me on a jog? It was highly unlikely that I'd hightail it to my childhood home on foot, in a storm, to dig for buried treasure.

When I returned to the house, I showered and dried my hair. Afterward, dressed in sweats and a T-shirt, I checked email. Max had sent me a curt message: *Call me. Got something.*

I reached her instantly.

"I'm in the car with Candace," she said. "I'm putting you on speaker. We're going to grab takeout. Have you eaten?"

"I've got soup."

"That's not enough, sugar."

"Don't mother me. What've you got?"

"Yaz Yazdani is a wunderkind."

"Don't let him hear you say that," I joked. "His ego will balloon to the size of New York."

Candace tittered.

"A friend of Yaz's was able to use facial recognition to see if an image of your guy appeared anywhere on the Internet in the last ten years, and voilà, success."

"Don't keep me waiting." I fetched a glass of water and settled at the kitchen table.

"Turns out he is a high-priced divorce lawyer on his third marriage. Neither of his first two marriages lasted three years. The third? Going on ten years. But the woman you described is not his dearly beloved. His wife happens to be an invalid in her fifties. Poor woman suffered a fall a year after they were married."

"Does he work at Bartlett Law?" I asked.

"No. His partnership is much bigger." Max rattled off a firm with six surnames.

"I wonder how Tammie knows this guy."

Max said, "Given his track record, I'm going with my initial guess—lover or ex-lover."

"Hey," Candace said, "didn't she see this guy leaving her former law office? I'll bet someone there called her and told her where to find him."

"To what end?" I asked.

"To follow him. To get the skinny and see if he's having an affair."

I squelched a chuckle. *The skinny.* She'd definitely watched too many crime shows.

Undaunted, she added, "What if the wife hired her to take pictures, you know, like you guys would."

"Tammie isn't a detective," I said, though Candace's theory held water. Given the bleak way Tammie had referred to her interior design job possibilities, maybe she did have a second job. Moonlighting made sense.

"What else can I help with, sugar?" Max asked, the reception cutting out.

"Yeah, what else, Aspen?" Candace chimed.

"Nothing." I gazed through the dining room door at the murder board. "I have to review my notes."

"Text us any questions," Candace said. "I don't have any homework."

I grinned. I could see her eagerly waiting by her cell phone. "Will do. *Not.*"

"Aww."

I glimpsed the engagement ring on my finger and tamped down the urge to blurt out the news over the phone. "You two have a good night."

At six, I switched on the television and listened to the nightly news. After ten minutes of depressing recaps and political negativity, I gave up. I poured the contents of a can of Amy's lentil soup into a bowl, zapped the soup in the microwave, and nestled into the leather armchair in the living room with my meal. I ate while reading a thriller by Meg Gardiner that I'd uploaded to the app on my iPhone. Meg had gone to Stanford like I had. I'd always found her writing compelling.

Around nine, as I was nearing a climactic point in the novel, the storm kicked up outside. Rain hammered the roof. Wind created a ghostly howl in the living room chimney. Perfect accompaniment to my reading.

Until something clacked. And then clacked again.

I bolted to my feet and ran to the front door. I peered through the sidelight into the darkness. All I could see was rain, illuminated by streetlamps.

The clacking continued. I roamed the house, peeking out each window. Outside the master bedroom window, I saw a shutter that was loose. No way was I going to be able to sleep until I fixed it. I threw on my raincoat and cap, grabbed a screwdriver from the set of tools I found in a kitchen drawer, and headed outside.

I skirted the house and, bracing my cell phone between my teeth so I could aim its flashlight at the offending shutter, I examined the problem. The top hinge was loose. Guessing that the threads of the screws holding it in place were stripped bare, rather than try to repair the darned thing I unscrewed the lower hinge and yanked. The shutter pulled free, the force causing me to stumble into a bush.

Cursing under my breath, I set the shutter on the ground and stomped toward the front porch. Halfway there, I froze. A sedan was driving down the street. Slowly. I ducked and waited. The sedan sped up as it passed the house.

Breathing in short spurts, I sprinted to the porch and into the house. I slammed the door and locked it. I peeked through the sidelight. Waiting. The sedan didn't reemerge.

However, something else sent a shiver through me. I spotted a car parked in the driveway across the street. Not just any car. It was black and boxy, like Brandt's RAV4. And someone wearing a brimmed hat was sitting in the driver's seat. The glow of a cigarette flickered behind the darkened windows.

Was Kurt Brandt out on bail? Already? He couldn't have afforded it on his own. Not if his wife had taken him for everything he'd had.

Chapter 31

Too restless to sleep, I wandered into the kitchen, made a cup of tea with honey, and opened my laptop's search engine.

I typed *Kurt Brandt*, added a *plus* sign, and added the word *casino*. I was curious to know more about his previous employment and who his benefactor might be. A few links came up for him. I clicked on LinkedIn. In his biography, Brandt described his early career, first as a dealer at a casino in Reno, Nevada, after which, in the 1970s, he'd moved into the technological side of the business, whatever that meant. Computers weren't in vogue yet. Maybe being deft at counting cards was considered *technology*. Unsatisfied with his rise in the ranks, Brandt returned to college, got his degree in electrical engineering, and was hired at General Motors in the 1980s. That must have been where he'd met my grandfather. No more references to casinos appeared. He had no apparent connections to the mob.

Trying to figure out the identity of his wealthy benefactor was fruitless, so I returned my focus to William Fisher. He was easier to track online. He had a business. He had a website, which was quite professional and forthright. He'd received stellar recommendations on Yelp from his former employer and other clients. I discovered that he'd been arrested once for a bar fight, but he'd been released on his own recognizance. No jail time.

Next, I did a deep dive on his son, Johnny Fisher, who was in prison for murder. He failed his first consideration for probation. He cried foul and racial profiling. There were a number of newspaper articles about the murders of the policemen, with pictures of Johnny included. He was a beautiful young man, with lustrous black hair and strong Native American features, like his father. He looked proud, not defiant. Recently, a reporter had decided to tackle Johnny's story. He wrote that none of Johnny's friends had a bad thing to say about him. Johnny was a stand-up guy. He never caused trouble. The reporter had included a picture of the girlfriend who had turned on Johnny. Currently, she was working as a waitress in San Jose. Clad in a tight purple dress, her hair streaked with purple dye, her mouth turned down in a churlish frown, she appeared untrustworthy. Was that the best photo the reporter could find, or had he been biased against her?

Learning nothing new that could help me point a finger at any of the main suspects, I gave in to fatigue and went to bed.

I slept fitfully, waking every two hours and checking the driveway across the street. The SUV hadn't budged, but I could still see the top of the driver's hat. Brandt. I was sure of it. He was no longer smoking. Smart move if he happened to doze off. I wondered whether I ought to call the police but decided against it. Brandt was making no move to come closer.

In the morning, feeling wiped out and looking ragged, I took a shower, dressed, and drank a cup of black coffee. I followed that with scrambled eggs and a glass of orange juice. I hoped the sugar and caffeine would kick in soon.

Before leaving the house, I checked the neighbor's driveway. The SUV was gone. Maybe I'd been wrong. Maybe it hadn't been Brandt. Or perhaps he'd moved to another vantage point. To confirm my suspicion, I called Detective Sergeant Quincy. He was quick to reply that yes, sadly, Brandt had made bail. He didn't know who had posted it. He suggested I hire protection. I said I didn't think I'd need it. Brandt wanted me to find his treasure and hand it over.

Thankful for a brief respite of sunshine before the next storm hit, I headed to Starbucks and picked up two lattes. Waiting for my items, I felt a deep ache in my gut, a searing need to be at the lake. To see the whitecaps skipping across the water. To drink in the heavenly mountain air.

"Aspen?" the counter clerk said, checking the name on the latte cups tucked into a carry box. "Are you Aspen? Your order is ready."

I thanked her, grabbed the box, and strolled to the Prius. It was time for the meetup I'd arranged with Tammie.

After setting the carry box on the passenger floor, I drove to Sharon Heights and parked on her cul-de-sac. Tammie was talking to Mia on the stoop. Mia looked slim in body-hugging jogging clothes. Tammie was dressed to the nines in a shimmery blue dress, spiked heels, and a broad-brimmed blue hat. I moved toward them with the lattes.

Tammie caught sight of me and gasped. "Aspen, oh, gee, I

apologize. Emergency meeting at Vasona Lake. I can't stay. Chat later?"

My cell phone jangled. I pulled it from my purse and glanced at the screen. "Wait. Don't go yet, Tammie. Give me a sec. I want to ask you one thing. But I have to answer this." Olga Payne was calling. "Good morning, Olga."

"Herman wants to talk to you," she said.

"Herman—"

"Yes. He has a lead for you," Olga said. "It's about Viraj. The debt thing."

"The debt thing," I repeated.

"He was very cryptic."

"Okay." I held up a finger to Tammie to stay put.

Mia said, "Bye, Mother. I've got to get a three-mile run in before I pick up Giselle." She trotted to her shiny blue Celica, waving. "Bye, Aspen."

"Thank you, Olga." I ended the call.

"Was that a lead?" Tammie asked.

"I hope so. Listen, we need to talk. I . . ." I hesitated. "I haven't been a good friend. I'd like to help you if I can."

"Help me?" Creases formed between her eyebrows.

"I'd like to be a proxy for my mother. I know she used to lend you money. If you—"

"I don't need help. I'm good. But it's sweet of you to offer." Tammie pecked my cheek and glanced at her watch. "Sorry. I've got to run. Later."

"Take the latte. I can't drink two." I pressed one into her hands.

She accepted it and darted to her Jaguar, glancing over her shoulder at me as she slipped inside, brow still furrowed and eyes narrowed. Was I reading guilt into her look? To be truthful, she appeared awfully dressed up for a meeting at a county park.

Hearing the same alarm bells that had gone off in my head yesterday, I hurried to the Prius, made a quick U-turn, and followed Tammie.

While driving, I tried Herman Hoek. The call rolled into voicemail. I set the phone aside and concentrated on Tammie. If she'd really intended to go to Vasona Lake, she would have headed to the

280 freeway. Instead, she had taken the same route as she had yesterday, through the Stanford Shopping Center, right on El Camino Real, and left on University Avenue. But this time she didn't drive to Bryant Street. She veered left on Kipling and parked. She got out and started running, her tight skirt preventing her from taking long strides. I found a parking spot three cars away but stayed in the car, idling. Tammie entered the Blue Moon Café, a chic eatery with exterior bistro tables bordered by a wrought-iron fence.

Knowing her destination, I eased out of my parking spot and drove to another around the corner. I climbed out of the car and moseyed to a footwear store on the opposite side of the street. After entering, I positioned myself by the window display so I could observe Tammie. She was seated at one of the patio tables. She glanced left and right but not in my direction. A few minutes later, a man in a gray pin-striped suit approached—the lawyer with the strong jaw and shoulder-length hair that Tammie had followed yesterday. He plopped into the chair opposite Tammie and leaned forward on both elbows. He wasn't happy. Even in profile, I could tell he was glowering at her. A waiter set down two glasses of water. When the waiter moved away, Tammie said something. The lawyer removed an envelope from the inside of his suit pocket and slid it slowly across the table. Tammie lifted it, inspected the contents, and smiled. The man held out his hand. Tammie pulled an envelope from her purse and handed it to him. He opened it and removed what appeared to be photographs and a roll of film. In addition, Tammie picked up her cell phone, swiped to what I presumed was the camera app, and displayed it in his direction. She tapped the screen and showed him the cell phone again. He nodded, satisfied.

I sighed, disheartened. *Extortion* was such an ugly word, but that had to be what had gone down. Tammie had given him the photos she'd taken of him in exchange for payment. Was that how, with the lack of interior design clients, she was enhancing her bank account?

How many others had Tammie extorted? And for how long? A moment from Sunday night flashed in my mind. At Tammie's condo. I recalled how Mia had asked her mother to show me photos of her projects, but Tammie had diverted the conversation. Had she been trying to keep me from seeing photos of her other marks on her cell phone?

Racing to the Prius, I drove around the corner, idled by the curb, and decided to call the D.A.'s office. If I was right, Tammie had made a similar business deal with him. I located the telephone number and tapped it in. When the D.A.'s administrative assistant asked what my query was in regard to, I hung up. The man would never admit to me that he was being extorted.

I drove to the rental house, thinking about Tammie the whole time and wishing my mother was around to advise me. I pulled into the driveway and searched for signs of Brandt. His RAV4 wasn't anywhere in sight. He wasn't, either.

The house was cold when I entered. I tossed my latte cup in the garbage, kicked on the heat, poured myself a glass of water, and tried Herman Hoek again. His phone rang once. Twice.

At the same time, Max was calling me, so I ended the first call and answered hers.

"What's up?" I took a sip of water.

"I've got big news."

"Don't keep me waiting."

"Your grandfather's gun *was* the murder weapon."

"Holy—" My breath caught in my chest and a shudder ran down my spine. The questions that had plagued me the other day returned full force. Why had the killer put the gun back in the hope chest? How had he . . . *she*, I revised as a possibility . . . known it was there in the first place? "The forensics team is certain?"

"Positive. The corresponding microscopic markings are consistent with two bullets having been fired from the same firearm."

"Even after all this time."

"That's the beauty of this particular science. What do you want me to do?" Her voice brimmed with energy.

"First, I have to figure out who could have known about the existence of the gun."

"Rosie knew."

"Yes, I know, but she did not do this."

Max sniffed. "Then one of her friends."

203

That was what Evers had thought. Antoine Washington came to mind. Who else? "I'll talk to her."

"Grill her," Max ordered.

As if I could grill my sister. No, I'd have to tread lightly. She'd held on to the secret about our mother's last words for fourteen years. What else had she kept to herself?

"Listen," I said, "I need you to help with another thing."

"On that personal matter?"

I smiled. How well she knew me. "Yes. I'd like you to check out Tammie Laplante's financial records. See how much debt she might be in. Has she refinanced her townhome? Is her car leased or paid for? Et cetera."

"What are you looking for?"

"An explanation for why she would be extorting men who are having affairs."

"Oho." Max chuckled. "That was why she was following the attorney. Okay, sugar, I'm on it. Be safe."

My heart ached, wishing I could rule out Tammie as a suspect in my parents' murders, but I couldn't. Had she been extorting people for years? Had she wanted out of that crazy life? Had she gone to my parents' house hoping to find the one coin that could bolster her bank account so she could stop?

Please let me be wrong.

Next, I contacted Nick. He had a quick moment to chat. His murder case was heating up. He'd already narrowed it down to two suspects.

"How are you holding up?" I asked.

"I'm hanging tough. How about you?" he replied, his voice warm and caring.

"I'm exhausted, but I've uncovered new clues."

"Any other altercations with your ex or Brandt?"

"Nothing from Damian. Brandt was arrested," I said.

"Good."

I didn't add that Brandt was already out on bail and that I'd seen him in his SUV, lurking in the neighbor's driveway. "I miss you," I murmured.

Nick chuckled. "Be honest. You miss the lake."

I caressed the diamond on my engagement ring. "Nope. You."

"And the lake."

"And the lake," I echoed. "And Candace. And Cinder. And my job. And—"

He laughed out loud. "Got it. You're lonely. Me, too. Did your aunt contact you about the ballistics findings?"

"She did." I cocked my head. "Did it take all your willpower not to call me yourself?"

"Yep."

After blowing him a kiss goodbye, I tried Herman Hoek again.

A man answered. "Who's this?"

It didn't sound like Herman.

I said, "Mr. Hoek?"

"No. I repeat, who's this?"

I bristled at the guy's crisp tone. "I'll tell you if you tell me first."

"Detective Sergeant Quincy, Atherton Police Department."

I sat taller, on full alert. "Detective, it's Aspen Adams. What are you doing there? Has something happened? Where's Herman? He wanted to talk to me about—"

"He's been attacked."

"Attacked? By whom?"

"We don't know. I'm working with Palo Alto P.D. on this. A dark sedan was seen burning rubber down the street."

"A Honda Civic?"

"The witness couldn't tell. She didn't catch the plates, either."

"Is Herman . . ." I couldn't say the word.

"No. He's not dead, but he's in bad shape. He's on the way to the hospital."

"Which one?" I asked.

"Stanford."

Chapter 32

Stanford Health Care was consistently ranked as one of the leading hospitals in the nation. That didn't make me feel any better as I entered. I wasn't squeamish. Heck, I could climb into Dumpsters filled with slimy things, and I'd seen enough dead bodies to make me puke, but hospitals? The urgent way people moved unnerved me.

Tamping down my unease, I asked reception for Herman Hoek. The woman said he was out of emergency and had been assigned a room. I took an elevator and strolled along a corridor toward the room number she'd given me. I paused when I spotted Quincy outside the doorway talking to another man dressed in a blue wool suit and white shirt with blue tie. His subordinate or a plainclothesman from Palo Alto P.D., I figured. When Quincy saw me, he beckoned and the other man strolled away.

"You made good time," Quincy said.

"As did you. Is Herman okay?"

"He'll survive. His wheelchair probably saved his life. The attacker couldn't find a good angle to wield the blow."

"Wield the blow?"

"To his head. The attack seemed random. The perpetrator used a metal flower vase."

The hefty one I'd seen on Hoek's bookcase.

Quincy said, "Palo Alto P.D. tells me there have been a rash of attacks in the area in recent weeks. However, this might have been a case of iguana-napping. When a neighbor heard Hoek scream 'Lulu!' he pounded on Herman's door. The killer must have given up on his quest to steal the lizard and fled through the window."

I cocked my head. "You don't believe that about the iguana-napping, do you?"

"The jury is out."

If only Herman had had a guard dog.

"Why did Palo Alto P.D. bring you in on this?" I asked.

"Evers's card was on Hoek's kitchen counter. Tell me again about your relationship to Mr. Hoek." Quincy nudged his rimless glasses up his nose.

I explained that Hoek had rung Olga Payne, who'd contacted me. "I think he figured out what Viraj Patel wanted to tell me. I called him a few times over the last few hours. His voicemail machine kept answering for him." I motioned toward the room. "May I see him?"

"Yes, but I'll warn you, it's worse than we thought. Concussion. Grade three. He can count to ten and tell us who he voted for a few weeks ago, but because he lost consciousness, there's no telling the damage. There's quite a lot of swelling, causing pressure on the brain, so he has partial amnesia."

"Does he remember yelling Lulu?"

"No, that was information the neighbor provided. Hoek can't remember anything for the last twenty-four hours. He doesn't know who did this." Quincy added, "He has a visitor already."

I peeked into the room. Olga Payne, dressed in a white winter coat and white hat, stood to the right of Hoek's bed. She was holding his hand. She raised her chin when I entered, her smile tight.

"Viraj was listed as Herman's emergency contact," she said, adding that with Viraj dead, she had taken the call.

Hoek, awake and staring straight ahead, looked pretty bad. His head was heavily bandaged. The skin on his face was mottled and his eyes were rheumy. Tubes were attached to his arms.

I moved to the other side of the bed.

"The doctor said not to press him," Olga advised me. "His memory should return, but not for quite a long time."

"I know. I spoke to the detective outside." I took his hand as Olga had. "Hi, Herman."

Without moving his head, he acknowledged me with a blink. "Computer."

"Computer," I repeated. "You like to work with a computer."

"Lulu."

"That's his iguana," I said to Olga.

"Lulu is fine, Herman," she assured him. "A neighbor is watching her."

His eyelids fluttered. "Computer."

I said, "You told Olga you found something on the computer."

Olga threw me a reproachful look.

"Viraj," Hoek rasped.

"It had to do with Viraj's computer?" I asked.

"Please, Miss Adams, stop." Olga glanced over her shoulder as if the police might pop into the room and haul us away.

"Hacker," Hoek said.

I patted his hand. "Yes, you're a hacker. So was Viraj. You two were friends."

He pressed his lips together. I leaned into the silence, heart pounding as it dawned on me that he might be trying to say he'd hacked into Viraj's computer. "Did you find something in Viraj's cloud backup?"

Hoek blinked again. Rapidly. He wasn't trying to signal with Morse code. He was agitated.

"Did it have to do with a debt?"

"Don't—" He licked his lips.

"Okay, I won't."

"Remember."

Aha. *Don't remember.*

"That's okay," I said. "You don't have to remember right now."

Olga looked relieved that I would let the matter go.

But I couldn't. "Did the debt have to do with someone named Antoine Washington or William Fisher? Or Kurt Brandt? Or Tammie—"

"Stop," Olga begged.

"I can't."

She *tsk*ed. "You do not take instruction well."

"I never have."

Hoek turned his head ever so slightly. His gaze landed on me. "Brandt," he said with a lot of effort. "Brandt. Plant. Gant."

What was he trying to tell me? That Brandt had been involved in Patel's deal for the teardown deal in Mountain View? Or was he merely repeating words that rhymed? The other day, he'd told me he knew someone named Gant. He'd said Brandt's name first, though. I pictured Brandt, following me for days. He could have figured out where Hoek lived. He could have attacked him. But why? Did he think Hoek knew where the treasure was?

"I'm so sorry this happened to you, Herman," I whispered. "Rest. Get well."

Hoek smiled and closed his eyes.

I gazed at Olga. "You're a good woman to help him out."

"Who else does he have?"

"A sister. She's the one who gave him Lulu."

Outside Hoek's room, the plainclothesman in the blue suit had returned. Quincy was nowhere to be found. On my way out of the hospital, I called Atherton P.D. and asked to be put through to him, but apparently he couldn't be reached. I told the dispatcher that Quincy might want to look into Kurt Brandt for the Hoek incident. Brandt was out on bail. Brandt wanted answers. The dispatcher promised she'd give Quincy the message.

Near the emergency room exit, I caught sight of Ilona Isles sitting on a padded bench, her face tear-streaked, her hair tangled. Clad in jeans with dirty knees and a plaid shirt stained with green smudges, she looked like she'd just finished gardening.

I hurried to her. "Ilona, it's Aspen." I patted my chest as if she might not remember me. "What are you doing here?"

"Aspen." She held out both hands, motioning for me to sit beside her. I perched. "It's so good to see a friendly face. Ted. My husband." Her voice caught. "I told him he works too hard. He needs to slow down. He had a heart attack."

"Is there anything I can do?"

She shook her head.

"How about a glass of water?" I asked.

"That would be nice."

I filled a plastic cup from a nearby cooler and returned to her.

She sipped the water and rested the cup on her thigh. "Why are you here?"

"A friend had an accident. He was attacked."

"Oh, no!"

"He's going to be fine. So will Ted." I patted her shoulder.

"I hope so. He's never been in the hospital. He seemed freaked out." She chewed her lip. "It's so cold in here. Not cold, chilly. It's . . . impersonal. What if Ted has to stay overnight?"

"Bring him something like a photograph or a pillow. And bring him a clock. So he can tell the time." That was what my grandmother had done for Grandpa Gray. "Things like that will help orient him."

"I hadn't thought of that."

To take her mind off her worry, I said, "Hey, talk about coincidence, the other day I went to the house of a woman named Viola Isles. In Atherton. Near the Circus Club. Do you know her?"

She shook her head. "I don't think I do."

"I thought it was funny, you both having the same last name, seeing as I'd just met you. A friend of mine is redoing the guest room in the Isles house. She said she'd met you briefly. Tammie Laplante."

"We did meet. At an ASID meeting. She has an excellent reputation. Your mother would be proud of how—" Ilona wheezed, as if the air had been knocked out of her. She clutched my wrist and held on fast. Tears streamed down her face.

"It's okay, let it out," I coaxed, but my mind was shooting off in another direction.

About Tammie. Had I jumped to conclusions about her? Maybe the man she'd met at the Blue Moon Café had hired her to redo his house and the photographs were ideas for the renovation. Maybe he'd paid her in cash. No extortion. Maybe Tammie was fine financially and my concern was unwarranted. Except why would she have tailed him and taken photos?

• • •

As I jammed the Prius into gear and tore out of the hospital lot, I decided to follow my aunt's suggestion and contact my sister.

As if Rosie had predicted the call, she answered before the first ring completed. "I'm coming to Atherton," she announced.

"What? No." I hadn't meant to sound so sharp.

"I spoke to Candy."

"I ordered you not to—"

"She told me what Max found out. About the gun being a match."

I tamped down an exasperated sigh. When had my sister ever followed my instructions?

"I can come down and help you dig deeper," she went on.

"No, Rosie, take a breath."

She exhaled but not because of my command. She was smoking. "You think you can do it all yourself. Like always."

"No, that's not it. It's—"

To be truthful, I didn't want to worry about her ruining whatever I was on the cusp of learning.

"It's because I'm a bull in a china shop," she grunted.

Yep. That captured it in a nutshell, but I didn't agree out loud.

"What have you learned so far?" She took another drag on her cigarette. Or joint.

"Something that probably isn't related to the case but makes me sad." I told her about following Tammie and how she might be shaking down guys for cash.

"Never be surprised by what people will do for the almighty dollar," Rosie quipped. "How is she finding her marks?"

If they are marks, I mused.

"She must have a Joe steering her toward them."

I repeated Candace's guess. "A former coworker from the law firm where she'd served as a bookkeeper, I suppose." That would make sense, seeing as the two men she'd followed worked in the legal field.

"Does Mia know?" Rosie asked. "I sure hope not. She's devoted to her mother. In her eyes, Tammie can do no wrong. Mia has put her mother so high up on a fricking pedestal, Tammie probably needs oxygen." She snickered at her joke. "I guess that sort of thing happens when a dad is missing in action. If Mia learns about her mom's, uh, second profession, I don't know what she'll do. She's such a rules follower. A real stickler. Remember in high school, when she dropped out of my life?"

"I've often wondered about that."

Rosie hooted. "Mia saw me snort some coke and that was it. Boom! She dropped me like a hot potato. 'We are no longer friends, Rosie!'" my sister said in Mia's higher-pitched voice. "'You'll become a drug addict. My mother warned me.'"

"Tammie warned her about you?"

"No, Tammie warned about the dark side of getting hooked. On anything. Hey"—Rosie made a sucking sound with her tongue—"d'you think Tammie was already into this extortion crap then? When we were kids? Maybe she knew about getting hooked on something because she was hooked on the high of rolling people. A con game like that can work like a drug." Rosie snickered. "Good little Mia. Incorruptible to the core. Truth be told, she was sort of prissy, you know? Never tolerated anyone having faults. Like *moi*." After a long inhalation followed by a lengthy exhale, she said, "Whatever you do, Aspen, don't tell her about Tammie. Let Tammie tell her the truth. It won't come off well if you tell her, you know? No one likes a tattletale."

Especially my sister.

Chapter 33

Headlights strobed my eyes as I swung onto El Camino in the direction of the rental house. Squinting to relieve fatigue, it dawned on me that I hadn't eaten all day, so I dropped by Safeway to pick up a premade dinner from the deli counter. Standing in line, waiting my turn, I decided turmeric chicken salad with asparagus sounded right.

My cell phone jangled the moment I was in my car and pulling out of the parking lot. Quincy was on the line.

"Thanks for the heads-up," he said. "We tracked down Kurt Brandt. Sadly, he's not our guy. He was at a movie—the latest Marvel heroes film—and has the proof on his cell phone app."

"That doesn't mean he didn't scan his ticket and leave."

"True. However, when I asked him about Mr. Hoek wanting to talk to you about a debt, he swore he's been debt-free his entire life."

"I didn't get that impression."

Quincy went on. "He insisted that he didn't know Herman Hoek. Never heard of him."

My aunt said if she had a penny for every time a suspect vowed this or that, she'd be a billionaire.

"What about the dark sedan the witness saw driving off?" I asked. "Was that captured on any traffic cameras in the area?"

"Nope. And Brandt drives a RAV4."

"He could have a second—"

"We'll have to wait until Mr. Hoek is a little clearer on the facts," Quincy said, cutting me off again. "Gotta go."

As the connection went silent, a slim woman on foot darted out in front of me. Not in the crosswalk. I slammed on the brakes to avoid hitting her. She threw me a nasty look, even though I had the right-of-way. I waved my apology. She flipped me off. Nice.

Watching her continue on, I flashed on Mia, slim and beautiful in her jogging outfit. Mia, whom my sister said was incorruptible. Had she written the letter in the hope chest I'd found, the one in a youthful scrawl with the *M* engraved at the top? The author of the letter had begged Mom to help her mother. She'd said her mother was sick and that she'd hated what her mother was doing. Had Tammie been extorting people for years, as Rosie had suggested? Was she hooked on it? Did her craving for money have nothing to do with my parents' deaths? Rosie had warned me not to tell Mia anything.

Given the pleading letter in the hope chest, I suspected Mia already knew what her mother was up to.

• • •

I sat at the kitchen table, my dinner on a plate and a glass of chardonnay in hand. I took a sip of the wine, relishing the flavor and eagerly anticipating the momentary calm that would come from the alcohol.

Setting the glass aside, I scrolled through email messages. One from my aunt: *Nothing yet* and another from Candace: *Miss you.* I decided not to call her. I would cry if I did. I wanted so much for this mystery to be behind her and her mother. Healing was in both of their futures if I could—

My cell phone trilled. The sound startled me. I dropped the cell phone onto my dinner. "Dang it," I muttered. Checking the screen as I wiped it off, I saw the name: *Damian.* Swell. Not what I needed.

"What?" I answered with a bite.

"I'm sorry for the other night."

Apparently he didn't remember his apology. Evenly, I said, "You should be."

"I was . . . not myself."

He had been every bit *himself.* That was what had been so bad about it. I had never seen the signs when I was in the throes of love. I'd been blinded by hope.

"I was a fool to let you go. If only you—" He halted.

"If only I *what?*"

Silence.

"If only I hadn't spent long hours at the clinic?" I goaded. "If only I hadn't cared about my patients first and you second?" That had been one of our regular arguments, usually started by Damian after he'd been on hiatus and had found himself with way too much time on his hands. "If only I'd dedicated my entire life to making you happy?"

"That's not what I was—"

"Sure it was. You always blamed me for your bad behavior. And in some ways, it was my fault. I should have seen the truth earlier." I had lied to myself. I'd wanted him to be the flawless man I'd fallen in love with.

"Forgive me."

"I forgive you, Damian. But I also forgive myself for staying in our marriage a year too long." Twelve months of horrid spats. Vile exchanges. Bitter tears. "I've moved on. It's time for you to do the same. Go to New York. Make it the best life you can dream up. I want you to find the happiness you deserve."

"Without you." His voice cracked.

"Without me."

He ended the call and my heart wrenched. I hadn't lied to him. I had moved on. I was blithely in love with Nick and on the path to finding the happiness *I* deserved.

As I was washing my dinner dish, the cell phone rang again. *Serenity.* Holy heck. Who knew I'd set myself up for reunion week by coming to the Bay Area? I answered. "How are you?"

"Damian called an hour ago." Her voice was barely a whisper, as if she raised it she might break whatever trance she was in. "He wants me back."

I couldn't believe it. Had Damian called me to test me? Had he planned on moving ahead with Serenity no matter what? Had he hoped to throw the news in my face? Luckily, I hadn't taken the bait.

"It's stupid, I know, but I told him yes."

"He's moving to New York, Serenity. Did he tell you that?"

She didn't answer.

"Serenity, I love you," I said. "Think about this decision. You have a career, friends, and family. Here. In the Bay Area. They love you. Promise me that you'll make good choices for yourself."

Again, no response. Only a *click*.

I tossed the cell phone aside and yawned. "Bed. Sleep. Do not answer phone. Do not even look at phone."

Taking my sage advice, I tiptoed to the front door, peered through the sidelight for any sign of Brandt's SUV or a dark-colored sedan. Seeing nothing, I gave in to fatigue and strode to the bedroom.

215

Chapter 34

Eight hours later, I was ready to face a new day, despite the fact that it would be drizzly and bitter cold. According to the forecast, a new storm was fast approaching. I dressed in jeans and a fleece pullover and settled at the kitchen table. With a glass of juice in hand, I contacted my aunt.

"So far you've found nothing on Tammie?" I asked.

"Actually, last night I had nothing. This morning, I've got results. Darcy is a mastermind when it comes to deep diving into a person's financial records. Especially at two a.m."

Adrenaline coursed through me. "What did she find out?"

"Your pal Tammie Laplante is in hock to the tune of two million dollars."

I gasped. "For what? Her townhouse should be nearly paid off."

"She refi'd that to buy her daughter's condo. In addition, she pays for her granddaughter's nanny, and she's paying off her daughter's college loans. All covered by one loan from a private lender."

"Not a bank?"

"Nope."

"Is the lender Kurt Brandt?" I asked, trying to connect the two.

"No. Somebody named Yates."

I settled in my chair. "No wonder she's extorting people. She doesn't have enough income to cover that kind of debt." I sighed, realizing my mother must have been clueless as to Tammie's extracurricular activities. If she had known, she would have ended the partnership and never would have given Tammie another loan.

"If I've taught you anything, it's not to overextend yourself," Max said.

"Yes, you have." As did my mother and father. They'd all drilled into me the value of a dollar. I said, "Tammie wants her daughter to have the life her ex-husband refused to provide."

"That's no excuse."

I ran a hand along my neck, once again stunned by how little I knew about Tammie. All those years of seeing her working alongside my mother. The countless Christmases. And birthdays. And graduations.

After thanking my aunt and ending the call, I shuffled into the dining room. I stared again at the murder board, wondering anew whether Tammie had killed my parents to get her hands on the treasure Kurt Brandt sought.

If it were true, I couldn't fathom how my mother had felt at the end. Had she seen Tammie crouching over her, not Rosie? If so, she must have suffered acute betrayal.

Anger surged within me as I tapped in Tammie's number.

She answered, breathless. "What's up?"

"I need to see you. Now."

"I'm with a client. How about—"

"Now," I demanded.

"What's wrong?"

"I need to ask you a few questions. Where are you?"

"The Youth Science Institute at Vasona Lake, but Aspen, can't it—"

"No, it can't wait." I threw on a jacket, grabbed my keys, and hurried to the Prius.

Plowing through traffic, windshield wipers flipping occasionally to remove the drizzle, I made it to Blossom Hill Road in less than thirty minutes, though not without a few scares. The roads were slick. A semi swerved from one lane to the next, pumping its brakes. A madman in a yellow Lamborghini believed it was his mission to cut in and out of every small opening on the freeway. By the time I reached the lake, my nerves were ragged.

Tammie was right. The lake, which was really a reservoir, was no Lake Tahoe. No ring of mountains. No pines. No startlingly blue water. Not to mention it was about the size of an inlet at Tahoe. How I ached to return home. But I couldn't. Not yet. Not when I felt in my bones that I was close to the truth.

I parked between Tammy's Jaguar and a silver Mercedes. The one other car in the lot was a blue Accord. I clambered out of the Prius and shoved my cell phone and car key into my pocket. Because of the inclement weather, no one was on the lake. A security guard paced near the restrooms. His car must have been the Accord. I acknowledged him with a chin hitch. He did the same.

A gust of wind hit me. I staggered, recovered, and made a beeline across the slick grass to the Youth Science Institute, a rustic one-story building with a red-tiled roof. The door was ajar.

Tammie, dressed in a forest green sweater over leggings tucked into leather boots, was standing outside with a very tan man who looked eons warmer than she in his burnt orange parka, the hood pulled up.

I skidded to a stop. "Tammie."

She apologized to her companion.

He smiled genially. "No worries. I'll catch up with you tomorrow. You close up." He strode toward the parking lot.

Tammie cocked her head. "What's so urgent, Aspen?" She folded her arms to brace herself against the cold. "Are you okay?"

Anger at her fake concern spiraled through me. "I know what you're up to."

"What are you talking about?"

"You're extorting men. I've seen you."

She glanced over her shoulder and refocused on me.

"How long have you been doing this, Tammie?"

She pressed her lips together.

"Why are you in so much debt?" I asked.

"I'm not."

"Two million dollars."

Her face paled. "How . . . Why . . ." She inhaled, her nose narrowing with the effort, and exhaled through her mouth. "Fine, if you must know, yes, I've overextended myself. I can't manage funds well. With Mia's college debt and her condo payments and the nanny's salary and trying to make payments on my townhouse and the Jag, I'm three months in arears."

"To a private lender. Is that because the banks turned you down?"

"How do you know—" Her eyes narrowed. "Did Serenity's mother tell you that?"

"Extortion, Tammie. Why? There had to be another way."

She raised her chin proudly. "I'll have you know that I've only extorted those who've deserved it. Men who cheat on their wives. Men with very deep pockets. Like my ex-husband."

"Did you kill my mother because she found out about your secret job?"

"What are you talking about? What kind of accusation . . ." Tammie pivoted and marched toward the water, arms outstretched. "How dare you."

I chased after her. "Mia wrote my mother. Years ago. I found a letter from her in Mom's hope chest. She was worried about you. She wanted my mother's help. She didn't like what you were doing. Did Mom—"

"I loved your mother." Tammie whirled around. "Like a sister. I never would have harmed her."

"She's dead, Tammie."

"Not by my hand. How could you even think that? Aspen, what's gotten into you?" Tammie reached for me. "Come here. Whatever you believe you've learned—"

I recoiled. "Don't."

Out of the corner of my eye, I spied the Accord in the parking lot and suddenly images of Mia and her shiny blue Celica reeled through my mind.

Mia, in her warm-up clothes.

Mia, with her shaved head, protesting for a woman's right to choose.

Mia, who was never considered a suspect in my parents' murders, and therefore was never questioned.

Had she broken into my parents' house to rob them in order to bail out her mother?

I thought of the evidence found at the crime scene. No foreign hair. Viraj Patel claimed to have seen a tall, thin person with short hair running through the neighborhood the night before my parents' death. Mia was a runner as well as lean and tall and at the time, thanks to her protest over women's rights, she'd been bald. I also thought of the minute corner of a foil candy wrapper found at the scene. Mia chewed gum with regularity. As a girl, her favorite had been Doublemint.

My stomach churned with anxiety.

Why had Mia selected my parents as her target? Not for the silver. The paltry amount we'd owned wouldn't have paid for a semester of college, let alone a portion of her mother's debt. Tammie must have told Mia about the silver dollar—the insurance policy. Yes, that had to be it. Also, from Tammie, Mia could have learned that my parents were out of town. She entered without breaking in because she'd known where we'd kept the spare key. Over the years, Rosie and I had accessed it in front of her numerous times.

I drilled my gaze into Tammie and whispered, "Mia."

Chapter 35

"What about her?" Tammie pivoted and headed toward the Youth Science building. "I've got to close up."

"She killed my parents."

She drew up short and faced me, hands on hips. "Are you out of your mind? Where are you coming up with such ridiculous ideas?"

"The pieces fit."

"Impossible."

Quickly, I told her my theory about Mia the runner, and Mia the bald protestor that a witness might have mistaken for a man, and Mia our childhood friend who knew where the spare key to my parents' house was hidden, and Mia the daughter whose mother had probably told her about my parents' schedule and the existence of an incredibly valuable silver dollar.

"Be honest, Tammie. You suspected her, didn't you?" I stated. "That's why you made up that phony alibi for the two of you."

"What phony alibi?" She raised her chin. "Mia and I were college hunting at the time."

"Wrong. She was twenty when my parents died."

"I told you she took a couple of gap years."

"Wrong again. The truth is, she didn't start college until a few years later. Well into her twenties. I saw the diploma on your office wall."

"I've heard enough." Tammie fanned a hand. "It's all lies. I need you to leave before I—"

"Mom, move away," Mia ordered.

I whirled around and fear ricocheted through me. Mia, in black running suit and black tennis shoes, marched toward us, a gun aimed at my chest. A Glock, to be exact, the same gun Kurt Brandt carried. Her hair was spiky and damp, her eyes pinpoints of resentment.

"How'd you find me, Mia?" I asked, trying to keep my voice neutral even though my heart was pulverizing my rib cage.

"Mom texted me. She was worried about you. She said you were agitated. She said you were on your way to see her. I came to protect her." Mia brandished the gun. "Can't have you going all crazy now, can we? Let's take a hike. To the lake."

"Mia," Tammie said, wariness in her tone. "Where'd you get the gun?"

"What're you going to do, Mia?" I asked. "Shoot me and dump my body in the water? There's a guard on duty."

"Not anymore," she said. "I told him I heard a kid screaming along the multiuse trail. He took off like a shot."

I glanced at the parking lot. There were four parked cars—Tammie's, Mia's, mine, and the Accord—but the guard was gone.

"Mia, sweetheart," Tammie said, her voice wavering. Did she truly not know what her daughter was capable of? "Tell me where you got the gun."

"At a gun store," Mia replied glibly.

"When?"

"Two years ago."

"Why?" Tammie asked.

"Because my sweet husband threatened me with a knife."

"He what?" Tammie squawked. "You never told me."

"I said he wasn't a nice guy, Mom. Did I have to go into detail? Don't worry. I've been taking self-defense classes."

Tammie blanched. "Mia, for heaven's sake, he takes care of Giselle every other weekend. Have you informed someone that he's dangerous?"

"Yes."

"How could the court award him joint custody?"

"He had a better lawyer than I did." Mia coughed out a laugh. "We sure can pick 'em, can't we, Mom? Bad men who screw blondes. Sounds like a good name for a country western song." She glowered at me. "Move."

I didn't budge. The water was a hundred yards away. If she shot me here, now, the guard might hear the sound and return before she could drag me to the lake. She couldn't take the chance.

"I said move." Mia whipped my head with the gun.

I sank to my knees, the ground coming up to meet my face. In the nick of time, I thrust out my hands and caught myself short of a face-plant. Pain roiling in my head, I pushed to a stand. Blood trickled from my ear down my neck.

Before I could prepare to ward off another blow, Mia whacked me again. On the arm. Automatically my other hand went to protect it. She flailed again. Connecting with my fingers.

I yowled. Had she broken my index finger? It didn't matter. Right now, I had to engage her. I had to get her to focus on me. On my words. Using all the composure I could muster, composure drilled into me when working with twitchy patients, I said, "Mia, the ballistics on my grandfather's gun and the murder weapon match."

"So?"

I didn't let her vile gaze rattle me. "Fourteen years ago, you took the gun from the hope chest in my parents' bedroom and used it to kill them, didn't you?"

"Don't be asinine," Tammie rasped.

"I'm guessing you knew where to find it, Mia," I went on, "because Rosie showed you. She showed a lot of people."

Tammie gaped at her daughter. "Mia, tell her she's wrong."

Had Tammie really not known what had gone down? Had Mia kept the secret all this time? What had she told her mother that would have made Tammie provide a fake alibi?

Mia grinned, her lips pulling hideously against her teeth. "Yeah, okay, Aspen, let's talk. About Rosie. Man, your sister was a piece of work. Always getting into trouble. Always wanting me to join her at every idiotic turn."

"Like snorting coke?" I asked.

"Coke, pot, uppers, downers. No, thanks."

Mia could judge all she wanted, but unlike Mia, Rosie hadn't killed anyone.

"I'll always remember that day Rosie bragged to me about your grandmother." Mimicking Rosie, she said, "'Grandma Patrice is so clever. So gifted. So artistic.' Man, she couldn't stop driving it home that I didn't have a grandmother like that."

Tammie moaned. After her parents checked out, she'd never again made contact with them.

Mia said, "Rosie absolutely *had* to show me the gun box."

"She must have shown you how to open it, too," I offered.

"What's a puzzle box good for if you can't open it?" Mia asked in singsong fashion.

"So, you took the gun from the hope chest . . ." I said.

"In case I needed to use it at a pawn shop when I tried to hawk the silver. I'd heard those guys could be shady."

"A knife would have worked just as well," I countered.

"I liked the idea of a gun."

Mia punched me in the stomach. I'd anticipated the jab and had steeled my abs. Even so, I doubled over. Shook it off.

Tammie groaned.

I studied Mia's face. Blank. Devoid of guilt. Devoid of emotion or any feeling. When had she become cold?

"I think you're lying, Mia," I rasped as another theory came to me. Evers had mentioned in his notes that my mother's office had been tossed. He'd thought the killer had been looking for a document of some kind. "You never intended to rob them of silver."

Mia gazed past my shoulder, as if she were looking at something far away. If only I could devise a way to disarm her, but out in the open, with no weapon, it seemed impossible. When she returned her focus to me, her eyes flickered. Was she trying to concoct a story?

After a long moment, she said, "You deserved better, Mom."

Tammie shook her head. "What are you talking about?"

"Lily denied you. Over and over again."

"Denied her what?" I asked. "Money? Not true. My mother loaned your mother a lot of money over the years."

"With interest," Mia hooted. "Written in blood."

"That's an exaggeration."

"Oh, yeah?" Mia thrust the Glock in my direction.

I flinched, hating myself for the kneejerk reaction, but my ear still throbbed. My hearing was definitely messed up. And my stomach, arm, and fingers ached.

"Your mother was a control freak," Mia said. "The last time Mom borrowed money, Lily made her sign a loan document."

"A promissory note," I said. "For how much?"

"A half million."

I scoffed. "Try again. My parents didn't have that kind of cash."

Tammie said, "Yes, they did. Your mother refinanced—"

"Your mother"—Mia cut in—"always thought she was better than mine." She shoved the nose of the gun into my throat.

I gagged.

"Lily kept Mom under her thumb. She treated her like an assistant. She didn't let her shine. Mom didn't have freedom of expression. She didn't have autonomy."

"Sweetheart, you're wrong," Tammie said, her voice soothing, as if she were speaking to a toddler. "I was a full partner."

"Bull."

"I had been for at least a year before Lily—"

"Bull, bull, bull!"

As Mia glared at her mother, I remembered my cell phone.

Shivering, pretending I was cold, I slipped both hands into my pockets. I felt my cell phone and pressed the Home button to activate it. I tapped in my password, praying I'd gotten it right. I'd done it blindly numerous times while driving. It wasn't a difficult one—four nines in a row. Next, I clicked the Messages icon above the Home button and selected the topmost name. The last person I'd texted was Nick. I typed in what I hoped were the letters *SOS*. If they were one letter off either way, like *DPD* or *AIA*, would he understand my plea? Would he think to triangulate my location? Following the fiasco that had occurred months ago with my news anchor friend, we'd made sure he could track me.

"Mia," I said, drawing her attention. "If you hated my mother so much, why did you reach out to her for help all those years ago?"

She slapped me with her free hand. "Shut up."

"I saw your letter in the hope chest."

She slapped me again. "I said quiet."

Cheek stinging, I pressed on. "How old were you then? Thirteen? Fourteen? You wrote that your mother was sick."

Tammie cut a hurt look at her daughter.

"You didn't mean she needed to go to the hospital," I continued. "You thought she was sick, as in addicted, because she was extorting people and couldn't stop. How did you figure it out? Did she take you on a couple of her jaunts?"

Tammie winced, conceding that she had.

"Mia, I'm sorry to tell you this," I said, "but your mother still can't stop."

"Enough, I said. Shut up." Mia clocked me with the gun on the jaw. Blood spurted inside my mouth. Pain scudded through me. Had I lost a couple of teeth thanks to the hit?

"Turn around, Aspen. Hands up."

This time, I obeyed.

"Walk. To the water. Now. And, Mom, leave."

Chapter 36

I didn't see the guard. Didn't see anyone. I felt woozy but forced myself to stay focused. Mia pressed the icy muzzle into the hollow of my neck. As she did, the truth became clear.

I said, "That night, you went to my parents' house to get the promissory note." Had Mom filed it in my father's office? That would explain why both hers and my father's offices had been tossed. If Mia had found it, that also explained why Ulyssa Thaller didn't have a record of it and why the value of my parents' estate was less than it should have been; they'd refinanced the house to help out Tammie, but she'd never been forced to repay the loan. Again, I became suspicious of Tammie playing innocent. She had to have known what Mia had done. How else could Mia have come up with the paperwork to absolve her mother from debt?

"You believed that if you could destroy the note," I went on, "then my mother would have nothing to hold over your mother's head. Tammie wouldn't have to pay the loan with interest. She could leave the business and start fresh."

Mia dragged the barrel of the Glock to the spot between my shoulder blades. "Good guess." I heard a click. She'd released the safety.

"Sweetheart," Tammie began. She had stuck to Mia like glue.

"Mom, I told you to leave. Aspen"—she poked me—"keep walking."

Fearful that this time she really would shoot, I moved cautiously ahead. "After you found the note, however, you decided to search for my parents' insurance policy. The silver dollar. Your mother had told you about it, hadn't she?"

Tammie choked back a sob.

"I get it, Mia," I continued. "You were angry at my mother. You wanted justice. Revenge. Why not rob her of everything you could?"

I flashed on the cherrywood puzzle box, the one Mia's daughter had thought contained a treasure. Mia must have stolen the box and given it to her mother, which meant she must have told Tammie about the robbery. Had she lied, saying that she hadn't been anywhere near the place when the murders had occurred? Had Tammie bought the lie?

"Am I close, Mia?" I dared to glance over my shoulder. Her jaw was trembling. I'd struck a nerve. Maybe she was second-guessing her decision to kill me.

"Don't look at me." She kicked the hollow of my knee. I buckled but recovered.

Come on, Aspen. Get her to talk. Get her to unload the burden she's been carrying around for years.

Softly, I said, "Mia, I'm not going to walk any farther. I'm going to turn around."

"No!"

"Yes. I'm turning slowly."

"No!" She whacked me on the right shoulder.

Searing pain spiraled down my arm. Even so, I pivoted. Mia leveled the gun at me, but she didn't pull the trigger. Her eyes were fluttering, her jaw twitching.

In a soothing voice, I said, "You scoured the dining room, thinking that was where they'd hidden their wealth. Where there's silver, there must be gold. But you didn't find the coin, did you?"

I was certain she hadn't. If she had, her daughter wouldn't have thought the treasure was in the cherrywood box.

I continued. "Frustrated and sensing you had spent more time than you ought to in the house—I mean, someone might notice you skulking about, right?—you gave up on the treasure and decided to take the silver. You might as well have something for your trouble. Plus, that would make your incursion look like a simple robbery. No one would suspect that you'd taken the promissory note. But, to your surprise"—I let the silence hang for a moment—"my parents showed up."

Mia whimpered. Tammie covered her mouth, fighting tears.

"Walk me through what happened next, Mia," I said. "Dad entered first. What did he—"

"He roared at me," she shrieked. "He scared me. He demanded to know what I was doing. He . . . He . . ." She scraped her lips with her teeth. "Before I knew it, the gun went off."

"Shooting him was an accident?"

"Yes!"

"Except you shot my mother when she threw herself on top of my dad."

"No. Listen." Mia blinked. "Lily yelled at me, too. 'What have you done, Mia? What have you done?'"

Mia used her hands to replay the event, but even though the Glock was no longer pointed at me, I wouldn't charge her. I had to time it right.

"See, I couldn't explain to her why I was there." Mia's voice quavered. "I wasn't wearing a mask, but I was dressed in black, and the silver and the note were in a pillowcase by my feet, and . . ." She rubbed her neck with her free hand. "Lily begged me to call 911, but I couldn't. The police would arrest me. My mother would be so ashamed. So I . . . I . . ."

"You killed her."

"No, that's not what happened," Mia cried.

I flashed on my mother's last words to Rosie: *You'll never get it.*

"No, it's not," I whispered. "You're right, Mia. First, you hovered over my mother and demanded that she tell you where the silver dollar was. Mom wouldn't say, so you threatened her. She wouldn't relent. She said, 'You'll never get it. I've hidden it where you'll never find it.' Or something like that, am I warm?"

Mia hiccupped.

"You spotted items in the cabinet with the medals and curios, and it dawned on you that she'd displayed her other prized items in the master bedroom. On the bureau. You demanded to know which one. She wouldn't say. But believing that she had betrayed herself by saying she'd hidden it, you killed her and gleefully went in search. When you picked up the cherrywood box and shook it, you felt you'd found what you were after."

"Gleefully?" Mia spat, nostrils flared. "I wasn't gleeful."

"Of course you weren't," Tammie said.

No fingerprints flashed in my mind. Now I understood why that clue had bothered me.

"You were wearing gloves for your foray, Mia, weren't you? But, even so, you cleaned up afterward. Now I know why. To protect your mother, like you always have. Because you didn't want *her* fingerprints to be there. You were worried she'd be suspected of murder."

"No." Tammie blanched.

"No," Mia echoed.

"Yes," I said. "What I don't understand, Tammie"—I swiveled my aching head in her direction—"is why you didn't break open the box the moment she handed it to you? Mia must have demanded that you do so."

Tammie's chest rose and fell. "Because I knew what was inside, and I knew it was worthless."

"How's that for irony?" Mia snapped. "Your mother, in her dying moment, stuck it to my mother one last time. All she had to do was tell me where the valuable coin was. If she had—"

"You still would have killed her," I cut her off.

Mia heaved a sigh and her face went slack, as if drained of all emotion. "Enough chitchat. Move."

"One last question."

"No," she barked.

"Did you attack Herman Hoek?"

"Who's that?" Tammie asked.

I stared at Mia. "Answer the question. You overheard me mention Herman's name when I was on the phone at your mother's place. You overheard me say that he had information for me."

Mia grunted.

"You've been following me." I wasn't paranoid. I had picked up on a tail, as elusive as it may have been. Mia had followed me in her blue car. "You must have persuaded the nanny to work a lot of overtime."

Mia didn't respond.

"You took note of who I was questioning. You left a *Go Home* message on my windshield at Big Box after I met with Antoine Washington, didn't you? And you knew I'd visited Herman Hoek."

She didn't deny it.

"Hoek said he had information about a debt," I said. "I'm presuming he found out about your mother's gigantic liability. If he invited scrutiny from the police, your mother could have become the primary suspect in my parents' murders. But no, Mia, you set off to protect your mother yet again."

"Mia?" Tammie whispered.

With pain zinging through me, I landed on another thought. At the hospital, when I'd asked Hoek if any of the suspects' names had sounded familiar, he'd muttered *Brandt*. Seconds later, he'd added the word *plant*, the same word Patel had said to his fiancée. The two men had been trying to suggest the name Laplante.

"Did you tell him you were there to avenge your mother?" I asked.

If Mia had revealed that she was Tammie's daughter, Hoek might have been trying to implicate her by saying *plant*, not knowing that Mia's surname was Smith.

"Mr. Hoek is going to live," I said. "He has a concussion and he can't remember what happened, but he will in time."

I glimpsed Mia's blue car in the parking lot, and one more piece of the puzzle fell into place. Viraj Patel had seen what he'd thought was a green car driving through the neighborhood looking shifty, but he had been color blind. He could have mistaken the color of Mia's blue car for green.

"Did you also kill Viraj Patel and set fire to his house?" I asked.

"No," she said. "Don't be absurd." But the tremor in her voice suggested she was lying.

A moment at the storage facility the other day flashed in my mind. "Your mother heard me talking to Patel on the phone. I'd uttered the word *debt* out loud. She went to fetch water for us and contacted you, didn't she? Which leads me to you, Tammie." I peeked at her out of the corner of my eye. "You're not innocent, no matter how much you try to fake it. You knew what your daughter had done because you were keeping her in the loop."

"I didn't mean to, I . . ." Tammie stammered. "Mia kept asking how your investigation was going. I thought she was curious because you girls used to be such good friends."

I didn't say what a load of bull, but I thought it.

"One thing mystifies me, Mia," I said, remaining focused on her. "Why did you return my grandfather's gun to the hope chest? Why didn't you take it with you to protect yourself when you went to hawk the silver?"

Mia lifted her chin defiantly.

"Wait." I held up a hand. "I've got it. Because you thought if Rosie leaked anything about the gun, and the gun was found in its puzzle box, then she would become the main suspect. Who else besides her would have known about it? You could deny, deny. Very clever."

A siren wailed in the distance. Hope leaped up my throat.

Mia stared wild-eyed at me. "What did you do?"

Lying, I said, "I called the police before I came here." How I prayed that the police car was truly heading in our direction.

Within seconds, however, the wail receded and grew faint. The vehicle was continuing on toward the Santa Cruz Mountains. Dang it. Did Mia or Tammie realize that?

Bluffing, I said, "Why don't you give me the gun, Mia? If you do, when they arrest you, I'll ask them to be merciful." I held out my hand. The pain in my shoulder made it hard to keep my arm from shaking. "You'll serve time, but you'll—"

"No!" Tammie shrieked and dove at me. "My daughter will not go to prison. Ever." She clawed my face.

I howled and grabbed her in a bear hug.

Tammie yelled, "Mia, run!"

But Mia didn't budge. She aimed the gun, looking uncertain about taking the shot.

"Mia, go!" Tammie repeated. "Run!"

"Mom," Mia screamed, "get out of the way."

Using all my weight, I yanked Tammie to the ground. Neither of us lost our grip. We tumbled on the grass, away from Mia. Ten feet. Twenty feet. I dug my heels into the grass and clambered on top of Tammie, pinning her beneath me. "Tammie, give it up. This won't end well."

"Yes. It. Will." Tammie writhed to get out from under me.

Mia yelled, "Aspen, get off her or I'll—"

Grunting, Tammie propelled me to the left, winning the advantage.

At the same time, Mia fired. The bullet hit Tammie in the arm. Blood spurted. Tammie yelped like a wounded animal. I shoved her off of me. Mia sprinted toward us, Glock raised. I extended my right leg and connected with her ankle. She stumbled and careened backward. I scrambled to my feet and dove at her.

Gripping her wrist, I squeezed until the Glock fell from her grasp. I nabbed it, straddled her, and pointed the gun at her.

"Aspen, no," Tammie wailed.

"Don't worry. I won't kill her. Do you know why?" Through clenched, bloody teeth, I said, "Because I want you to spend the rest of your life in prison, Mia, thinking about how you not only destroyed my family's life, but how you ruined your daughter's life, as well."

Heavy footfalls. Fast approaching.

I dared to take a peek. Not the guard. Not the police. A man in a black overcoat was hurtling toward us. Over his shoulder, I caught sight of a RAV4 in the parking lot. Kurt Brandt.

He thrust his gun at Tammie to keep her at bay and eyed me. "Are you okay, Miss Adams?"

"Yes. How did you——"

"You kept spotting me, so I resorted to putting a tracer on your car. When I saw you'd come here, I figured your mother must have found a secret place to stash the treasure. A place only you and she would know."

"Sorry, Mr. Brandt. My mother and I never came here. We always went to Tahoe if we were in the mood to see a lake." I smiled at him. "But I appreciate the backup. Would you mind contacting the police?" I rattled off Quincy's telephone number.

But Brandt didn't have to call him. A Los Gatos Police Department patrol car whizzed into the parking lot, lights flashing.

Nick, bless his soul, must have deciphered my SOS.

Chapter 37

As I watched the EMTs set Tammie on a stretcher and hoist her into their vehicle with a Los Gatos policeman standing at the ready to help, I reflected on how people told themselves lie after lie, and ultimately, started to believe them. That was how they survived. With blinders on. Tammie had lied to herself for years about her daughter, just as she'd lied to herself about the rationale behind her extortion scheme.

"How are you feeling?" Detective Sergeant Quincy asked. Minutes after he'd appeared, he'd peppered me with questions, following which he'd arrested Mia Smith and tucked her, handcuffed, into his Atherton P.D. vehicle. He offered me a bottle of water. "How's the head?"

"I'm okay." I had allowed the EMTs to cursorily check me out and declare me fit to drive. I was bruised and battered and I ached to my core, but I wasn't broken. I would go to the hospital of my own accord and get checked out fully after Quincy and I discussed everything. "How's Herman Hoek?"

"He's feeling better, but he's still not remembering much." Quincy smoothed the lapel of his jacket.

"I'm sorry to hear that."

"He doesn't remember Miss Laplante's daughter hitting him, although he does repeat in singsong fashion the words *Brandt* and *plant*."

I held up a hand. "I'm afraid I might have put that rhyme into his head."

"What he does remember," Quincy continued, "is earlier that morning, before he was attacked, he was combing Viraj Patel's backup data. He'd found a backdoor and was able to access Patel's files and information on his cloud account. He didn't remember what he'd found, so I had one of our tech guys scour it, and it turns out Patel had created a file for Tammie Laplante. In it, he'd recorded all of her outstanding debts. In addition, he'd located her private lender as well as the lawyer for whom Miss Laplante was, let's say, doing specialty work. Subsequently, we've contacted that lawyer, who feebly admitted

234

that he has been *in contact*"—Quincy mimed quotation marks—"with Miss Laplante. Needless to say, he clammed up and requested his own representation. I'm pretty sure he was taking a commission."

I thanked Quincy for his help in solving my parents' case.

He brushed my upper arm. "I know full well who did the solving, Miss Adams. I'm simply glad you have closure."

I mentioned Dale Warwick's death to him. "You might want to look into it." I explained Warwick's connection to William Fisher.

Quincy tapped his chin with his water bottle. "Interesting that you should mention that. We already have an answer in that matter. Warwick made a few enemies besides Fisher. Particularly in the gambling world, if you catch my drift. Fisher is blameless."

Despite the fact that Fisher had taunted me with the baseball bat, I was actually glad to hear that he was innocent. His son would need his father to continue to fight for his freedom.

"Whenever you're in town, stop by," Quincy added. "Say hello."

As he climbed into his SUV, I scanned the area for Kurt Brandt so I could thank him. He'd slipped away.

• • •

Feeling freer than I had in years, I swung by the hospital and got bandaged up in the emergency room. No stitches. No broken bones, although they insisted on splinting my finger. And they advised me to see my dentist when I got home. No teeth had fallen out, but one was loose. I returned to the rental house, packed my things, and leaving the house nearly as pristine as when I'd arrived, other than the shutter that I'd removed, I drove to Lake Tahoe.

As I was passing through Auburn, I found the energy to call my sister. Rosie picked up after three rings. She sounded groggy.

"Hey, little sis," she slurred. "S'up?"

Despite her state of mind, I plowed ahead, recapping the showdown with Mia and Tammie.

"I can't believe it," she said. "Mia?"

"Can pack a punch."

"You're okay?"

"Tougher than I look. Listen, Rosie, I don't mean this in a bad way, but when you sober up—"

"I'm not wasted." She coughed out a half-hearted laugh. "Yeah, okay. I'm halfway wasted. I'm not good at waiting for answers." She ended the call abruptly.

I worked the tension out of my shoulders, wincing as I moved the right one, and then phoned Nick. Yes, I'd spoken to him the moment I'd concluded with Quincy, but I wanted to hear his voice again.

"What do you want for dinner?" he asked.

"A kiss."

"And?" His voice was warm and sexy.

"Steak. Rare."

"Consider it done."

I hoped I could chew.

• • •

When I arrived at the cabin, Nick, Candace, and Max were waiting for me. Cinder, too. Nick held a tight leash on the dog so he wouldn't knock me over with his exuberance. Candace hugged me gingerly, as if I might break in two. Max stroked my cheek.

Nick waited his turn and kissed me gently on the lips. "You look pretty decent for a piñata," he murmured.

Smiling hurt.

Candace said, "Did you call Mom?"

"Yes. She and I will talk in a few days." I didn't mention Rosie's current state of health. "She was very excited to hear that the case was solved. She—"

"Whoa," my aunt cut me off and pointed at my hand. "Is that what I think it is?"

I held out my arm, the ring sparkling in the foyer's light. "It is."

"You and Nick are engaged?" Candace squealed. "When? Why didn't you tell us until now?"

"I wanted to do it in person."

Max said, "Congratulations."

Candace peppered Nick and me with questions. How? When? What did Nick say? Did he drop to one knee? She wanted specifics. A few minutes into our account, Max received a text and had to leave. She kissed me on both cheeks, whispered that she was as pleased as punch that I was alive, and forbade me to come to work tomorrow, advising me to take a day off to let it all sink in.

When Candace had exhausted a list of questions, she said, "I'm going to call Waverly. Is that okay? I want to tell her the good news."

"Sure."

In the kitchen, Nick stroked my back. "How was your sister really?"

"Not good." I ran a hand through my ragged hair.

"Wine?"

"A goblet, please."

Cinder, now off his leash, brushed my leg with his nose. I pulled a piece of dog-friendly jerky from a jar and handed him one. "Pillow," I said, pointing to the living room, but he didn't listen. He wouldn't leave my side. "Fine. Sit by the door. Not under foot." He understood that command and hunkered down.

Two hours later, after enjoying every bite of a delicious dinner of baked potato, asparagus, and grilled steak—the trick was cutting my steak into small pieces—I felt as if my jeans had suddenly become two sizes too small. I switched into my sweats, threw on a parka, and ambled to the back porch. I nestled into one of the patio chairs, inhaled the scent of pine, and let the cool breeze lick my face. Tahoe. Heaven. Home.

Nick passed through the kitchen door and let the screen door swing shut. "I solved the ski resort murder." He handed me a snifter of brandy.

"Good for you. Who did it?"

"His ex-wife," he said. "He'd jacked her in the divorce settlement. She wasn't pleased."

"Isn't it amazing what people will do for money?"

"Glad I split mine down the middle with my ex."

I took a sip of the brandy. It burned my throat but in a good way. I peered up at him.

He bent to kiss my forehead. "I'm glad you're safe," he said, his voice thick with emotion.

"Me, too."

Chapter 38

Nick left at midnight. In the morning, I slept through my alarm. When sunlight forced my eyes to open, I lumbered out of bed to take Candace to school. Luckily, she'd roused herself and had eaten a hearty breakfast.

As I was driving home, a gaping yawn nearly made me drive off the road. My aunt was right. I needed sleep and time to regroup.

My cell phone rang. Happy to have something to focus on, I answered.

"I thought you'd like to know," Quincy said with no preamble, "that Tammie Laplante was arrested as an accessory in your parents' murders. She has already lawyered up." I heard him moving papers around on his desk. "With the same lawyer who helped her with her, um—"

"Second job," I said.

"Exactly. She has secured a separate lawyer for her daughter's defense. And a third lawyer to take on the custody battle."

"Mia's husband can't get sole custody of the child," I exclaimed. "He went after Mia with a knife."

"So I've heard," Quincy said. "Miss Laplante has put in her two cents about the husband and, as it turns out, the girl's gestational surrogate mother is weighing in. It seems Miss Laplante has reached out to her. The woman has wanted to be part of the girl's life from the beginning. Miss Laplante thinks this might be the best solution until Mia is released from prison."

"Is the surrogate fit?" Silently, I chided myself for never having questioned Tammie about the woman, figuring that, by contract, she was out of the picture at birth. How could I be so disconnected? Both of my careers as psychiatrist and investigator required me to be more invested. More inquisitive. I made a promise to change that aspect of my personality going forward.

"The woman has three children of her own. She's a good mother with an upstanding reputation."

"Will Mia get parole?" I asked.

"I have no idea. She's looking at three murder charges. It will be up to the courts and her behavior once she's behind bars."

Worry shimmied through me. I didn't want her to garner an ounce of sympathy. She'd mercilessly killed my parents and had kept quiet all these years. "I'll need to be there for the trial."

"Already noted with the D.A."

• • •

Unable to sleep—I'd never been able to during the day—I idled around the house. Dusting. Cleaning. Sitting on the porch with a book I couldn't read. Making a grocery list. Setting an appointment with the dentist.

At three p.m., I picked up Candace at school. She, like Cinder, didn't want to leave my side, so we threw together a plate of treats and played a few hands of dominos.

At dusk, Nick showed up with takeout for dinner. Gluten-free pizza and salad. Perfect. We ate and chatted as if nothing untoward had happened in the past week. Life as usual. Candace didn't press me about her mother. I didn't raise the subject. When she retreated to her room to do homework, I told Nick about Quincy's recap. He listened attentively.

When I finished, he said, "Sounds like he's on top of things."

"I agree."

Someone knocked on the front door. Nick was on his feet in a nanosecond and beat me to the foyer. He peered through the peephole.

"Is it Rosie?" I asked, expecting her to burst in.

"It's your aunt and Yaz." He whipped open the door.

Max entered first.

Yaz, in all his colorful glory—purple mohawk, purple sweater, tie-dyed jeans, and silver-studded cowboy boots—followed. Cinder rushed him and demanded love. Yaz never failed to nuzzle the dog's ears. When Yaz rose, he said, "Hey, gorgeous. Congrats on finding resolution. Nothing like it in the world." Tracking down the driver who had killed the love of his life and making the guy pay had done wonders for Yaz's belief in the system.

"What's so urgent that you needed to come by?" I asked, acid blooming in my stomach right when I thought it might be subsiding.

"The gun," my aunt said.

"Sit in the dining room," I said to everyone. "I'll get us all something to drink. What'll it be? Wine? Beer? Tea?"

My aunt opted for ice water. Yaz accepted a pale ale from Nick.

After setting beverages on the table, I joined them, choosing the armchair at the far end, nearest Nick. He brushed my cheek with his knuckles and smiled.

"Okay, I'm ready," I said.

Max leaned forward on her elbows, the glass of water between her hands. "The lab sent your grandfather's gun on to Atherton P.D."

"Good. Let them keep it."

"You'll need to fill out some forms."

"You came all the way to tell me this?" I couldn't hide the crispness in my tone.

"And to bring you this." My aunt reached into her oversized tote. She pulled out the foot-square cedar gun box and set it on the table.

I shivered. "I don't want it."

Nick said, "Take it. Your grandmother made it."

"The gun was in it."

"It doesn't have bad karma," he said. "Put it where it was. In a week or so, we'll strip the insides. Make it a jewelry box. Candace might want it as a keepsake."

"She knows the gun was in it," I argued.

"Take it. We'll figure something out." Nick gave me a wry look. He was right. It was a keepsake.

Yaz passed the box to me. My hands shook as I held it.

"I'll be right back." I slinked down the hall, glimpsing Candace's room as I passed. Her door was ajar.

"What's that?" she called, catching sight of me.

"Nothing."

The word *nothing* worked like a charm with teenagers. It was the same as whispering near them. They would want to listen harder. She trotted out of her room and followed me into mine.

"Is the gun in—"

"No," I snapped and quickly apologized. "It's on its way to Atherton P.D. This is just a box."

"Well, duh," she said in that inane way teens spoke.

I opened the hope chest and started pulling out items, intending to stow the box where it had been before. At the bottom. Hidden. Buried.

"What's that thingie?" Candace asked.

"What thingie?"

"That little doodad there?" She pointed at the inside of the chest's lid. "It looks like a paper clip or something."

The doodad wasn't a paper clip but a handle to access a tiny compartment. Not big enough to hide a silver dollar. No reason to hold my breath. I set the gun box aside and slid open the compartment's lid. Within was a metal circle about the size of a quarter. No markings.

"What are you two up to?" Nick asked from the doorway.

"My grandmother, or possibly my mother, hid what looks like a slug for a slot machine in the top of the hope chest." I held it out to him.

He rubbed it between his fingers. "It's a magnet."

By now, my aunt had entered the bedroom. "Are you okay?"

Yaz followed her. "No tears."

"No tears," I said. "We've made another mini discovery. Candace found a hidden compartment in the top of the hope chest. Inside was a magnet."

Nick tapped my shoulder and grinned. "When I first started woodworking, I took lessons from an old guy who loved to make puzzle boxes, like your grandmother. Big ones, little ones, you name it. He enjoyed making people work to hide their valuables."

"Your point?"

"A magnet can open a secret drawer."

Candace sniffed. "We opened a secret compartment with that clippy thingie."

"That one was obvious," Nick said. "A drawer that opens with a magnet is completely concealed. The way it works is that you have to match up your magnet to another magnet hidden in the framework of the container." He handed the magnet to me. "It could be on the side of the hope chest or on the back or even underneath. Run the magnet all around. If there's a mate, this magnet will find it."

I rolled my eyes, not believing him, but to humor him, I did as he suggested.

"Slowly," he advised.

For a half hour everyone chimed in, telling me where I might have missed a spot.

When I was ready to give up, I felt a tug on the magnet. At the front of the chest. Near the bottom. A rush of excitement made me drop the magnet. I picked it up and placed it where I'd felt the tug. It clung.

"Use it like a drawer handle," Nick suggested.

Pinching the coin between two fingers, I dragged it toward me. A drawer, about one inch deep and twelve inches wide, opened up. The grain of the chest's wood had made it impossible to see the drawer's seam.

Inside lay a velvet pouch-style bag, folded in thirds. I removed the bag, unfurled it, and spilled out the contents—a letter, a piece of parchment paper, and a tinier velvet bag.

Nick nodded for me to continue.

Carefully, I turned the bag upside down. A thin plastic box fell out. It held a silver dollar, its face engraved with a picture of a woman, her hair wafting behind her.

Nick opened the letter and then the parchment paper.

"What do they say?" I asked breathlessly.

"One is a letter to your grandmother, and the other is a document, stamped for authenticity, describing the 1794 Flowing Hair silver coin—the image is of Lady Liberty—and the coin's worth at the time the document was authenticated."

"Which was?"

"Seven hundred and fifty thousand dollars."

Candace and Yaz whooped. My aunt clapped a hand to her chest.

A shiver raced down my spine. Tears sprang from my eyes. "We found it." I gazed at Nick. "We found my family's insurance policy."

Chapter 39

The next day, I contacted a coin collector in Reno and had him evaluate the coin. Indeed, the Flowing Hair silver dollar was real and worth more than it had been twenty-two years ago, when my grandmother had first had it authenticated. I decided then and there to sell it and deposit the money in a bank, after which I'd decide the next step. Deposit all of it in the trust? Give half to Rosie? No, that would not have been my parents' wish. She would run through her portion in a nanosecond. But she deserved to know.

First, however, I contacted Kurt Brandt.

When he answered, I said, "It's Aspen Adams. I wanted to thank you for coming to my rescue the other day."

"Right place, right time."

"Speaking of right, I'd like to make right by you. I know you're broke."

"I'm not broke." He snorted.

"But you said your wife took you for all you had."

"She did, but in the next year, I made a killing in a couple of card games. Pardon the choice of words. I'm flush."

I chuckled. That would teach me to presume. He had been his own benefactor when it had come to paying his bail. "Then why were you so adamant about finding my grandfather's treasure?" I asked.

"It's a matter of honor," he said. "A man always pays his debts. Gray understood that."

"How much did Grandpa Gray owe you?"

"What do you care?" He clicked his tongue. "You said you don't have any extra cash."

"It turns out that I do now."

He whistled. "You found it, didn't you? His ace in the hole. What was it?"

"A rare coin."

He whistled again. "Where'd you find it?"

"In my parents' hope chest."

"But I searched—" Brandt cut himself off.

I chuckled. "We all searched. It was well hidden and a fluke that we found it. I've cashed it in. I can pay you your due."

"Your grandmother wouldn't want you to," Brandt countered. "Not without a signed IOU."

"I want you to stop tailing me."

He guffawed.

"How much?" I asked.

"Eighty-four thousand, two hundred and forty-three dollars. That's on account of interest. Gray always insisted on paying interest."

I smiled. If he knew the amount down to the dollar, I would believe him. I asked for his bank account information and said I'd have my bank transfer the money to his. When our transaction was completed, I wanted him to send me a signed letter that we were all square. I gave him the detective agency address.

A text message appeared on the heels of our conversation. I thought Brandt was following up until I saw that it was from Serenity: *I said no to D.*

I texted: *I'm glad.*

She responded: *If I come to Tahoe for a visit, can I stay with you?*

I wrote back: *You bet.*

She replied: *XO.*

Chapter 40

A week later, as I was doing the Sunday morning crossword puzzle and making a list in my head of what I needed to buy for Thanksgiving dinner, I heard a car screech to a halt outside the cabin. Cinder sat to attention. Nick rounded the corner from the kitchen, chef's apron over his sweater and jeans. He'd come by at nine to make us brunch.

"Expecting anyone?" he asked.

"Nope."

Candace bounded down the hall, dressed in pink pajamas. "It's Mom. She called me a few minutes ago." Shoulders visibly tense, she flung open the door and stepped backward, hands folded in front of her, chin lowered.

Rosie, in a billowing plaid shirt over jeans tucked into knockoff Uggs, strode into the foyer. She clutched Candace in a bear hug and then held her at arms' length. "Look at you." She toyed with her daughter's hair. "Needs a trim."

"I got a trim two weeks ago."

"You've put on weight."

Candace wriggled free.

"It looks good," Rosie said.

Candace's shoulders relaxed. She lifted her chin and smiled that quasi-confident smile I'd grown to love.

Rosie regarded Nick, who looked ready to grab my sister should she lunge at me. "Calm down, big guy," she said. "I'm four days clean and counting. I'm not on the warpath." She gazed clear-eyed at me. "Can we talk?"

I hadn't told her about the coin yet. I'd been communicating with Ulyssa Thaller about how best to handle the proceeds of the sale. We hadn't come to a conclusion.

"Sure," I said.

"Alone?" She gave Candace a nudge.

Reluctantly, Candace trudged down the hallway, glancing meekly over her shoulder. She loved her mother, but it was clear she was still cowed by Rosie's domineering personality.

Nick hooked a thumb. "I've got bacon cooking." He disappeared into the kitchen.

Rosie moved into the living room and sat on the leather sofa. Air whooshed out of the cushion. I joined her on the couch so we could keep our voices low.

"Are you really clean?" I asked.

"Yep. It's hard." She raised a knee laterally, resting the ankle on her other leg, and propped an elbow on her thigh. "Doing my best, but you know . . ."

"You have urges."

"I'm fighting them."

"We got the answer, Rosie. We found out who killed them. It wasn't your fault. You can move on."

"I get that. And I'm glad. And I . . ." She fought tears. She despised tears. "I want to be a good mom to Candy. I do. I'm going to try. But, well, I'm not sure I can stay clean long enough." She lowered her chin. "I'm going to try to go six months. If I make it, then Candy should come home."

We sat in silence for a long moment.

I spoke first. "How about a clinic?"

"Too expensive."

"If we could afford it . . ." I hesitated. We had the money now. Would Rosie waste the opportunity? "If we could afford it, would you do it? Detox. In-patient. Six months."

She shrugged. "Maybe."

"Where there's the will," I said.

"Aye, there's the rub. The *will*." She chortled low and gruff. "I was thinking if I did get through this, you know, maybe I'd contact Antoine. You said he's a good guy now. We had something special once upon a time. What do you think?"

All I said was, "We can afford it."

• • •

After I told Rosie about finding the coin and how Ulyssa Thaller thought we should invest and distribute it, Rosie and Candace went for a walk.

Nick exited the kitchen and drew me into an embrace. "Throw on a parka. Let's go outside."

The air was crisp, clean. Inspiring. We stood at the wood railing, his arm slung around my shoulders, our gaze focused on the sliver of lake we could see through the pines. A gentle wind created whitecaps that scudded across the surface of the water. Cinder plopped down at the top of the stairs, his ears perked, listening for a critter.

Nick nuzzled my ear. "We have to talk about something."

I molded into him, loving his warmth. "What?"

"A date for the wedding," he said. "And where we're going to live. For Candace's sake, I think we should live here. And lastly, do you want to have—"

I rested my finger on his lips. "We have all the time in the world to discuss these things." Time I hadn't been sure I was going to have when staring down the barrel of Mia's gun. "How about June for the wedding?"

"June." He jutted his chin. "I like June."

"And living here would be great, if Candace is still with me."

Nick raised an eyebrow. "Do you think Rosie can do it?"

"I hope she can."

"But Candace might not do well moving back."

I frowned. He was right. But I couldn't think about that right now. Baby steps. "We'll discuss where she's going to live as we get closer to that day, okay?" I wanted Candace to have some say in the next phase of her life. "As for your final question."

"I didn't complete it."

"I'm pretty sure I know what you were going to ask. Do I want to have children?"

Nick's mouth quirked up on one side. "So, now you're a mind reader?"

I wiggled my hands like a psychic would. "I've had my moments."

Wind whisked through the pines. Cinder spotted a squirrel and dashed after it.

"So, do you?" Nick asked.

I kissed him on the lips. "If you do."

About the Author

Agatha Award–winning, nationally bestselling author DARYL WOOD GERBER writes suspense novels as well as cozy mysteries. She is best known for her Cookbook Nook Mysteries, featuring an admitted foodie and owner of a cookbook store in Crystal Cove, California, and her Fairy Garden Mysteries, featuring a fairy garden shop owner in Carmel, California. She also writes the French Bistro Mysteries, featuring a bistro owner in Napa Valley. Under the pen name Avery Aames, Daryl writes the Cheese Shop Mysteries, featuring a cheese shop owner in Providence, Ohio. Her suspense novels, including the Aspen Adams novels, *Girl on the Run,* and *Day of Secrets* have garnered solid reviews.

As a girl, Daryl considered becoming a writer, but she was dissuaded by a seventh-grade teacher. It wasn't until she was in her twenties that she had the temerity to try her hand at writing again . . . for TV and screen. Why? Because she was an actress in Hollywood. A fun tidbit for mystery buffs: Daryl co-starred on *Murder, She Wrote* as well as other TV shows. As a writer, she created the format for the popular sitcom *Out of This World.* When she moved across the country with her husband, she returned to writing what she loved to read: mysteries and suspense.

Daryl is originally from the Bay Area and graduated from Stanford University. She loves to cook, read, golf, swim, and garden. She also likes adventure and has been known to jump out of a perfectly good airplane. She adores Lake Tahoe, where this series is set, and she has a frisky Goldendoodle named Sparky who keeps her in line.

Visit Daryl at www.darylwoodgerber.com, and follow her on Bookbub at http://bookbub.com/authors/daryl-wood-gerber, on Goodreads at http://goodreads.com/darylwoodgerber, and on Amazon at http://bit.ly/Daryl_Wood_Gerber_page.